What people are saying about

Another
F-Word

"**Ruth and Darrell Wilson** are excited at the birth of their son Rory, but as little Rory grows, his father is bothered that his son's interests aren't in line with his perceived notion of those of other boys. Darrell tries to force Rory to participate in sports activities and doesn't hold back on criticizing and degrading him when he doesn't show interest. Ruth, trying hard to accept that Rory is different, demands a divorce from Darrell due to his treatment of their son. Things are better for Rory at home but school is torment because of the bullying he receives. As Rory matures, he excels at science and meets others who help him understand he is not alone. As he enters college, he begins to find friendship and acceptance and is able to acknowledge and stand up for who he is.

Lissa Brown does an excellent job portraying the challenges gay boys face as they grow up and become men as well as those of a loving parent trying to understand and accept their offspring. She realistically depicts the rejection, bullying and outright hate gays and lesbians face and shows how family dynamics can influence the adults they will become. This is a story teenagers and adults would benefit from reading as it reveals the perspective of a gay person dealing with a rejecting parent and bullying from peers, as well as their inner and outer struggle to recognize their own self-worth."
—Christy Tillery French in *Midwest Book Review*

"**This book was so realistic** I read it cover to cover in one sitting. It is a very heart- wrenching story that is so commonly happening daily in our world. This is one of the many reasons we will combat bullying forever for all kids.... Everywhere. Thank you for your work to bring awareness to this horrible thing in our society!"
—Kirk Smalley, President, Stand For The Silent

"We are allies. We are friends. We are family; but we cannot understand what our LGBTQ students go through. Lissa Brown has opened the door so we can start to understand. Her description of Rory Wilson's life, from young, sensitive boy to out and empowered young adult, is riveting. His turmoil at school, with his family and with his friends is graphically painted by Ms. Brown as the hopeless picture many of our students live through. It is a must-read for every Gay-Straight Alliance Advisor. We cannot be allies for those we don't understand. Thank you Lissa Brown."
—Barb Silvey, Gay-Straight Alliance Advisor, Spokane, Washington

"A very honest, raw, and heart-wrenching reality for many LGBT children is exposed in Brown's Another F-Word through a young man's innocent eyes. Many lessons are learned and emotions exposed through a mother's quest and a son's pilgrimage through childhood. The story ends with an unpredictable twist from one of the first bullies Rory ever encountered. Unconditional love comes full circle when a tragic event places Rory in the same room as someone he thought he would never see or hear from again. Brown is able to take us on the journey with compassion, through heartache and triumph as Rory and his family continue to learn from one another and focus on moving forward.

This is an amazing novel for LGBT youth, parents, educators, and leaders to use as a guide to what a young LGBT person may be experiencing and how they may be able to support them. It's not just another f-word; it is another family that you will care about or even become part of one day."
—Crystal Simmons, President, Adam Foundation, Inc.

Another F-Word

Another F-Word

a novel by

Lissa Brown

Copyright© 2013 by Lissa Brown
Cover illustration from shutterstock.com
Book design by Luci Mott

This book is a work of fiction. Names, characters, locations, and incidents are products of the author's imagination or used fictitiously. Any resemblance to actual events or places or persons, living or dead, is coincidental.

ISBN-13: 978-1481908450
ISBN-10: 1481908456

Acknowledgments

It might not take a village to write a book but I've learned it takes lots of people helping the author before a book reaches publication. Since the topic of this novel is one I've learned about second-hand, the technical assistance I received from Joe Fazio, Dave Gonzalez, Mike Barringer and Jeff Everette was extremely important. That is not to ignore the many rich conversations I've had with psychologists and others who work with parents and kids on issues confronted by gay boys. I learned a great deal from those as well. In addition, I drew on the many bullying incidents I witnessed as a middle and high school teacher.

As a writer, of course I read. One particular book, *In My Own Country,* by Abraham Verghese, provided some important insights into issues surrounding the initial reluctance of some medical facilities to treat people with HIV or AIDS. Perry Deane Young's book, *God's Bullies: Power, Politics and Religious Tyranny,* gave me a better understanding of how some people who are committed to doing God's work can twist scripture to justify hatred of LGBT people. Unfortunately, I observed first-hand the work of some of them as they turned decent, well-meaning North Carolinians into instruments of their bigotry in their effort to codify discrimination against LGBT residents of that state.

I will be eternally grateful to Rev. Marcia Cham and other members of the clergy who gave their all to bring sanity to sometimes hateful discussions leading to the tragic passage of Amendment One to the NC Constitution.

Steve Johnson and Bill Gillenwater allowed me to tour their men's resort so I could use it as a setting for a scene in the book. I'm grateful for their trust and friendship in permitting me to do that.

I owe a debt of gratitude to several PFLAG activists who provided me with stories about their own handling of their children coming out. That organization offers a wonderful service to parents and others who need support as they learn to accept their gay children, siblings and friends.

Wes Nemenz of The Trevor Project provided a wealth of information about suicide among LGBT kids and I thank him for that.

Barb Silvey shared her insights about how an effective Gay-Straight Alliance functions.

Lee Hirsch's powerful documentary film, *Bully*, is a must-see for anyone trying to understand the subject. Through that film I began a dialogue with Kirk Smalley, one of the co-founders of Stand For The Silent. Sadly, the organization grew out of Kirk's grief when his 11-year-old son Ty took his life.

Catherine Tuerk's book, *Mom Knows: Reflections on Love, Gay Pride and Taking Action* gave me a clearer understanding of how difficult it is for parents to come out to others about their gay kids and introduced me to groundbreaking work on gender non-conforming behavior exhibited by some boys and girls.

On the technical side, I am very grateful to Linda Marsh for her thorough editing of my manuscript. It is better because she put her hands on it.

I'm fortunate to belong to a small critique group that worked over much of this book as it spun from my imagination. Marcia, Ingrid, Ree, Sally and Terri gave me the courage to continue with this book and their advice, mostly heeded, has made a huge difference in my writing.

Equality North Carolina hosts an annual conference that deals with many of the issues covered in this story. It's an excellent source of information and I appreciate their effort to produce a quality experience.

I've been part of North Carolina's High Country Writers for many years and have learned much from critique sessions with fellow writers. Their encouragement plays a major role in my decision to write books and essays.

To my partner of 30 years who lovingly puts up with my long periods of seclusion while I write and the hastily prepared suppers

I throw together half an hour before she gets home, I can only offer the promise of more to come. Does anyone see a problem with eating baked ziti three days in a row?

Lastly, I must thank the anonymous driver of the small truck that bore the bumper sticker "Santa Hates Jewish Kids" for starting me on the path to write this book. My strong reaction to that horrible message and several days of brooding about it provided the impetus to consider the irreparable damage some adults do to children. After days of trying to figure out the motivation of someone who would put that on their truck, I knew I had to tell the story of Rory Calhoun Wilson.

Readers who have bought my books and urged me to continue writing make me want to keep telling my stories and I shall do it as long as they are willing to read them. I am very grateful to all of you.

Lissa Brown
Zionville, NC
www.lissabrownwrites.com

**Sticks and stones may break my bones
But names will never hurt me.**

How many of us grew up hearing that rhyme from parents, teachers
and others who tried to console us when people hurt our feelings?
The sad truth is that names do hurt. In extreme instances, those
who are targeted by bullies come to believe their lives are not worth
living. To everyone who has been stung by the harsh words or actions of a bully, I dedicate this book.

Another
F-Word

Chapter One

"Papaw, are ya supposed to say grace if ya just eat a cookie?" six-year-old Rory asked his grandfather as soon as they'd said the amens. Rory's Saturday lunch at his grandparents' ramshackle Tennessee farm was the highlight of his week. This was his special time alone with them.

"We thank the Lord whenever we eat, son. Now, you know the rules. You have to eat somethin' before you start askin' questions."

Rory shoveled mashed potatoes into his mouth and swallowed without chewing. "Okay, Papaw. Now?"

"Have some barbecue, first, while it's hot."

Rory ate another mouthful before putting his fork down on the plate. "What's a faggot, Papaw?"

Grady Wilson shot a worried look across the table to his wife. "Where'd you hear that word, Rory?"

"I heard Daddy say it to Mama. He said he'd just as soon not be around to watch a little faggot grow up in his house. Was he talkin' about me, Papaw? Is Daddy goin' someplace else to live?"

The pained look on Rory's face tugged at his grandfather's heart. At the same time, fury threatened to heat Grady's blood to the boiling point, but first things, first.

"I don't know what your daddy meant by that, Rory," he lied. "I bet you heard wrong, anyway. Maybe he said maggot. Those are bugs that hang around bad meat and such. They're real pesty this time of year. Yep, I bet that's what he said. I'm sure your daddy ain't goin' anywhere."

While Rory continued eating, Grady and Lily Wilson had a wordless conversation over the tops of their eyeglasses. Rory seemed to accept the explanation. He continued eating and wiped his mouth after each bite of food. He couldn't stand to be messy.

Unlike most boys his age, Rory was well-mannered and never had to be reminded to wash his hands and face or comb his hair. In fact, his comb was like an extra digit.

"Lord, Rory, you'll be bald before you get to high school at the rate you're combing your hair," his grandmother had once scolded. "Besides, I'm tired of sweeping blond hair off the bathroom floor," but her smile had softened the sting of her words.

Grady hardly ate after Rory's question and his plate was half full when Rory and Lily finished.

"Something wrong with my barbecue?" Lily asked. She stood with her hands on her hips spoiling for a fight. It was a posture Grady had come to love and fear from his tiny wife.

"No, it's good as ever. I just don't seem to have much appetite today." He got up from the table.

"What's for dessert, Meemaw?"

"Guess."

Grady usually enjoyed watching the guessing game, but not today. He walked out to the porch and sat on the glider to ponder Rory's question.

"I bet we're havin' ice cream."

"Nope, guess agin."

"Banana puddin'?"

"Un-uh. Ya got one more guess. Better make it a good one or ya won't git any."

Rory wrinkled his brow, placed a finger on his cheek, and struck a thoughtful pose as he spoke slowly, "I wonder if it's cobbler." A smile spread over his face as he saw his grandmother approaching the table with a Pyrex dish and three bowls.

"Ooh, blackberry! That's my favorite. How'd you know?"

"I know what my only grandson likes. Why, these blackberries are almost as big as your eyes, Rory Calhoun Wilson."

***

Darrell and Ruth Wilson had desperately wanted children but after four years of trying, their thoughts had turned to adoption. They'd been researching agencies for a few months when Ruth missed a period. She told no one.

After another month went by, Ruth made an appointment to see her gynecologist. Dr. Triplett took his time examining her. "Get dressed and I'll be back," he said. Ruth looked at him expectantly but his face gave no indication of what he'd found.

In a few minutes he returned with a smile that spoke volumes. "Am I?" Ruth asked.

"Nearly three months. I'm surprised you haven't experienced morning sickness. You are most definitely pregnant, and everything looks just fine."

"Do I have that glow?" she asked. "They say pregnant women always have that look about them."

"I don't know if it's a glow, but you look happier than I've ever seen you."

Ruth floated to her nearly new, dark blue 1989 Ford Bronco and drove home on auto pilot. She fantasized about a conversation she'd love to have with her mother, but a horrible collision on a rain-slicked, mountain highway had ended Ruth's parents' lives prematurely.

She headed for the Food Lion, taking a couple of turns before reaching the state highway that did double duty as Craggy Grove's major road. The town was quiet, and as she gazed at the rundown shops and fast food eateries to her left and right, she imagined she could roll a bowling ball down the road and not hit anything or anyone.

Tonight's dinner was going to be special, and that meant dipping into her mad money jar so she could buy steak, Darrell's favorite. She picked out two good-sized ribeyes, mushrooms, onions, baking potatoes and green beans. She drove a few blocks beyond the city limits and stopped at Ricky's Liquor Locker for a bottle of cheap champagne, but remembered pregnant women weren't supposed to drink alcohol.

Every time that phrase, pregnant women, crossed her mind she smiled to herself. Finally, at the age of 27 she was one of them!

She made a U-turn and returned to town, slowing to make a tight turn into the Rite-Aid parking lot. Usually, it took her no time at all to pick out a Father's Day card for her father-in-law, but this time she searched for two cards. She agonized over the choice of Darrell's first card.

When Ruth returned to their five-room ranch house on the outskirts of town, she had just enough time to prepare dinner. She scrubbed the potatoes and put them in the oven, setting the timer for one hour. If Darrell was on time, she'd have everything ready to go on the table when he walked in the door. He liked that. She folded the cotton napkins into a fan-shape she'd learned from Martha Stewart's magazine and took out the Sunday dishes and silverware.

Before putting the onions and mushrooms into the skillet, she addressed the Father's Day card. "To Darrell, my dear husband and father-to-be, with all my love, Your pregnant wife, Ruth." As an after-thought, she added the date, June 18, 1989 since this was an historic milestone in their lives. She propped it between his glass and plate.

Ruth checked herself in the small mirror on the wall next to the pantry as Darrell's car pulled into the driveway. She slid the steaks into the broiler and grabbed a cold Budweiser on her way to the door.

"Hi, darlin'. How was your day?" She kissed him and handed him the beer.

"Oh, the usual," he answered. "How about yours?"

"Same here." She hoped he didn't notice the grin on her face.

"Wash up. Dinner's ready."

"Umm, is that steak I smell? Did I do something good, or did you do something bad?"

"Can't I fix steak without a special reason? Hurry now."

Darrell released his clip-on tie, opened the top button of his shirt, and rolled up his sleeves to bare his arms as he walked into the kitchen. He spotted the fancy table setting. "Am I in trouble? Did I forget an anniversary or something?"

"No, I'd have hit you on the head with the beer if you had."

Darrell hip-bumped Ruth away from the sink so he could wash his hands, and she was in too good a mood to object.

"Sit down, honey."

Ruth heaped the onions and mushrooms on his steak and brought the rest of the food to the table. Darrell reached for her hand and bowed his head. He dispensed with the blessing quickly. He could be grateful and still not have to eat cold food.

"What's this?" He pointed to the envelope.

"Open it."

He slid his knife into the corner and tore it open. Father's Day? He looked quizzically at Ruth. His eyes filled as he read, and he got up and walked to her side of the table. "This isn't a joke, is it? You wouldn't kid about this, would you?"

Ruth smiled in answer.

"Stand up. Let me look at you."

Ruth stood and he placed his hand on her abdomen.

"I can't believe it," he almost choked with emotion. "I never thought this would happen."

"Well, the good Lord had other ideas." They embraced for a moment and then she pushed him away gently.

"Eat your dinner while it's hot. I'll tell you all about it."

Darrell cut into his steak while Ruth talked. She was too excited to eat more than a few mouthfuls, so she speared what was left of her steak and put it on his plate.

"Are you sure you don't want this? You're eating for two, now."

"I've got plenty of time to feed this child. You go ahead."

Chapter Two

When Ruth reached the 19th week of her pregnancy she went for an ultra-sound. She took new interest in the plastic alphabet blocks and stuffed Sesame Street characters that adorned the waiting room. Soon, she thought.

Once inside the examining room, she put on the gown and waited. She shivered and wondered why it was always like a refrigerator in there. She bet if the doctor and nurses had to get naked, they'd turn up the heat.

Dr. Triplett cautioned her, "Depending on the baby's position, you know I might not be able to give you a definite answer about its sex."

Within a minute, he said, "I hope you have some boys' names picked out." He pointed to something on the computer screen.

Knowing the baby's gender made it seem that much more real. Ruth beamed at the fuzzy image. "That's my son," she giggled to the nurse who was assisting Dr. Triplett.

She couldn't wait to call Darrell from the car. "It's a boy, darlin'. The doctor showed me, but honestly, I wasn't sure what I was looking at." Realizing how stupid that might sound, she corrected herself. "Well, I can guess what he was showing me," she laughed, "but I really couldn't tell it apart from all the other things. The image moved and was all blurry."

Darrell had said he didn't care whether it was a boy or girl, but Ruth suspected he really wanted a son. Given the difficulty she'd had conceiving, and the unlikely prospect of a second pregnancy, she truly didn't care.

"Lord have mercy!" Lily had exclaimed when she heard about the baby. "If this isn't the best news of my life." When Grady showed up the weekend after the ultrasound with a drivable replica of Dale Earnhardt's #3 race car, everyone knew he, too, had harbored a secret wish for a boy.

At supper one night he asked, "Give any thought to what you're gonna call the little feller?"

"We've been kind of superstitious about that, actually," Ruth said. "It took us so long to get pregnant we were afraid we might jinx the baby if we made too many plans."

"Is somethin' wrong?" Lily asked, worry furrows spreading across her forehead.

"Oh no, the baby's fine, and I'm fine," Ruth answered quickly.

"What do you think we should call him?" Darrell asked.

"Oh, son, that's not for us to say. That's for y'all to decide."

"Come on, Mama, you must have a favorite name for a boy."

"Well, if you really want to know, I always had a name in mind in case we had another child after you. I'd have named it Rory Calhoun Wilson."

"Rory Calhoun Wilson? I get the Wilson, but Rory Calhoun? Wasn't that the name of some movie actor?"

"Not just any actor." She expressed an exaggerated sigh. "Didn't I ever tell you how I spent the last two months before you were born?"

"Uh uh."

"Well, when I was seven months along, Dr. Clawson told me I had to stay in bed until you were born because my blood pressure shot up. Louise Crockett and the other Baptist church ladies worried I wouldn't stay put, so they came to see me every day and brought magazines and books. Can you imagine lying flat on your back for two months? I nearly lost my mind and would have, I'm sure, if it wasn't for Rory Calhoun, that handsome devil. Evelyn and Iris knew how much I loved Rory Calhoun, so they drove to Elizabethton each week to buy every movie magazine that had something about him. One night a week I watched reruns of his TV show, The Texan, and that was the high point of my week, believe me."

"I'm surprised you didn't name me after him," Darrell joked.

"Well I would have, except you remember my daddy was named Darrell, and he passed the year before you were born. Aren't you tickled it wasn't my mother? You'd have been called Shirley."

Grady chimed in, "Johnny Cash would have had to do a song about a boy named Shirley."

Ruth and Darrell smiled at each other. They did that a lot those days.

"Anyway, where was I? Oh yeah, there I was readin' about Rory Calhoun and watchin' him on TV for two months. You were a big baby, and I had a hard time with you, so I was happy to call you Darrell after my daddy. I didn't give any more thought to Rory Calhoun for some time."

"When did you start thinking about him again, Mama?"

"Well, I thought it might be nice if we had another baby. I made a bargain with your daddy that if I was willin' to go through that bed rest again, I'd get to name the baby Rory Calhoun. Grady worried if it was a girl she'd have a hard time in life, but that was the deal. I guess the good Lord didn't think we needed another child, though."

Ruth listened to her mother-in-law's story. She kind of liked the name Rory. It was different, and Calhoun was a good Southern name.

After Lily and Grady left that evening, Ruth looked up Rory Calhoun on the Internet. No wonder Lily was so taken with him. He'd had dark, rugged good looks that would appeal to any woman. She wouldn't mind a bit if their son turned out to look like that.

Christmas had been quiet that year. At eight and a half months pregnant, Ruth's back pain had been severe. It was the price she paid for gaining too much weight.

Darrell had given Ruth a baby book with a blue cover and pictures of animals. It was titled, "My Life, by...," with space for the baby's name.

"I guess we should be thinking about a name for our son," he'd suggested and handed her another gift, a baby-naming book.

For the next hour they'd perused the book and tried out a variety of names. Nothing had felt right until Ruth said, "Hon, since this is going to be your parents' first and possibly only grandchild, what do you think about naming him Rory Calhoun Wilson? I was so touched by your mother's story."

"You won't believe this. After that night when she told us about her two months with Rory Calhoun, I couldn't get that name out of my head. I even dreamed about it one night. I thought you'd think it was silly."

"I looked him up on the Internet," Ruth said. "He was gorgeous, a real man's man with dark curly hair and a rugged face that must have earned him a fortune. Let's do it."

"Okay, but let's not tell Mama until she meets him."

On New Year's Eve they snuggled on the sofa as they watched the ball drop in Times Square and kissed when the giant numbers 1990 lit up the screen. Surely this would be the best year of their lives.

Chapter Three

Grady wasted no time addressing the issue of Darrell's language around Rory. He brought Rory into the house instead of dropping him off in the driveway. Rory ran in letting the screen door slam behind him and charged into his mother's arms for a hug.

"Did you have fun with Papaw and Meemaw?"

"I did, Mama, but I missed you. Did you miss me?"

"Of course I missed my little darlin'. You must have been gone for five whole hours."

Grady followed Rory in. Ruth stood to kiss him on the cheek.

"How're you, Daddy?"

"Doin' all right. Is Darrell here?"

"He went to the filling station. He should be back any minute. Want some coffee?"

"Naw, thanks. I'm coffeed out for the day." He smiled with genuine affection at his daughter-in-law. If he'd had a daughter, she couldn't have been dearer to him.

"I'll be right back, Daddy. I left my gardening tools out there. Rory, want to help Mama?"

Rory didn't need to be coaxed. He loved anything to do with the garden. He even loved to weed. They'd had a week-long burst of unusually mild weather, and the crocuses were up. Rory checked on them every half hour during daylight hours. He loved seeing the changes from the moment they poked their green arms out of the dirt until the flowers showed off their purple and pink garments.

Grady heard the car and slipped out the kitchen door to greet Darrell in the carport.

"Hey, Daddy. It's good to see you." Darrell knew from his father's face that something was bothering him.

"I need to talk to you."

"Okay. Let's go in."

"I think it would be better if we went for a walk. I don't want Ruth and Rory to hear us."

"Did Rory do something bad today? Is Mama okay?"

"No, Rory's fine, and so is your mama. Let's walk."

Darrell called to Ruth, "We'll be back shortly."

Ruth raised her eyebrows and Darrell shrugged. As soon as they were out of earshot, Grady got to the point.

"Rory asked me a question today that shook me to my roots. Wanted to know what a faggot was. Said you didn't want to stay around and see a little faggot grow up in your home."

Darrell's face turned red as he listened.

"Asked me if you meant him, and if you were goin' away."

"What'd you tell him?"

"What could I tell him?" Perspiration poured down Grady's forehead and disappeared into his bushy eyebrows. "I lied. Told him he prob'ly heard wrong, that you musta said 'maggot' because they're plentiful this time of year. Said I was sure you weren't goin' anywhere."

"Shoot, Daddy, I never meant for him to hear me."

"Well, he did. What in hell's got into you? If I had the strength, I'd hike your butt to the woodshed."

Darrell cleared his throat and recoiled at his father's reprimand.

"He acts more like a girl every day, Daddy. He won't play ball like the other boys his age, and he dresses up in Ruth's clothes and high heels when he's not playing with the flowers in the damned garden."

It took enormous effort, but Grady kept quiet.

"A few weeks ago he came prancing into the living room while I was watching TV. He had on one of Ruth's shawls and an artificial rose tucked alongside his ear and her high heels on. He danced around like he expected me to applaud."

"What'd you do?"

"I told him to take off those clothes. Said boys don't dress like that. 'I like to wear Mama's clothes, Daddy,' he said." Darrell spoke in a falsetto voice imitating Rory. "'It's not Halloween. No need for you to wear a costume,' I said. Ruth believes we shouldn't make an issue of it, but I think she's wrong. I hate to say it, but I suspect something's weird about Rory. He still sleeps with a doll, for cryin' out loud. And another thing. I wanted to sign him up for T-ball and when I took him down there, he cried and didn't want to get out of the car. I was so embarrassed I turned around and took him home."

"Well, not all boys like sports, you know."

"Yeah, but real boys don't like to wear women's clothes."

"You can't be tossin' words like that around where he can hear you. It ain't right, Darrell. It's probably just a stage he's goin' through. He'll get over it. I don't like to take sides, but I think Ruth's right. He's a good boy. Let him be."

As Grady drove back to the farm, he thought about what Darrell had said. He wondered if that would be the last time they'd have this discussion.

Chapter Four

Over the years Ruth and Darrell's marriage had settled into an easy rhythm and except for a few difficult months adjusting to sleep-deprivation after Rory's birth, they seemed to be content with one another. Fights between them were rare and short-lived until Darrell's derogatory comments about Rory started getting on Ruth's nerves.

He grumbled about Rory's dressing up in Ruth's clothes and spending so much time playing with Ashley, a neighbor's daughter. "He never wants to play ball or do things with the other boys," he complained to her repeatedly. She knew that some men looked at their sons as rivals for their wives' affection and chalked it up to that.

Tonight, after Darrell and his father returned from their walk, Grady didn't come back into the house, something Ruth found odd.

"What's going on with your dad?"

"Later," he answered and shifted his eyes in Rory's direction. He hoped Ruth would forget it.

That night, Darrell settled in bed with a copy of *Field and Stream* while he waited for Ruth to finish in the bathroom. She climbed in next to him and turned to face him. "So, what did your daddy have to say today?"

"Hon, I'm trying to read."

She playfully reached over and snatched the magazine out of his hands. "You can read later. Tell me."

"He was worried about something Rory said to him today. Rory asked him what a faggot was."

"Oh, no. He must have heard you the other day."

"There's no doubt he heard us. He told Daddy he heard me say I didn't want a faggot growing up in this house. He asked Daddy if I

25

meant him, and if I was going away."

"Oh Lord, Darrell, what did Daddy say to him?"

Darrell told her how his father had handled it.

"I told you it was a hateful thing to say. You must never say anything like that again about Rory. He might be a little different, but you're his father. No matter what, he has to know you love him. You do love him, don't you?"

"Of course I love him. I just can't stand the way he acts sometimes. You baby him and let him do all those girly things. That's probably why he is this way."

"What do you mean 'this way'? What's wrong with the way he is? Not all men are macho, you know. This world needs more sensitive men. If we had a few more, maybe we wouldn't be in all these damned wars." Her face turned red and she pushed the covers off. "Look at your precious Elvis, for heaven's sake! He wore makeup, and some of his outfits were fancier than anything I have in my closet. And he was partial to pink Cadillacs! No one ever said he wasn't manly."

"Quiet down or Rory'll hear you," Darrell cautioned.

"Rory is a sweet, gentle boy. He might be a little more sensitive than some of those roughneck boys in his class, but at least he's considerate and thoughtful. And he doesn't talk trash like some of the kids. Why, the other day I stopped at the post office and Sally Wheeler got out of her car as I was pulling in. I parked next to her and noticed the twins in the back seat. They didn't see me, cause they were too busy hitting each other. I heard one of them call the other one a f---ing liar. Six years old, same age as Rory, talkin' like that!"

"Boys do that, Ruth. I'd almost rather hear Rory cuss every now and then instead of always being so polite."

"I hope I'm around the day he says that word to you. Let's see how pleased you'll be." Ruth got out of bed and stomped toward the living room. "I wouldn't mind one bit if there was one cultured male in this house," she hurled back over her shoulder.

Chapter Five

"Come on, son. Careful not to spill your drink." Darrell and Rory inched past several sets of knees on the way to their seats. Darrell held two hot dogs and a beer and juggled them as he sat down. "Here's your hot dog, Rory," he said and handed him the naked frankfurter. Rory didn't like mustard or chili on his hot dogs; he said it burned his tongue.

Darrell was on a crusade to introduce his son to all of the things he believed would make him more masculine. Rory was eight years old, and he'd spent most of that time hanging around with his mother and Ashley. Darrell knew he had to hustle to undo the female influence if he was going to mold Rory into a real boy.

The cars inched toward the line for the start of the race at Bristol Motor Speedway. Rory pushed his long, stringy hair out of his eyes and adjusted his headphones. The noise was unbearable, even with ear protectors. He dug into his jeans pocket to see if he had tissues he could stuff in his ears.

Rory finished his hot dog and pulled a book out of his backpack.

"Put it away," Darrell shouted over the noise.

Rory did as he was told. The last thing he wanted was for his father to launch into his favorite topic: what boys are supposed to like and do. Truth was, he'd only agreed to accompany Darrell to the race because his mother said he had to.

"Daddy wants to spend time with you, Rory," she'd urged. "You should be glad he wants to take you places. Some kids' fathers are never around and when they are, they're glued to the TV."

The drivers revved their engines, and the crowd responded to the rush of adrenaline. People stood and some pumped their arms in the air. Rory was aware of someone talking in his earphones, but the voice was drowned out by the roar of the engines. A cloud of gas fumes floated over the grandstand, and he held his nose.

Darrell slid Rory's left earphone forward and yelled in his ear, "See that guy with the flag?" and he pointed to the starter. "When he waves it, those cars will shoot out of the line and start trying to gain the advantage."

Rory wasn't sure he'd heard his father, but he nodded. He tried to appear interested, but all he could think of was the birthday party he was missing. He'd been very disappointed when Ruth called Ashley's mother to say he wouldn't be able to make it. "Darrell wants to have some male bonding time with him, so he's taking him up to Bristol for the race," she'd told Jane.

Rory had helped pick out Ashley's present, a pretty pink sweater with white trim around the collar and sleeves.

"Be sure you tell her I helped pick it out," he'd urged Ruth.

For the next two hours, Rory watched his father jump up and sit down and pump his arm into the air as he shouted encouragement that his favorite driver, Dale Earnhardt, couldn't possibly hear above the commotion. The only thing that excited Rory was when a car spun out and occasionally hit the wall. "Is he hurt, Daddy?" he'd ask. He was sure nobody could smash into a wall at those speeds and not be seriously injured.

During a bathroom break, Darrell explained that the drivers wore harnesses and helmets and protective suits, so they didn't usually get hurt. He filled Rory in about pit stops and why they had to change tires. "Quit worrying and enjoy the race," he said as they headed back to their seats.

Rory stood and sat when his father did, although he didn't understand why. It seemed little enough to try to please Darrell, so he did it.

Mercifully, the cars began the last lap. The crowd was on its feet, and Darrell propped Rory up on his seat so he could see the finish. No one was happier than Rory to see that checkered flag come down. That meant they could soon go home.

"Well, son, what'd ya think of your first race?" Darrell asked while they sat in bumper-to-bumper traffic and snaked toward the race-way exit.

Rory's ears were still ringing. "It was good, Daddy, real good." He was old enough to know the difference between the truth and a lie, and also wise enough to know it was sometimes easier to tell some-one what they wanted to hear.

Rory knew lying was wrong, but guessed he wouldn't go straight to Hell for pretending to like that noisy, smelly place. Likely, his pun-ishment would be that he'd probably have to go to another race.

Chapter Six

"Did you have fun at the race with your daddy?" Ashley asked as they sat on the swings behind her house a couple of days later.

"I'd rather a' been at your party. Did you ever go to the races?"

She shook her head. "What's it like?"

"You'd hate it. It's so loud it hurts your ears. It stinks too. It's like sittin' in traffic behind a hundred smelly buses. I don't know why my daddy likes it. The cars go round in circles, and sometimes they crash into each other or smash into the wall. I'd never want to ride in one of those cars. It's worse than some of the carnival rides I been on. All the people go around sayin, Boogity, boogity. Don't know what it means. Maybe they all pick their noses or somethin."

"Did you tell him you didn't like it?"

"No way. He'd call me a sissy again. I think he hates me."

"Parents don't hate their kids, Rory. Mama says they're just mean sometimes."

"Did you get good presents?" Rory steered the topic away from the race.

"I'll tell you something if you promise not to tell," Ashley offered.

Rory looked expectantly at her.

"Cross your heart and I'll tell you."

Rory drew a cross over his chest.

"When I opened your present everyone said it was real pretty, but Rebecca said she bet you picked it out 'cause you wanted to wear it. She thinks you're really a girl."

"Well, she's stupid," Rory answered. "Who cares what she says?"

"I told her to take it back."

"Did she?"

"She said she'd take it back if I saw proof that you were a boy. Her brother said he thought you didn't even have a weenie."

"I do too," Rory answered, suddenly feeling he was being backed into an uncomfortable corner.

"I'm your best friend, right?" Ashley asked.

Rory nodded.

"Well, I can tell Rebecca I saw it."

"Okay," Rory answered hesitantly. He didn't see much harm in that.

"Rebecca's pretty smart, and I hope she won't know I'm lying," Ashley said. "I don't want to go to Hell." Rory recognized Ashley's scheme-hatching look.

"What if you go by those bushes," she pointed to the hedges that separated her yard from her neighbor's, "and pee, and I happen to walk by and see it?"

"If I got caught peeing in your yard, Mama would kill me."

"She'd never find out. It's just you and me out here. Then I wouldn't be lyin' when I told Rebecca I saw it." She let that thought sink in for a few minutes as her feet took running steps backwards to make the swing go higher.

Ashley was the only real friend Rory had. She never poked fun at him or called him names. Just recently, she'd stuck up for him when two of the neighborhood boys ran after him with sticks.

Rory knew it was wrong to let a girl see his private parts. His mama had yanked him in the house once when he ran outside without his pants on and told him God did not want anyone but his mama and daddy and the doctor to see his privates.

But Ashley's like a sister, he thought. If nobody's around and Mama doesn't find out, maybe I can take a chance.

"Are you sure nobody can see me behind the bushes?"

"Let's go see." She stopped swinging and walked over to the shrubs with Rory a couple of steps behind her. "You stand there and face the bushes," she instructed. "I'll go around to the other side."

Rory stood facing the bushes.

"Nope, I can't see you from here. Are ya gonna do it?"

The fear of losing Ashley's friendship outweighed his mother's caution. "Okay, but be sure nobody's around."

Ashley's plan to take a casual stroll and chance upon Rory as he was urinating into the bushes quickly vanished as curiosity got the better of her. She came around and stood next to him as he unzipped.

"You don't have to keep lookin'. You saw it."

"Yeah, it's little. Are all weenies that little?" she asked.

Rory finished and zipped up. "Uh huh, they are 'til you grow up. My daddy says when I'm a man it'll be a lot bigger."

Unknown to Rory and Ashley, Ashley's mother had watched the whole episode from her second floor window. She punched in Ruth's phone number.

"Hey, Ruth. This is Jane. How're ya doin'?

"I'm just fine, Jane. Are you all right?"

"I was until a few minutes ago. I hope you're sittin' down, girl."

"What's wrong?"

Jane described what she'd witnessed.

"I'm goin' to give him such a whippin', Jane. I'm so sorry. He knows better than to do that. Did you talk to Ashley yet?"

"Not yet. I hope this isn't the start of somethin' new with these kids. I figured I had a few more years before I had to put a chastity belt on Ashley. I guess I shouldn't be surprised, though. Kids nowadays are so curious about everything."

"Let's talk again tomorrow and compare notes. We'll see if they tell the same stories. Thanks for lettin' me know, Jane. Oh, and I hope he didn't kill your hydrangea. If it dies, I'll dig up one of mine. See ya."

Ruth knew she'd better handle this before Darrell got home or there'd be hell to pay. She walked down three houses to where the children were playing in the yard.

"Rory, time to come home," she called.

When they got home Rory asked, "Can I stay out here and play in the garden 'til Daddy gets home?"

"No, you need to come in. I want to talk to you." She sat on the sofa and patted the seat beside her. "What did you and Ashley do today?"

"Oh nothin' much. We played on the swings and messed around."

"What do you mean, 'messed around'?"

"She told me she liked the sweater, and I told her about the race me and Daddy went to."

"Did you do anything that you should be ashamed about, Rory

Calhoun?"

Rory knew he was sunk. His lower lip began to quiver and his face got red. Next came the tears.

"Well, what did you do? Tell me right now."

In between sobs, Rory managed to get out his story, at least part of it. "I peed in the bushes."

"And who saw you do that?"

More sobbing. "Ashley."

"Why was Ashley watching you pee?"

A torrent of sobs prevented Rory from talking for a few minutes.

"I'm waiting, Rory. Why was Ashley watching you?"

After fits and starts, Rory told her about the remark one of the girls made at the party and Ashley's plan for remedying the situation.

Ordinarily, Ruth would have spanked Rory and punished him, but this story gave her pause. She knew what Darrell thought of Rory's behavior, but until now she'd never heard anyone else question it. Why would the children at the party say such hateful things about him? Had she been putting her head in the sand?

"You know that was an ugly thing to do, don't you, son?"

"Yes," he sniffed. "But I didn't want Ashley to have to lie for me. Then it would be my fault if she went to Hell."

Ruth tried to understand the logic of his eight-year-old mind. With Ashley's help, he'd convinced himself it was the right thing to do to save her from eternal damnation. It was hard to argue with that.

"I understand that you wanted to protect Ashley since she was going to help you," she began. "But it's wrong to show your privates to her, and you are never to do it again. Do you understand?"

"Yes, Mama. I won't do it ever again. I promise."

"Well, then, go get washed up for supper. Your daddy will be home soon."

"Do you have to tell him?"

Good question, Ruth thought. She knew Darrell would hit the ceiling. She didn't want to add fuel to his argument that something was wrong with Rory, and she surely didn't want to give him a chance to say "I told you so."

"I have to think about it. I don't know," she answered.

After washing his hands, Rory came back to the kitchen where Ruth was fixing dinner.

"Mama, please don't tell Daddy, please. He hates me already."

She stopped what she was doing. She'd never seen that look of terror on Rory's face.

"Daddy doesn't hate you, Rory. What a thing to say! He loves you just like I do."

Rory continued to plead. "Please, Mama, don't tell him."

Ruth's heart went out to the boy, but Darrell was her husband and she shouldn't keep things like this from him. Or should she?

"I'll think about it. Go play in your room while I fix supper."

Chapter Seven

Rory usually dove into spaghetti and meatballs with gusto, but he barely picked at his food that evening. He gnawed at one meatball, hardly making a dent in it, and sucked a few strands of spaghetti into his mouth before wiping the red sauce off his lips and chin.

Throughout supper Rory had only one thought: I have to get away from home before Daddy hears what happened. Where will I go? The only place he could think of was his grandparents' farm.

But they surely would want to know why he'd run away. If they found out, they would be ashamed of him, and he couldn't stand that.

"What's the matter, son? You hardly touched your food."

"Nothing, Daddy. I'm just not hungry." He looked at his mother pleadingly.

"Well, I guess I'll have to eat your dessert then. Ruth, I'll have his share."

"What're we havin', Mama?"

"It's banana pudding, one of your favorites."

"Can I eat mine tomorrow?"

"I reckon I can save you some. If you're through playin' with your food, you may be excused." Rory slid out of his chair without moving it away from the table.

With Rory gone, Darrell asked, "What's with him?"

"Oh, I guess he's just tired. He's been kind of cranky all afternoon," she answered. "I'll check his temperature later. Maybe he's coming down with a bug."

She'd never consciously lied to her husband before. Months later, Ruth would recall that day as a turning point in their marriage. She'd also eventually admit that it was the first time she started to acknowledge that Rory really was different from other boys, though it would take years before she stopped denying the obvious.

Rory's suffering tore at her. She put the last of the dishes away and went to his room.

"What in the world are you doing?" She quickly closed the door when she saw Rory's clothes piled on the bed.

"I don't want to be here when you tell Daddy what I did. He'll be glad when I'm gone anyway."

"And just where do you plan to go?"

"I'm goin' to Papaw and Meemaw's house."

"Their house is six miles from here. How are you fixin' to get there?"

"I can walk."

The whole time they were talking Rory continued taking clothes out of drawers. He'd nearly emptied every drawer and covered the bed.

"Stop doing that and sit down, Rory."

Rory shifted a pile of underwear over and sat on a corner of the bed.

"I've decided not to tell him."

Rory's shoulders slumped in relief. He got up, slid between her knees and hugged her around the waist. "Oh, Mama, thank you, thank you. I was so scared. I prayed to God and Jesus that you wouldn't."

"But," she shook a finger at him, "if you ever do a thing like that again I'll have to tell him. Is that clear?"

"Yes, ma'am. I promise. I'll never do it again."

"Now, put those clothes back in the drawers. You're not going anywhere except into the bathtub, and then if your appetite comes back, I might scrape up some banana pudding."

Ruth bent down and kissed the top of Rory's head. She lingered a moment and held onto him, knowing she and her son were embarking on a difficult path.

Chapter Eight

Jane was one of a few other college-educated women in Ruth's small social circle and they discussed topics that neither dared bring up with most of their neighbors, like politics and religion. Ruth had picked Jane and Phil out as fellow Democrats the first time she met them. Jane had made an off-handed crack about Dan Quayle, and Ruth and Darrell had laughed.

Jane and Phil had relocated to Craggy Grove from Pittsburgh when he got a promotion. It took a couple of years before they began to feel that people in the community stopped blaming them for what some still called the War of Northern Aggression.

"If I didn't have you for a friend, I think I'd go stir crazy in this place," Jane confided one day over Diet Cokes in Ruth's kitchen. Jane had come from an entirely different world. Most of her Pittsburgh friends enjoyed theater and the other arts. When she moved to Craggy Grove, the nearest theater was a fifty-minute drive in either direction. There was no symphony, unless you counted the two closest universities, and the local library was lucky to stay open with donations of dog-eared Danielle Steele novels.

"You'll get used to our slower way of life," Ruth counseled. "You need to learn to relax. You Yankees are always in a rush. Things get done if you slow down too, you know. You've been here almost, what, four years? It's not all bad livin' in a small town. At least you don't have to fear for your life when you go out at night, and you have to admit, people are friendly."

"True," Jane agreed.

"Oh, I nearly forgot. How's your hydrangea?"

"It seems to have survived the extra watering," she answered.

"What did Ashley tell you the other day?"

"She said Rory had to go to the bathroom and she told him not to go home, that he could do it right there. When I asked her why she was watching him, she said she wanted to see what a weenie looked liked. She'd never seen one."

"I guess that's normal at that age," Ruth offered.

"If we were still in Pittsburgh, Rory'd probably have demanded to see her business too. Kids up there are faster about those things. Let's hope we're a few years away from that. I'm not taking any chances with Ashley. The minute she enters puberty, I'm putting her on the pill."

"Did she say anything else?"

"No, that was it. Of course I read her the riot act and threatened not to let her play with Rory if it happened again. I tried not to make too big a deal out of it. In fact, I even forgot to tell Phil about it."

"Good, don't," Ruth responded.

Jane looked at her strangely. "Why?"

"Because I'm not planning to tell Darrell. Phil might mention it to him."

"Why don't you want Darrell to know?"

"He gets on Rory's case somethin' awful, and I don't want Darrell to torment him about it."

"Okay, I won't say anything. What'd Rory say?"

"Pretty much the same story."

Changing topics, Jane asked, "What's on your agenda for the day?"

"Agenda? I don't have an agenda. Remember, I'm Southern. We just go through our days lazing around, doin' nothing much. I might sit on the porch and sip a Mint Julep or two and fan myself."

Jane poked Ruth on the arm. "Very funny. Okay, Scarlet, I've got to go do some laundry since I don't have any slaves to do it for me." She got up and put her Coke can in the recycling box next to the trash can. "See you later."

Jane was a friend, but not yet close enough that Ruth could share her feelings about Rory's problems. Ruth missed having the kind of close girlfriends she'd had before she got married.

For the past few days, Ruth had been doing a lot of searching on the Internet about homosexuality. She'd found a site run by an organization called PFLAG, Parents, Family and Friends of Lesbians and Gays, that welcomed questions. She'd typed, "At what age do boys begin to exhibit signs of homosexuality?" She'd also found another site that claimed homosexuality could be cured if the person accepted Jesus Christ and chose abstinence. She had her doubts about whether that could work since most of the articles she read said that homosexuality was genetic.

A few days later Ruth got an email from a woman at PFLAG. Instead of an answer to her question, the woman wrote she'd be happy to talk with Ruth and provided her phone number. She lived in southwest Virginia and had a gay son. Ruth printed the message and tucked it into her jewelry box. Over time she forgot about the email and the paper got pushed to the back of the box. She wouldn't think of calling that woman for several years when she was desperate to talk to someone.

Chapter Nine

Rory hated Mondays. He prayed for illness every Sunday night so he wouldn't have to go to school the next day. Sometimes he got lucky and developed diarrhea and his mother would keep him home. His tormented school life grew worse, the older he got.

Now in sixth grade, the incessant bullying was more than he could stand some days. After an especially rough time on the school bus one afternoon, Rory questioned the school's zero tolerance policy. From what he'd experienced, it seemed like nobody took it seriously.

He didn't think it was an accident when Mr. Starnes called him Miss Wilson in class the other day. Even though the teacher said it was a mistake, he had the same kind of nasty smile on his face that the kids do when they call him names. Rory sensed his teacher cared more about being popular with the bullies than making them stop picking on him.

As long as Rory got good grades, Ruth had no reason to suspect all was not right in school. Parent-teacher conferences were uneventful. Darrell didn't bother to go, and no mention was made of Rory's not getting along with other children.

"Who did that to you?" Ruth demanded one day when Rory came home from school with a black eye.

"Nathan Powers."

"Did you hit him first?"

"No, ma'am. He just walked over and hit me on the playground. You can ask Ashley."

"Did you hit him back?"

"No, I did like you told me. I walked away."

"Come in the bathroom where the light's better."

Upon closer examination, Ruth saw there was no serious damage. It looked far worse than it was.

"What did Mr. Starnes say when you told him?"

"I didn't tell him. I didn't want to be a squealer, Mama. Then Nathan'd hit me worse the next time."

"What's wrong with that boy that he'd hit you for no reason?"

"He just picks on kids. Ashley says his daddy beats him up and that's why he's mean."

"I'm going to have a talk with Mr. Starnes and find out why they don't do somethin' about that."

"Aw, Mama, don't do that. It'll just make things worse. I'll stay away from him." Ruth remembered her own school experiences and knew Rory was right about situations like this getting worse when parents got involved. Teachers can do only so much to protect kids. They can't be everywhere; bullies have a way of knowing where to go to avoid watchful adult eyes.

At supper that night, Darrell demanded all the details of how Rory got a shiner. When Rory told him he'd walked away after getting hit, Darrell hit the roof. "Dammit, son, you have to learn to fight back when somebody pops you one."

"Darrell, there's no need to cuss at the supper table. Besides, Rory did the right thing by walkin' away. Jesus says to turn the other cheek, remember?"

"I'm sure Jesus didn't mean you should let yourself be used as a punching bag by some bully, Ruth."

Rory continued eating while his parents argued. This wasn't the first argument he'd witnessed over something that involved him.

After supper Darrell told Rory, "Get in the car. We're goin' to the WalMart."

"What for, Daddy?"

"You'll see. Wait for me in the car."

"What's this all about?" Ruth asked.

"I'm going to buy boxing gloves and teach him how to fight. We won't be gone long."

"Oh Lord, Darrell. This is crazy," Ruth said, but she knew it was useless to try to talk him out of it.

The first boxing lesson didn't go too badly. Darrell had bought a punching bag, and Rory didn't mind standing on the metal base while he swung at the bag.

"Picture Nathan's head where the bag is," Darrell coached. "Just pound away at it for a while."

After standing too close and getting hit with the rebounding bag a couple of times, Rory seemed to get the hang of it. He didn't exactly punch the bag. It looked more like he was slapping it from side to side. If it didn't get any worse than this, it probably wouldn't hurt, Ruth hoped.

But the next lesson did. Darrell held his hands up in front of his chest and urged Rory to hit them. Rory took a couple of open-handed slaps at his father's hands and stopped.

"What's the matter with you?" Darrell shouted. "You can't hurt anyone like that."

He took Rory's gloved hands and folded them into fists. "Now keep them closed like this. That's how you punch. Men don't slap. That's what girls do. Come on. Hit me hard with your fists."

Rory picked up one hand and brought it down like a hammer toward Darrell's hand and missed completely.

"No, do it like this." Darrell got behind Rory and put his son's hands into a boxing stance and showed him how to shoot his arm straight out in a punch. Rory's frustration was nearing the level of his father's. He put all his strength behind one punch and swung as hard as he could, missing his father's hands and losing his balance.

Ruth heard the bang when Rory hit the floor, and she came running into the makeshift gym.

Darrell was yelling, "For pity's sake, Rory. Can't you do anything right? Get up."

"Maybe that's enough for one night," Ruth urged. "He's got homework to do."

"That's right, stick up for him like you always do. No wonder he's such a sissy." Darrell stalked out of the room.

Rory looked pathetic with his skinny arms and those big red boxing gloves. The purple shiner added an almost comic element.

"He doesn't mean it, son," she said, but she knew he did. Plus, it was clear that Darrell blamed her as much as the boy for Rory's weakness.

Rory pushed the gloves off his hands and flung them across the room. They landed in the corner next to the punching bag. He went to his desk and sat in the chair with his shoulders drawn inward. "Mama," he said in a voice barely above a whisper, "I'm no good at this. It's just something else he hates me for."

She heard the defeat in his voice but felt powerless. She put an arm around his shoulders and squeezed gently, then left him to his homework.

Chapter Ten

The boxing lessons continued with slight improvement in Rory's performance. Once his father showed him how to stand, he was less likely to lose his balance. He'd even managed to land a couple of passable punches on his dad's hands. But the strain was showing on Rory.

Ruth often checked on Rory before she went to bed. He'd always been a quiet sleeper, but lately she noticed he tossed and turned a lot. He'd even begun talking in his sleep and grinding his teeth. Ruth tried to understand what he was saying, but his words were garbled.

Despite the bullying in school and at home, Rory appeared to maintain an even disposition. He could still lose himself in the garden as he planted and weeded. He'd enlisted Ashley's help and it was good to watch the two of them together. Ashley adored Rory, and he was very fond of her. Wouldn't it be nice if they ended up being sweethearts, Ruth thought one afternoon as she watched them. She and Jane kidded that they could end up related by marriage one day.

***

One morning Ruth noticed large spaces in Rory's garden where somebody had pulled up flowers.

"Who did that?" she asked Rory after school.

"I did."

"Why? Was there something wrong with them?"

"No, I was gonna pull them all up, but I changed my mind."

"Why would you do that? You love flowers." She walked over to him and took his chin in her hands. "What's the matter?"

"Daddy's always making cracks about my flowers, so I got mad and thought it would be better if I didn't grow them anymore. I thought he'd like me better if I quit growing things."

"What made you change your mind?"

"I remembered you said if somebody does something hateful, I shouldn't be hateful back. If I'd dug up something beautiful that makes people happy, that would have made me as hateful as Daddy, so I stopped."

Ruth puzzled over Rory's behavior for several days after that conversation. On the one hand, she was pleased to hear Rory had absorbed something she'd tried to teach him. But she knew he truly believed his father hated him.

**

Darrell hadn't talked about boxing for several weeks. It appeared he'd given up, and Rory again felt his prayers had been answered.

Then, one night as Darrell ate the last forkful of dessert, he said, "How about boxing after supper, Rory?"

Rory's face flushed. "I don't know where my gloves are."

"Well, they have to be here somewhere. I'm sure you can find them."

"I haven't seen them in a long time. Maybe they got thrown out by mistake."

Ruth jumped in. "Why don't you fellas do something else? Play cards or watch TV."

"Don't go buttin' in, Ruth. This is between Rory and me." Darrell turned to his son. "Did you throw those gloves away?"

No answer. Rory studied his plate, hoping his father would let it go.

"I'm talking to you. Did you throw those gloves away?"

"May I be excused?" Rory addressed his mother.

"No, you may not," Darrell roared. "You did, didn't you? Tell me the truth or you'll get a whippin."

"I hate boxing!" Rory's face glowed red, and he glared at his father. "You just make me do it so you can hit me. Go ahead! Hit me and get it over with. You know you hate me!"

Rory's outburst shocked everyone, especially himself. It was the first time he'd talked back to his father.

Darrell recovered quickly and jumped out of his chair. He grabbed Rory by the arm and dragged him to his room, yelling as he went. "Don't pull this martyr crap with me. You took perfectly good boxing gloves and threw them away. I paid for them with hard-earned money, you ungrateful brat!"

Darrell took off his belt and hit Rory as he cowered on the floor next to his bed. He got three or four licks in before Ruth came up behind him and grabbed the belt. "Stop it this minute! You are totally deranged. You'll kill him. Why don't you pick on someone your own size? What kind of maniac are you to beat a child?"

"No kid is gonna talk to me that way," Darrell bellowed and stomped into the kitchen and out the side door to the carport. In his haste, he forgot his keys and came back to get them.

"Go somewhere and cool your head," Ruth said. "When you get a hold of your temper, if that ever happens, come back."

She walked back into Rory's room where he remained crumpled on the floor. Strangely, he wasn't crying. Ruth knelt down beside him. "Are you okay?"

"He didn't hurt me. I didn't let him."

Ruth knew that could not possibly be true. "Come on, get up." She offered him a hand, which he brushed aside. "You're going to have to apologize for what you said, you know."

"I'm not sorry. When I'm bigger, I'm gonna hit him with a belt. We'll see if he likes it."

Something changed between Rory and his father that night and neither seemed to want a repeat performance. For several months they spoke little and kept their distance.

Chapter Eleven

Rory's body began to fill out and he'd grown five inches during sixth grade. No longer the skinny little boy, he was rapidly approaching adolescence. Some days he spoke in a high-pitched voice, and other times he croaked when he talked. His moods began to reflect the turmoil his body was experiencing. He preferred to spend time alone in his room with his books and music and less time with his parents.

At the end of the school year, there was a watered-down graduation for sixth-graders, and families were invited. Grady and Lily were wearing their best church clothes when Ruth and Darrell picked them up. They arrived at the school as Mr. Starnes was lining up his students for the procession into the auditorium.

Rory looked so mature in his jacket and tie. Most of the boys wore sport coats. It was amazing to see the difference in their sizes. Rory stood a full head taller than most of the other boys, and nearly all of the girls were taller than the boys.

As the Wilsons passed the line of students in the parking lot, they heard an unmistakable, "Hey, faggot" and turned in time to see one of the boys poke Rory in the ribs. Mr. Starnes stood not two feet from where this took place. Although he didn't react, he had to have heard it.

Darrell turned on his heel and strode toward Mr. Starnes. Grady lurched after him but couldn't keep up with his son.

"Are you in charge here?" Darrell demanded.

"Yes, I'm Mr. Starnes," and he stuck his hand out. Darrell pushed the hand aside. "If you're in charge, why do you tolerate that kind of behavior from these kids?"

"I'm sure I don't know what you're referring—"

Darrell cut him off. He pointed to the boy he'd seen jab Rory in the ribs. "He just called my son a faggot and you stood there and said nothing. So much for the no-tolerance policy for bullying." Standing inches from Starnes' face, Darrell's face was redder than his tie.

"Can't we discuss this somewhere else?" Starnes pleaded, aware that every student's attention was focused on them.

"What's the matter? Are you afraid the kids will see what a coward you are?"

Grady reached for his son's arm, but not soon enough. Darrell landed a punch square on the teacher's jaw, and Starnes dropped to the asphalt. Grady, Ruth and Lily rushed to tend to him.

Pandemonium broke out, and the students began shouting and carrying on. Stunned, the teacher got to his feet, rubbing his jaw. "You're going to have to answer to the authorities for this, mister."

He motioned to one of the girls. "Go get Mrs. Whitlock and tell her to call the sheriff." When she hesitated, he said, "Go quickly, Frannie."

On his feet again, Starnes returned his attention to his charges while the Wilsons walked into the school. "Okay, settle down. The show's over for now. Get back in your lines," he ordered.

"Mrs. Whitlock, some man hit Mr. Starnes, and he said to tell you to call the sheriff," Frannie reported a few minutes later.

"Oh Lord," the principal sighed. She was about to signal the music teacher to begin playing the processional. She ran as quickly as her 4-inch heels would allow to the playground where she saw Mr. Starnes rubbing his jaw.

"Frannie told me what happened. Are you okay?" The back of his shirt was soiled from his fall. She brushed him off.

"I'll live. That guy who just walked into the auditorium socked me in the jaw. I want him arrested."

Mrs. Whitlock steered him away from the students, knowing from her 26 years as a principal that there was always more to the story. "You can't mean Mr. Wilson, Rory's daddy. I think that's who just walked into the auditorium."

"Yes, that's who hit me. I'm sure of it because he mentioned his son," Starnes answered.

"What prompted this?" she demanded. "Was there an argument about Rory?"

"No, not an argument. He accused me of allowing someone to bully the boy and before I could explain anything, he knocked me on my butt in front of the kids."

"We need to discuss this after the graduation. I'm not going to call the sheriff and turn a simple disagreement into a full-blown circus. Come to my office after the ceremony and we'll figure out something."

Starnes wasn't satisfied with her response but knew she was right about the timing. Mrs. Whitlock re-entered the school, and within minutes Mr. Starnes heard the piano.

"Okay, boys and girls, straighten up these lines and no talking. Let's go." He led the students to the auditorium and paired them off, a girl and a boy, pausing to let two walk partway down the center aisle before he let the next pair begin. Rory was the last boy in line. By the time it was his turn to walk down the aisle, there were no more girls left and he walked alone. He smiled as Darrell stepped into the aisle to take his picture.

Mrs. Whitlock offered the usual graduation platitudes about its being a beginning, not an end. The glee club sang a couple of numbers, and the sixth graders sang the school song. Everyone was relieved when the music teacher struck up a rendition of "Pomp and Circumstance" and the students filed out of the auditorium.

Mrs. Whitlock invited parents and other guests to join the students in the cafeteria for punch and cookies, and everyone peeled themselves off the sticky chairs and escaped the steamy auditorium.

"Do you think we should stay?" Ruth asked.

"Of course we should," Lily commented.

Grady's eyes questioned whether that was a good idea, and Darrell remained silent. Lily and Grady knew Ruth'd had words with him before they took their seats.

"Rory'll be expectin' us to be there," Lily continued. "We don't have to stay long."

They followed the crowd outside where several of the fathers and grandfathers stood smoking. "We'll meet you in the cafeteria," Ruth said to Darrell and Grady. Grabbing Lily by the hand, she said, "We need to hit the powder room."

As soon as they left the men, Ruth said, "Lord have mercy. I have never been so humiliated! I don't know what's gotten into that man. I think he's lost his mind."

"Maybe he reacted to that awful word, Ruth. Remember the time he said it and Rory overheard him when he was a little boy?" Ruth nodded. "Grady took Darrell to the woodshed over it. I'll never forget it. I thought Grady would burst a blood vessel."

"Could be," Ruth replied. "I guess he thought it was okay for him to call his son that, but not anyone else."

By the time Ruth and Lily rejoined Darrell and Grady outside, Darrell reported that Mrs. Whitlock had approached him and asked about what had happened in the parking lot. She told him she'd be meeting with Mr. Starnes after the festivities ended and asked if she could call Darrell later.

Rory hadn't said anything about Darrell's hitting his teacher, but that evening Ruth overheard him replaying the scene aloud in his room.

"So, Mr. Starnes, you think it's fine for kids to call each other faggot? How'd you like it if I called you a faggot? Are you a faggot, Mr. Starnes? Let's see how tough you are. Come on, faggot, defend yourself."

Ruth thought Rory sounded deranged. Then she heard him imitate the teacher.

"You're such a big, brave guy. I guess only you can call your kid a faggot. I heard about you, Mr. Wilson. No wonder your son thinks you hate him. I've heard that you pick on him all the time. Are you a wife beater too, or do you just pick on defenseless kids? Is that the best you have to offer? Your punch feels like fairy dust. Come on, Mr. Wilson, you can do better than that."

Ruth was stunned. She'd wondered if Rory remembered his father saying that. Now, she had an answer. She listened for a few more minutes and finally knocked on the door.

As Rory opened the door, Ruth smelled something burning. She looked quickly around the room. "What's that smell?"

He pointed to the metal wastebasket and Ruth saw it was filled with charred paper.

"What in the world?"

"I burned the graduation program and some other school papers."

"Are you crazy? You could have set the house on fire. What's the matter with you? If you didn't want that stuff, you could have torn it up. Why'd you have to burn it?"

"I just felt like it. I'm glad to be outta that place. I'd like to burn the whole school down with Starnes and some of those rotten kids in it. That'd teach them a lesson."

"Rory, what kind of talk is that? If I ever catch you doin' this again, I'm goin' to give you a whippin' you'll not soon forget. Do you hear me? Well, what do you have to say for yourself, young man?"

Rory stood and glared silently at his mother.

Chapter Twelve

Rory's mood improved after school got out. He began to act more like himself. To everyone's relief, Darrell had apologized to Mr. Starnes in Mrs. Whitlock's office the day after the graduation, and they'd shaken hands. Mrs. Whitlock had told Darrell that Mr. Starnes was only a second-year teacher and that she'd work with him about his responsibility to enforce the anti-bullying policies. She had persuaded Darrell not to take the matter any higher, and Mr. Starnes had agreed not to press charges.

During the summer Ashley and Rory spent hours rehashing Darrell's assault on Mr. Starnes.

One day Rory observed, "I don't get it. Daddy picks on me worse than anybody, but he went berserk when he heard somebody else do it. He hasn't said anything about me letting Matthew call me names. It's gotten so I almost don't hear Matthew anymore. Sometimes I wonder if faggot should have been my middle name. Rory Calhoun Faggot Wilson, or maybe Rory Faggot Calhoun Wilson. Which sounds better?"

"Not funny," Ashley answered.

Summer was Rory's favorite time of year even though it was short in Craggy Grove. The growing season lasted only from early May to mid-October. The tradeoff was delightfully cool mountain nights when other parts of Tennessee sweltered.

He devoted several hours each day to his garden, raising vegetables that outshone many professional farmers' crops. On Saturday mornings he took some of them to the local farmer's market to sell. The rest went into the Wilson larders, Ruth's and Lily's.

He had a bumper crop of peppers and tomatoes that summer

and with the money he made at the market, he bought an industrial grade telescope. He and Ashley dissected every plant they could get their hands on, and with special approval from the Craggy Grove librarian, they borrowed botany books from the university through inter-library loan.

Rory came alive in his garden. His intuitive understanding of plants produced lush flowers, and local cooks thronged to his stand to buy produce they knew would enhance their recipes.

"I don't know how you do it," Ruth had said to him many times. She tried to figure out what he did to get such spectacular blossoms.

"I just love 'em," he replied. "It's like having pets that grow in the ground. They know I'm waiting for 'em, so they come up happy."

He'd heard there was a Future Farmers of America club in his new school, and he planned to join it. At least there was one thing to look forward to in junior high school.

A few weeks into the summer, a woman approached Rory as he worked his garden. "Are these your mama's flowers?" she asked. "They're awful pretty. I wish mine would grow like that."

"They're mine, ma'am. I grew 'em from seed. My mama says I've got green thumbs," and he held up his hands.

"Land sakes, child. Your mama's right. I'm Mrs. Pruitt, president of the Johnson County Garden Club."

"I'm Rory Wilson. I'm mighty pleased to meet you, ma'am."

Mrs. Pruitt pulled a camera out of her purse. "May I take some photographs of your lovely flowers?"

"Yes, ma'am. I don't mind."

As Mrs. Pruitt got into her car she called to him, "Have a lovely day and thank you."

"Who's that?" Ruth asked as she came down the front steps.

"She just drove up. She's from the garden club."

"You're becoming a tourist attraction, Rory. Maybe you should think of charging people to look at your garden."

"Aw, Mama, I like having people enjoy my flowers. I wouldn't take money from 'em."

Ruth tousled Rory's hair and smiled at him. He was such a delight to have around during the summer, very different from the moody boy who shut himself in his room when school was in session. If he was the target of school bullies, that would explain why he was sullen and depressed much of the time during the school year. She'd tried to talk to him about it a couple of times, but he let her know that door was closed to her.

She worried about what would happen to him in junior high school. Her recollection of her own experience in junior high school could be summed up in one word, meanness. Teachers had mistaken her fear of speaking out in classes as shyness. The truth was she had been terrified of being harassed by the other kids. Ruth had been chubby as a young teen and stuttered when she had to speak in class. The scars of those awful years remained.

In early July, Jane called with surprising news. "Congratulations to Rory. That's a great article in *The Mountaineer*."

"What article?"

"The one about his flowers. The photos are great."

"I have no idea what you're talkin' about, Jane."

"You're kidding. If you've got a minute, I'll bring it over."

"Sure, come on."

Ruth was stunned to see a photo essay about "Local Boy with Green Thumbs" in their hometown paper. There were photos of Rory's dahlias, including one beautiful close-up that looked like a bee's-eye view. Another photo featured his morning glories and purple clematis which he had trained to cover a trellis. Mrs. Pruitt, the garden club president, was quoted praising Rory's amazing horticultural talent. There was even a quote from Rory about how much he loves gardening and his enjoyment at being able to share the beauty with neighbors and others in town.

"Rory never said a word to me about this," she said. "I wonder why. I'll have to get some copies of the paper."

Ruth drove to the Food Lion and bought three copies of *The Mountaineer*. On her way home, she stopped at the farmer's market. She parked her car on the grassless dusty patch that passed for a parking lot and walked over to Rory's stand.

"Are you the local boy with the green thumbs I read about in today's paper? Can I get your autograph?"

Rory's face was a question mark.

Ruth opened the paper and held up the two-page spread with the article and photos. Rory's eyes opened wide. "How'd that get in there? Let me see that."

"Were you planning to surprise us?"

"Mama, I promise I didn't know anything about it. Look, they even have me talking. I bet that Mrs. Pruitt had something to do with this. She's in the article, and she took pictures of my flowers that day she came by."

"But how did they get a quote from you for the story?"

"Last week some guy stopped to look at the flowers. He asked me a bunch of questions. He must have been a reporter 'cause what I said to him is in here. Can they put your words in the paper without askin' you?"

"Yes, I believe they can. This is exciting. Nobody in our family's ever been in a story in the newspaper."

"They mention our street in the story. I guess more folks will come by now," Rory said.

"Maybe you should put up a lemonade and sweet tea stand and sell drinks to the tourists. You could sell your produce, too, right in front of the house." Ruth left a copy of the paper with Rory.

She drove to her in-laws' farm and found Lily in the garden. "This is a nice surprise," she said. "What brings you to this part of the world?"

"I brought you something. Your grandson is famous," Ruth crowed and held up the open newspaper.

Lily took off her gardening gloves and reached for the paper. "Well, I'll be," she said. "Will you look at this!" She walked toward the house with Ruth in tow. "Grady," she called. "Wait 'til you see what Ruth brought."

Grady met them at the kitchen door. "Hey, Ruth. What's all the fuss about?"

"Our family's in the newspaper!" Lily proclaimed.

"Oh Lord, what did Darrell do now?"

"Grady, hush. It's not about Darrell. It's about Rory."

She handed Grady the paper, and he put on his reading glasses.

As he perused the story, he stopped often to read something aloud to them. When he finished, a mile-wide grin forced his eyes nearly shut. "That boy's something, ain't he?"

Lily peppered Ruth with questions. "How'd you get this in the paper?"

Ruth told them about Mrs. Pruitt's visit to look at Rory's garden and how she and Rory knew nothing about the story until Jane called her. She told them about her idea to sell drinks in front of their home to folks who come by to see the flowers.

"Be sure 'n let us know when he does it so we can come and buy some sweet tea. This could be the start of something, Ruth. He might open a restaurant one day or a flower shop."

"I could see him selling flowers, but that boy can't even boil water," Ruth replied.

"I'll have to pick up the paper when I go to town this afternoon. I want to show it to the boys in the barber shop." If pride was gold, Grady had just hit the mother lode.

As the day wore on, several people came to Rory's stand to buy his produce, and many commented on the article. He was uncomfortable with the attention and looked forward to three o'clock when his mother would pick him up. In Rory's experience, attention wasn't usually positive, so he'd developed a habit of shying away from being noticed.

On the way home Rory said, "Mama, lots of folks saw the story and came over to talk about it. They bought all my stuff." He held out a wad of bills. "Look what I made."

"That's wonderful, son. Maybe I'll let you put gas in the car, since you're so rich."

"I will if you need me to, Mama."

"I'm kidding, Rory. You keep your money."

Ashley was sitting on the front steps when Ruth pulled into the driveway. "See, you've got a fan waiting for you already," she kidded him.

Rory hopped out of the car. "How long you been waitin'?"

"Not long. About 15 minutes, maybe. Two cars came by and stopped to look at your flowers. I bet they saw the story. Maybe they'll wanna make a movie about you."

"Aw, it's not a big deal."

"Here, my mama picked these papers up in town. She thought you might want some extras. You should bring one to school when we go back. When the teachers ask us to tell about what we did on our summer vacation, you can show them this."

The mention of school cast a pall over the conversation. Rory associated school with misery. He wished it would be different in junior high school with some new kids. There'd be four seventh grades, and he hoped he and Ashley wouldn't be separated. She'd always protected him from bullies, except in the boy's bathroom. Rory had never told Ashley or his mother about twirlies, how the boys held his head in the toilet and then flushed it, a popular prank among sixth grade boys.

As they talked, Rory's father parked in the driveway.

"Are you gonna show your daddy?" Ashley asked.

"Hey, Daddy," Rory called, but his father either didn't hear him or chose to ignore the greeting.

"Guess not," he answered.

Everyone was excited about Rory's story in the paper, but a weight hung over Ruth as she thought about telling Darrell. The only way she maintained a semblance of peace these days was to avoid discussing Rory with him. If she'd have known how things would turn out between them, she wouldn't have kept trying to get pregnant. It was painful to watch Darrell turn from a loving father to a hateful one.

Lately, he had started drinking beer every night, and Ruth was sure he was smoking at least a pack a day. He used to have a beer with his supper and maybe one or two on a weekend while he watched baseball, but now he consumed a six-pack in an evening and fell asleep in his chair until Ruth roused him and told him to come to bed. If he was intent on killing himself, she thought, there were quicker ways.

"How was your day?" Darrell asked and reached into the fridge for a beer.

"Not bad. How 'bout yours?" she responded with little enthusiasm.

"What's for supper?"

"Fried catfish, mashed potatoes and Wilson home-grown green beans, courtesy of Rory's garden."

"Good, I'm starved."

Ruth turned off the flame under the boiling potatoes and wiped her hands on her apron.

Darrell had already parked in front of the TV to catch the evening news out of Johnson City. She picked up the paper and opened it to the story.

"You might find this interesting," she said as she walked over to his chair and held up the two-page spread.

He took the paper from her. "That's our house. Who put this in here?"

"A woman from the garden club stopped to admire Rory's flowers a couple of weeks ago. She was mighty impressed with him. We think she did it."

"Pretty nervy of her to have them do a story about our son without consulting us first, don't you think?"

"Is that all you can say about it? Aren't you proud of Rory's accomplishment?"

"I'd rather be reading about him making a winning touchdown or slammin' a home run, if you want to know the truth. I'll be the laughing stock of the town after this."

"Lord have mercy, Darrell. Is there anything Rory can do that doesn't cast a shadow over your manliness?"

He pointed to the front of the house. "Shh, they'll hear you." He tried to keep his voice under control but escalating fury cranked up the volume of Ruth's voice.

"I've had about enough of this," she shouted.

"You don't understand how men are, Ruth."

Ruth glared at him and tore off her apron. She went back into the kitchen and picked up her purse and car keys. When she opened the front door, Darrell called, "Where are you going? Aren't you fixing supper?"

"Rory and I are eating out. Fix your own damn supper."

Rory and Ashley jumped up at the tone of her voice and her language.

"Rory, you and I are going out for supper. Ashley, I expect your mama's about ready with yours."

"Yes ma'am. See ya," Ashley said and started down the street. She flashed Rory a sympathetic look as she turned to see Ruth's car backing out of the driveway.

Ruth's hands were shaking. "Are you okay, Mama?"

"I'm fine, son."

He knew she wasn't but let it drop.

"Feel like pizza?" she asked a few minutes later.

"Sure."

Ruth reached over and patted Rory's blond hair. By the time they got to the Pizza Oven, she took the last parking space. She'd calmed some during the 20-minute drive; her hands weren't shaking as much.

The Craggy Grove Little League baseball team was having a post-game celebration, which explained the full parking lot. Rory knew most of the boys seated at the long table in the back room and was happy they hadn't seen him come in with his mother. He spotted a few of them heading for the bathroom and turned his head to avoid eye contact.

Ruth ordered a medium pizza with sausage and onions and two Cokes.

Rory was relieved when four boys shoved their way out of the rest room and returned to the back of the dining room. He didn't think they'd bother him with so many parents around, but you never knew. He went to wash his hands.

Ruth returned from the women's rest room before Rory got back. She was reading the *Second Hand News*.

"Whatcha lookin' for?" he asked.

For the second time that day, she shocked him. "A new husband."

Rory smiled, more from embarrassment than anything.

"I'm sorry, son. You know I don't really mean that."

"I know," he answered, but in his heart he believed that might not be such a bad idea.

When Ruth and Rory returned home, she found a sink full of dirty dishes and Darrell lying in bed, watching a ball game. She turned the

TV off. When Darrell reached for the remote, Ruth stepped in front of him.

"We need to talk about our future," she began. "If you think your baseball game is more important than that, go ahead and turn it on."

He didn't move.

Usually, Darrell was the aggressor in their arguments and she'd wait until he'd finished shouting before saying anything. Not this time. She launched into a tirade that lasted at least five minutes and when she finished, Darrell sat there in shock. Her last sentence was the one that shook him: "If you're not prepared to start acting like a loving father to our son and quit bullying him, you can pack your stuff and find someplace else to live."

Darrell made a feeble attempt to justify his disappointment with Rory, but she refused to give an inch. "Whether he's manly enough to suit you or not, he's our son and he's entitled to a loving home. I will not stand for you abusing him and have him end up on a psychiatrist's couch for the rest of his life. Whatever he may be, he's ours, and you need to figure out how to make your peace with it."

As usual, Rory heard their fight through the thin wall that separated his room from theirs. His stomach churned each time he heard further evidence that he was the reason for their growing animosity toward each other. He always felt he needed to reach down deep to find ways to pacify his father.

After supper the next night, he sat with Darrell in the living room and suffered through a 13-inning baseball game, trying not to yawn. He was determined to make his father like him again. It would be good to have peace in the Wilson household, for however long it might last.

Chapter Thirteen

The best thing Rory could say about junior high school was that it only lasted three years. Also, he liked the fact that each subject was taught by a special teacher. He learned more about science in his first month in seventh grade than he had in all of elementary school. Miss Ebsen had been a real scientist before she became a teacher, and her specialty was botany. Difficult as Rory's days were, he was determined to survive until fourth period when Miss Ebsen guided him into the fascinating world of plant biology.

Rory went into her classroom one day during lunch when she was alone. He stood patiently while Miss Ebsen finished writing. When she looked up, he began, "If you're not too busy, ma'am, I wanted to show you something," and he reached into his pocket and withdrew the folded newspaper story about his dahlias.

"Oh, yes, I remember this story from last summer. This is quite an honor, Rory. How about telling the class about your gardening? I'm sure they'd like to know they have a celebrity in their midst."

Rory blushed. "Oh no, ma'am. I just thought you might like to see the article. I don't want to talk to anybody else about it."

"Why not? You should be proud of this. I bet your folks were tickled when they saw it." Her statement was more of a question, but Rory declined to answer it.

"A lot of the kids make fun of me because I like flowers," he volunteered. "I don't want to get them started." He was being as honest about the situation as he could without going into painful details.

"I see. Well, I certainly wouldn't want to cause problems for you. May I make a copy of this? I have a friend who teaches botany at the university, and I'm sure he'd like to see it."

"Yes, ma'am. That's fine."

A week later, as Rory gathered his books to leave the science room, Miss Ebsen asked him to remain. She waited until all of the other students were out of earshot and said, "Remember the friend I mentioned to you who teaches botany at the university?"

"Yes ma'am."

"I showed him the article, and he said he'd like to meet you. I also told him you're my best science student." Rory put his head down, not wanting her to see his red face.

"I could drive you over to the university after school one day if your parents say it's all right."

"I'll ask them tonight. Can I tell you tomorrow?"

"Sure. Do I need to give you a late pass?"

"No ma'am. This is my lunch period."

"Oh, my goodness. Hurry along, now."

Rory tripped along to his locker and retrieved his lunch. As he walked to the lunchroom, he pulled pieces of sandwich out of the bag and ate while he thought about Miss Ebsen's offer. Imagine, he mused. A professor wants to meet me. I never met a professor before. They're important people. I should wear a coat and tie when we go.

"Guess what, Mama," Rory called as he opened the kitchen door later that afternoon.

"You seem awfully excited about somethin'. What's goin' on?"

He related the details of his conversation with Miss Ebsen about the article and her offer to take him to meet her friend at the university.

"She said to ask you if I can go." He waited while Ruth dried her hands on her apron and turned off the water at the sink where she was peeling potatoes.

"Well, I don't see why not. That's real nice of her. When would you go?"

"She didn't say. She wanted me to get permission first."

"Other than your Future Farmers club meetin' and that dentist appointment next Tuesday, any day would be fine. Just let me know ahead of time so I don't plan an early supper."

Rory spent the next hour rooting through old papers in his room. He thought it would be a good idea to bring the science project he and Ashley had done in elementary school and the letter from one of the judges. He cut a path through the mountain of papers strewn all over the floor when Ruth called him for supper.

Darrell took his seat at the head of the table, and the three of them joined hands to say grace.

"Rory, your hands are all wet!" his father scolded. "Go dry them off."

When Rory was seated again, Darrell said grace quickly and picked up his fork. He couldn't stand cold food and his face reflected annoyance at the delay.

Suppers in the Wilson house were usually quiet these days. Ruth had long since given up trying to have civil conversation with her husband. Everything seemed to annoy him. If he wasn't picking on Rory for something, he was griping about his job and his boss. The less said when he was around, the better.

Ruth hadn't even considered telling Darrell about Rory's teacher's offer. Each time she made a conscious decision not to tell him something, she knew she was adding to the wall between them.

When Rory's principal called one day and said he wanted to meet with Ruth, she wondered why he didn't ask to see both parents. Maybe he'd heard about that incident at the elementary school graduation and figured Darrell was some kind of nut, she thought.

Mr. Stevens hadn't said it was urgent, and they set an appointment for the following week.

"Do you have any idea why the principal wants to meet with me?" she asked Rory that evening.

"No, I'm not in any trouble."

On the appointed day, Ruth drove to the school.

"Please Mrs. Wilson, come in." He turned to his secretary. "Let Mr. Molinaro know that Mrs. Wilson is here, please."

"I've asked Rory's guidance counselor to join us."

For a few minutes Mr. Stevens and Ruth chatted about the weather, an old standby topic in their mountain town. When Mr. Molinaro arrived, the principal made introductions and got up and closed the door. Ruth began to sweat.

"Rory's a real nice kid and a good student. All of his teachers say he's a fine boy. He's polite and well-mannered and is very coopera-tive," Mr. Stevens began. Mr. Molinaro nodded agreement. "So, I'm sure you're wondering why we've asked you to come in."

"Well, yes, I've been curious," Ruth answered trying to look at both men, which was difficult since they sat on either side of her at a long, polished wood table.

Mr. Molinaro began. "Has Rory said anything to you about other kids picking on him in school?"

Oh no, Ruth thought. That's starting again. She felt nervous as she answered. "He hasn't said anything specific, but to be honest, I'm aware that he doesn't have many friends. It worries me, but there doesn't seem to be anything I can do about it." She tore at a tissue she'd retrieved from her purse.

The men looked at each other. The guidance counselor contin-ued, "Rory's science teacher picked this note up after class last week and brought it to me. She's concerned for his safety." He handed Ruth a wrinkled paper and she read, "I'll be waiting for you after school you faggit. I hope your hungry cause I've got something for you to eat." She turned the paper over and saw Rory's name written on the reverse side. She dropped her head.

"Miss Ebsen went out front that day and made sure Rory got on the school bus without any problem. She did the same thing the next day."

"We think we know which student wrote this, but we can't be sure. I've asked teachers to give me papers so I can compare handwriting. Before I talk to the boy, I wanted to investigate to see if this is a seri-ous case of bullying or an isolated instance. I don't even know if Rory received this note. He hasn't said anything?" Mr. Stevens inquired.

"No, nothing."

He continued, "I've talked with Rory's teachers and it turns out Miss Ebsen isn't the only one who's noticed Rory isn't popular with the other boys."

"There's nothing wrong with not being popular," Ruth replied and smoothed imaginary wrinkles in her skirt. "Lots of kids aren't popu-lar. Some of them choose not to associate with students who behave like this," she said waving the note. "I've always taught Rory to stay away from troublemakers."

Mr. Molinaro cut in, "We're not saying anything's wrong with Rory, Mrs. Wilson. We're trying to head off potential problems if we can." His tone was softer and more sympathetic than the principal's.

"I'm grateful for that. I know y'all have a tough job dealing with kids this age. I remember when I was in junior high. I'm sure I wasn't pleasant to be around most times with raging hormones and all."

They smiled.

"Is there any reason you can think of why Rory wouldn't get along with the other students? He seems like a nice kid."

Ruth looked at Mr. Molinaro for a few seconds before answering. "Rory's a very sensitive child. He always has been." She hesitated.

She continued haltingly and looked down at the table while she put the tissue scraps back into her purse. There was nothing left to shred. "This isn't the first time I've run into this problem, and I suspect it won't be the last. Rory is just different in a lot of ways. I wish I could explain it better, but I can't."

Mr. Stevens offered a suggestion. "Rory's taller than almost all the boys in his grade. Maybe you could convince him to go out for basketball. It doesn't take a lot of skill to make our team." He smiled, and Ruth looked at him.

Can this man be so ignorant, she wondered. Sure, we'll put Rory on a basketball court so he can make a fool of himself. How'd someone so stupid get to be a principal? The idea was so ludicrous, Ruth didn't even respond.

"What will you do if you identify the student who wrote the note?" she asked.

"Oh, we'll take appropriate action, you can be sure," the principal answered.

"I wish you would drop it," Ruth said, surprised at her own quick reply. "Nothing has happened so far. Maybe it was just an idle threat. Whoever this boy is, he'll assume Rory squealed on him, and that could make it worse." She recalled many times when Rory urged her not to interfere when he'd been beaten up or harassed, saying it would make the tormentors retaliate.

Mr. Stevens countered, "I understand your concern, Mrs. Wilson, and I will take your suggestion into account, but we can't have the law of the jungle operating in our school. We have a zero tolerance policy regarding bullying here. Let me think about it."

"Will you let me know what you decide? We don't even know if Rory is aware of this note. Maybe the kid dropped it before he could give it to him."

"That's true. Let me sleep on it."

Ruth stood to leave, and Mr. Stevens took her hand. "We want Rory to have a good educational experience in our school. We take that responsibility very seriously, and we want you to know that."

Ruth muttered to herself as she left the building, "This guy should be selling detergent on TV. What a bullcrap artist."

The thought that crowded out all others as Ruth crossed the school parking lot was how desperately she wished she could home school Rory. She'd always opposed home schooling, but maybe she needed to reconsider it. She wasn't confident that she could give Rory a quality education, but at least she could protect him. She knew other mothers who home schooled their kids, and some of them only had a high school education and couldn't even speak proper English. The state didn't seem particular about that. Rory is a smart boy. He can probably learn anywhere, she thought. Darrell would be the biggest obstacle, though. She'd have to explain why she wanted to do it and that would surely be a call to arms.

After supper that night Ruth waited until Darrell was on his fourth beer in front of the TV. She knew it would be a matter of minutes before he nodded off. She stood in the doorway of Rory's room.

"Come take a walk with me."

Her tone told him this was not a suggestion, so Rory got up from his computer and followed her to the kitchen door.

Ruth reached for Rory's hand as they walked, and he pulled away.

"What's the matter? You too big to hold your Mama's hand?"

"Mama, I've got enough problems. I don't need kids seeing me holding my mother's hand."

"What sort of problems? Are kids pickin' on you again?"

Rory realized he'd put his foot in his mouth. "Nothin' I can't handle. You don't need to worry about it."

"Oh, I'm not so sure about that. I met with Mr. Stevens and Mr. Molinaro today."

Rory stopped dead in his tracks. "What about?" he barked.

"Why'd you go see them?"

"Cool it, Rory. I didn't request the meeting. They did. I told you Mr. Stevens called me last week."

"Oh yeah, I forgot. So what did they want?"

Ruth told Rory about the note they showed her. She watched his face carefully. It seemed obvious to her he had seen the note.

"It's no big deal. Nothing happened."

"Probably because your science teacher watched you get on the bus for two days. What if she hadn't done that? It makes me sick to think what that boy might have done to you."

"Nothin would have happened. You don't understand those kids, Mama. They talk trash all the time. It's just talk. I ignore it. If you think that was bad, you should see what they write in emails."

Oh, no, Rory thought. Now I've got two feet in my mouth.

"I'm going to get to the bottom of this, Rory. I want to see what they're writing. I've heard about cyber bullying. Some kids have even killed themselves over it. I'll put a stop to this, so help me."

"No way."

"What do you mean, 'no way'?"

"Just what I said. You're not going to snoop in my email. It's private."

"You're the one who brought it up, and I'm your mother. I have a right."

"Oh no, you don't. I'm not a little kid, Mama. I'm almost thirteen, and I have a right to my privacy." He looked down at her, another reminder that he was no longer her baby.

"Do you know who's saying nasty things on the Internet?"

"It's a few kids. They get their kicks out of writing dirty stuff. They're sickos, Mama. The best thing is to ignore them. They'll get tired of it. That's what my health teacher said. She told us some kids do it to make themselves feel important. It makes them feel cool if they can put somebody else down. They're jerks."

"Doesn't it bother you?"

"Nah, I usually don't even read it all. I delete it."

Fat chance of that, Ruth thought, though she wished with all her heart it was so. She used email occasionally but resolved to learn more about it. The first thing she wanted to know was whether there was a way she could get into Rory's email account. She'd ask Jane. Jane was pretty good with computer stuff. She monitored what Ashley looked at.

"So, what'd you tell Stevens? Is he gonna make trouble for me?"

"He's investigating it. He said when he finds out who wrote the note, he'll take 'appropriate action.' Those were his words."

"You have to tell him not to do anything, Mama. It'll just make things worse."

"I did tell him to leave it alone, but I'm not sure he'll listen to me."

"You did? Thanks. I hope he doesn't make a big stink out of it."

They walked a few minutes in silence, each weighing the words of the past 10 minutes.

"I just wish there was something I could do to help, Rory. It kills me to see people being hateful to you. Any mother would feel like I do, but I understand about not mixing in. Really, I do. Why do these kids pick on you?"

"Some kids are just mean, I guess," was all he said.

Chapter Fourteen

The planets must have aligned right. There had not been a single argument in the Wilson house for an entire week after Ruth's meeting with the principal. Darrell was especially attentive and even took Ruth and Rory out to the local Dairy Maid for ice cream one night. Ruth shared news while they sat on the bench behind the dairy bar and licked their swirl cones.

"I ran into Lurleen Thomas in the Food Lion today."

"Is she the one who lives down the street in the gray house?"

"Yeah, that's her. She's got red hair and bushy eyebrows. They're goin' to Elizabethton next week. Their landlord sold the house. They're movin' into a one-bedroom apartment. Jane thinks they're gonna live in one of those Section 8 complexes."

"What's Section 8, Mama?"

"It's for folks on welfare."

Rory knew about welfare. Some of the kids in his school were from welfare families, and they got picked on almost as much as he did. He'd felt sorry for them until some of them started picking on him too. He had thought they might not pick on others, knowing how rotten they felt when it happened to them, but it didn't work that way.

A couple of weeks later, as Darrell drove home from work, he spotted a moving van in front of the vacant house. "Looks like the new owners are moving into the Johnson's house," he announced as he entered the kitchen door.

Darrell twisted the cap off his beer. "What's for supper? I'm starved. It was so crazy at work today I never got a chance to eat lunch." He waved his bag lunch at Ruth.

Ruth put her finger to her lips. "Shh, it's a surprise. Wait a minute." He turned to leave and Ruth grabbed him by the shoulder. "Stay here," she urged.

"Rory, your daddy's home."

Darrell looked at her curiously. "What's goin' on?"

Before Ruth could answer, Rory entered the kitchen carrying a chocolate cake with 40 candles blazing away.

"Surprise," they called in unison. Rory put the cake on the table, and he and Ruth sang Happy Birthday.

"Blow out the candles, Daddy. Don't forget to make a wish."

"But my birthday's not for another week. Did y'all forget the date?"

"If we'd done it on the right day, you wouldn't have been surprised, would you?"

"Well, I guess not." Darrell turned to Ruth and kissed her. "Thanks, honey."

"Don't thank me. Rory made the cake and decorated it too."

Ruth removed the candles and Darrell took a closer look at the cake. "That's ole Dale's car, number 3. You remembered, son. That's real nice. Thank you."

Rory's smile spread from ear to ear. He felt proud that he'd done something his father liked.

"Let me get my camera."

Darrell returned in a minute. "You two stand by the cake."

"Okay, and then let me take one of the two of you," Ruth said. She couldn't recall the last time her husband and son posed together.

"Get closer. Look like you know each other." Darrell put his arm around Rory's shoulders and pulled him close. Rory still had the biggest smile on his face Ruth had seen in a long time. "Wait, don't move. Let me get another one," she directed.

Darrell was genuinely surprised and pleased to be on the receiving end of an early birthday cake. He'd been brooding lately about turning 40, but with the event only a week away, it didn't seem nearly so bad now.

"Let's eat cake," he said, reaching into a drawer for a knife.

"Before supper?" Ruth asked.

"Sure. It's not every day I turn 40 minus one week. I say we eat dessert first tonight. Rory?"

"Sounds good to me, Daddy."

"Oh, why not? I'm outvoted by the men, I see." Ruth took out three cake plates and they all sat down for chocolate cake. "Wait a minute." She hopped up and took out an unopened brick of cherry vanilla ice cream. "Okay, now we're ready." She scooped ice cream while Darrell cut his cake.

Ruth dipped two generous scoops of ice cream and placed them next to a hefty slab of chocolate cake on Darrell's plate.

"This is delicious, Rory. I didn't know you could bake."

"I learned how in school. The teacher said men had to know how to cook if they wanted to eat. I figured I wouldn't starve if I could bake a cake."

"He did it pretty much by himself. About all I did was wash the dishes and mop the floor after he was done throwin' flour all around the kitchen," Ruth said.

Chapter Fifteen

Pleasant respites like Darrell's surprise party became increasingly rare in the Wilson home as days and weeks passed. Strained silence ruled over the supper table most nights, interrupted from time to time by Darrell's criticism of Rory and Ruth, and the meal usually ended with Darrell's stalking out and driving around until he cooled down. Ruth was at her wit's end to explain Darrell's behavior and had begun to flirt with the idea of making some drastic changes.

When she was being completely honest with herself, she had to admit the love she once felt for her husband had been replaced by a sense of duty. Even that was difficult to justify some days. During infrequent phone conversations with her younger sister Rebecca, Ruth had hinted that the storm clouds were gathering. Who was she really preparing for imminent change, she wondered. Even pleasant memories like Darrell's fortieth birthday celebration couldn't erase the pain of living with his irascible moods and constant abuse of their son.

***

During the year that passed since the birthday party, Rory tried but couldn't forget the night of his parents' final argument. He relived the trauma of that miserable day in sweat-soaked dreams.

He'd been in school less than a week when he got off the school bus and walked to the side of the house to check his garden. Something caught his attention as he put his book bag on the ground. There on the tan vinyl siding, someone had spray painted in bold black letters, A FAGGOT LIVES HERE!

His lunch shot up to his mouth. He bent over and vomited, looked around to see if anyone had seen him, and leaned against a post in the shade of the carport. He didn't know how long he'd been there when he heard, "Hey, Rory, how come you took the bus today?" Ashley walked up the driveway.

"What's wrong? Are you sick?" She rushed to his side as he leaned over and vomited again. "I'll get your mama," she said, but Rory reached over and grabbed her arm.

"No!" he shouted. "She's not home." He pointed to the side of the house.

"Who did this?" Ashley shrieked.

"I don't know. We have to get it off before my daddy comes home. He'll kill me. I hope Mama didn't see it. She's over at Meemaw's and won't be back for an hour or so."

They went into the house to retrieve a bucket and mop and tried to remove the graffiti. It was useless.

"We need paint remover. I'll go home and see if we have some."

Rory sloshed water over the spot where he'd vomited while he waited for Ashley. Exhausted, he slumped down to the ground using a post to support himself. His heart sank when Ashley returned in a few minutes with her mother in tow. "She heard me scrounging around in the basement and made me tell her what I needed paint remover for. I couldn't help it. I'm sorry."

"Good Lord!" Jane exclaimed. "Has your mama seen this?"

"No ma'am. We were trying to get it off before she got home," he said. He pleaded, "Please don't tell her. She'll be so upset."

"I'm sure she will be, but this isn't something you should hide from your folks."

"Mama," Ashley begged, "his daddy will blame it on him. We have to get it off, please, Mama."

"Honey, this is serious." She looked at both of them. "People who do things like this are hateful and sick. They might not stop at words."

"Rory, come on over to the house with Ashley. I'm going to call your mama and warn her before she gets home. She can figure out how to deal with your daddy."

Rory burst into tears and Ashley squatted next to him where he sat with his hands covering his face. A series of thoughts ran through his mind. Why did God have to make me this way? Why can't I be like other boys? What's wrong with me? I wish I was dead.

Rory got up slowly and followed Ashley to her house.

Jane saw vomit on the front of Rory's shirt. "Take your shirt off. Let me toss it in the wash," she ordered.

"Take Rory in the bathroom and give him some mouthwash and a towel. I'm going to call his mother."

For a few minutes Rory sat on the closed toilet seat. Lord, he prayed, please take me now. It'll be better for everyone if I die before Mama and Daddy get home. If I'm not around, maybe they'll quit fighting. I'm ruining everybody's life. If you can't change me, just let me die, please.

He opened the medicine cabinet and saw only a bottle of aspirin and some laxatives, neither of which would do the job. He tugged on the cabinet door beneath the sink and found a box of wastebasket size trash bags. He sat on the floor with his back propped against the tub and removed one bag from the box. He put it over his head and pulled the tie close around his neck. His head began to sweat and the bag closed in on his face each time he inhaled. He took deep breaths until he felt light-headed. He experienced a strange calm as he thought of Ashley, the only true friend he had. She would find him and tell his parents what had happened. He should have said goodbye to her. He owed her that much. It was his last thought before he lost consciousness.

"Rory, oh my God, Mama! Come quick."

Ashley tore the bag off Rory's head and slapped his face repeatedly. "Rory, Rory, wake up!" she yelled. Jane reached the bathroom as Ashley scooped water furiously from the sink and threw it on Rory's face.

"What the hell? ... Oh my Lord!" Jane screamed. Rory started to regain consciousness. Jane and Ashley half dragged, half carried him into the nearest bedroom and hoisted him on the bed.

"Mama, he tried to kill himself," Ashley whispered.

"Rory, look at me," Jane shouted. She held up three fingers. "How many fingers do you see?"

"Three," he responded. He came around quickly, and Jane sat him up. She put her arms around him.

"Rory, we all love you just the way you are. It's okay to be different. You're a good person, honey. Nobody wants you to die. We're going to stay right here with you. Your mama is on her way." She instructed Ashley to get a glass of water.

They sat with Rory while he sipped it. Jane heard a car pull up. "You stay with Rory."

In a few minutes, Ruth entered the bedroom and sat down next to her son. His hair and undershirt were wet, partly from sweating, but more from Ashley's attempt to revive him. She leaned over and put her arms around him.

"It's all right, Rory. Mama's here. I won't let anyone hurt you."

"Daddy's goin' to be so mad at me," he said.

"You didn't do anything wrong, son. I'll handle your daddy. Don't you worry."

But Rory did worry, all the way down the block as they rode to their house.

Darrell's car was in the driveway, so Ruth knew he'd seen the words on the side of the house. She didn't want to leave Rory alone in the car, but she needed to talk to Darrell alone, so she turned the car around and drove back to Jane's house. Jane came out to meet them.

"Can I leave Rory here for a few minutes?"

"Sure, I'll stay with him. Call when you're ready and I'll walk him home."

"You're an angel, Jane."

Ruth tore at her cuticles until she drew blood. Her heart pounded, and she felt slightly dizzy as she parked the car and walked to the kitchen door.

After one of the most difficult conversations ever between Ruth and Darrell, Ruth called her friend to bring Rory home. Jane brought Rory in the front door so he wouldn't see the graffiti again. "Are you okay?" she asked Ruth. She'd never seen her friend so distraught.

"Darrell left. We're getting a divorce."

Ruth poured out the details and Rory was stunned as he listened. Ruth's description was so vivid that Rory almost felt he'd witnessed the confrontation between his parents. Over the years, he'd made it part of his own memory. Each time he recalled the conversation, he felt his mother's anguish.

As Ruth related it, when she got home, she had opened the door and found Darrell sitting at the kitchen table with three beer bottles in front of him. Two were empty and the third was half full. He wasn't drunk yet, but he was on his way. Ignoring her rule, he'd held a lit cigarette in one hand. Darrell always sweated profusely when he drank, and despite the 68-degree, air conditioned temperature, there were beads of perspiration on his forehead and wide wet circles under his armpits. His tie was on the table and he'd looked like he was spoiling for a fight.

"I suppose you saw it," she said as she put her purse down on the counter.

"How could I miss it? The whole freakin' world can see it; it's big enough."

He looked behind her.

"Where's the little pansy?"

"Darrell, stop it. He's over at Jane's. I didn't want you to jump on him. He's upset enough."

"That's right, take his part. You always stick up for him. How does it feel to have the whole town know your son's queer? Are you proud of him?"

Ruth lowered her voice and spoke deliberately. "Don't say another word about our son," she said. "He was so worried about what you'd do that he tried to kill himself over at Jane's this afternoon."

"That's one way to get your sympathy, I guess," he replied.

Ruth clenched her jaws as she spoke. "Ashley found him unconscious with a plastic bag over his head in their bathroom. If she'd waited a couple more minutes, he'd have been dead." She looked for a glimmer of compassion, but saw none.

The dam broke.

"You are the most hateful person I've ever known, Darrell. Any love I might have felt for you once is dead. I've worried that one day I would have to choose between my son and my husband. Today is that day, Lord help me, and I choose Rory. He's a good and decent person, something you once were before rottenness ate away at your heart." She stopped briefly to gather her thoughts before delivering the blow that would sever their marriage.

"I want a divorce. Pack your things and get out of here right now. Tomorrow I'm going to see a lawyer and do what I should have done a long time ago." She steadied herself by gripping the back of one of the kitchen chairs.

"Now, calm yourself before you go sayin' things you'll regret," Darrell pleaded as disbelief replaced anger. "You know you don't mean that. We can talk about this, maybe call Pastor Hodges." The suggestion that he was receptive to third-party mediation had worked in the past.

"I mean it, Darrell. I'm through. I won't stand by and watch you drive our son to suicide. I don't know what makes you so hateful, but I won't live with it anymore, and neither will Rory." Her voice was calmer now, increasing Darrell's fear that she was serious.

"How about if I go over to my folks' house for tonight? It'll give you time to cool down, and we can talk tomorrow."

"You can go wherever the hell you like. I'm not going to cool down this time, Darrell. This is the end of the road."

He got up from the table and started toward her, but quickly turned and left the kitchen. For a split second she had feared he might hit her and felt behind her for the knife drawer.

She heard him in the bathroom gathering his things. Within half an hour, he left with a small bag and several slacks and shirts on hangers.

Rory's eyes grew wide as he listened. "Mama, it's all my fault," he said when Ruth finished.

"No, honey, it's not your fault. Your father used to be a decent man, but something's changed him. He's not been a good father to you for a long time, and he's not been a good husband to me. I should have thrown him out a long time ago. We both need to be free of him. This thing tonight," she gestured toward the side of the house, "may turn out to be a blessing."

Ruth got up and went to the refrigerator and retrieved two Diet Cokes and one Mountain Dew. She handed Rory the Mountain Dew. "Here, son. Drink this slowly. It'll help settle your stomach."

After sipping her Diet Coke and hearing Ruth's story, Jane got up. "I really need to go. I have to throw something together for supper or I might be the one getting a divorce," she said. She hugged Ruth and tussled Rory's hair and patted his shoulder. "Remember, I'm just down the street if you need me. I'll see you tomorrow." She let herself out the side door.

"You need to eat something," Ruth said as she reached into the pantry and retrieved a can of Campbell's chicken noodle soup. Just a little something until your stomach calms down?"

Rory nodded his lukewarm assent. Ruth added a can of water and set the pot on the stove. "See if we have any crackers." She pointed to the pantry. "I think there are some saltines in there."

Rory pulled a box of crackers from the shelf and set them on the table. He handed his mother two small bowls and took two spoons from the drawer.

Ruth brought the steaming bowls to the table and sat down. She reached for Rory's hands across the table. Instead of bowing her head, she looked at him as she spoke.

"Lord," she began, "we thank you for this food and hope it helps heal the hurt that the world dumped on us. We ask you for strength to get through these difficult times, and let us always remember that our love for one another will see us through our troubles. In Jesus' name. Amen."

Ruth cried as she started to eat and then put her spoon down.

"Rory, you're all I have now. Please don't ever do that again. I'd die if I lost you." She reached for his hand. "Promise me you will not take your life, son. I couldn't bear it."

Rory's gaze met hers. "I'm sorry. I just felt so awful, Mama. Can you understand?"

Ruth nodded and wiped her eyes. She got up and fetched a tissue from the bathroom and tucked another in her pocket.

Rory blew on a spoonful of soup and for the first time that day, sitting in his mother's kitchen, he felt safe.

Chapter Sixteen

Several months later, after the divorce became final, Ruth was confident she'd made the right decision divorcing Darrell. He'd offered only token resistance and had been surprisingly reasonable in arriving at a financial settlement. The one thing she'd fretted about was the possible loss of Rory's relationship with his grandparents, but she needn't have worried.

The answer to that question came when Lily had called the day after the blowup to say Darrell had spent the night and told them about Ruth's wanting a divorce. Never one to pull her punches, she surprised her daughter-in-law.

"Ruth, you're doin' the right thing for you and Rory. Darrell's our son and of course we love him, but we don't blame you for wanting to end the marriage. I don't know where we went wrong in raising him." She cleared her throat. "But he's not the husband and father we hoped he'd be. Grady and me love you and Rory. I've never been one for sayin' much about it, but we think of you as our daughter. Me and Grady want you to know you're always welcome here. As for Rory, I don't think we could stop lovin' that boy even if he turned out to be an axe murderer. You tell him that for us. Well, you can say it better'n that, but you know what I mean."

Relief overflowed as Ruth replied, "Mama, it's so good of you to call. You know how much I love you and Grady. I'll be sure and tell Rory what you said." She was thankful that at least two good things had come out of marrying Darrell—Rory and her in-laws.

The road leading to and following the divorce was not an easy one for Ruth. No one in her family had ever dissolved a marriage, though she knew a few of them should have. Women in her circle believed that marriage was for keeps, "for better or for worse," as the vows put it. Well, she'd been seeing the worse side of marriage for several years, and it had taken her a long time to face the fact that the man she married was not the same one who got drunk most nights and bullied their son.

Ruth wasn't crazy about going back to work, but the alimony and child support Darrell paid barely covered the mortgage and utilities. She contracted with a university professor to edit a botany textbook.

While she worked on the book, Rory read parts of it and was fascinated. His interest in plants continued and he'd won second place in a science fair. The judges were impressed with his attempt to produce a strain of tobacco that would burn cleaner than the Burley variety popular in that part of Tennessee. They wrote, "This project demonstrates the type of out-of-the-box thinking that reflects maturity beyond this budding scientist's years." Rory's biology teacher sent a copy to Ruth with a letter of congratulations.

Not long after filing the divorce papers, Ruth talked with Jane.

"I'd never have gotten this far if you hadn't stood by me. This is the hardest thing I've ever had to do."

"No, it isn't, Ruth. The hardest thing was watching Darrell treat his son like dirt. I bet if you'd shot him, no jury would have convicted you. Even Darrell's folks said you were right to end the marriage. Now, what more proof could you want?"

"Thanks, I guess I needed to be reminded."

She looked at Jane in a strange way.

"What?" Jane asked.

Ruth smiled. "You'll find this hard to believe coming from me, a dyed-in-the-wool Southern Baptist."

"Oh?"

"I've not told this to another living soul. A couple of days after I made Darrell leave I went to see Preacher Hodges, thinking he'd help me work this out."

Jane's eyebrows raised in surprise.

"Oh, I know what you think, but I needed him to pray on this with me, to be sure the Lord wanted me to take this step. I told him what had happened and how Darrell acted with Rory and all. He's got four sons and a daughter, so I thought he'd see my point about needing to protect Rory."

Jane's expression said a lot and it all began with, "I told you so."

"Do you know what that man had the nerve to say to me?"

Jane waited silently.

"He told me a woman's place is with her husband no matter what. He quoted a bunch of scripture at me, stuff I'd heard all my life in Sunday School. I asked about a mother's duty to protect her child, and he shocked me.

"He said Rory isn't a normal boy. He said I needed to bring him in so he could work with him before he turned into a homosexual. The preacher said he worried Rory was headed that way, and that it's an abomination in the eyes of the Lord."

"What did you say?" Jane asked.

"I got up from my chair and told him I came to him for help and all he did was tell me my child is an abomination. I asked him what kind of preacher he is and where's his Christian love of Rory? I was so mad I could have pulled every hair out of his head.

"He put his hand on my arm but I pulled away from him. I said I needed to find a church where the preacher understands that we're all God's children, and I stormed out of his office."

Jane started to speak, but Ruth went on, "I didn't go to church for two months after that. Finally, I figured I'd show him I was a bigger person than he was, so I took Rory one Sunday. We sat with Lily and Grady. Preacher Hodges looked at me and I thought he was glad to see me. Well, he was glad to see us, all right. Do you know what that hateful man did?"

"What?"

"He started sermonizing about how evil homosexuality is, what a wicked lifestyle it is and how nobody who is homosexual will go to heaven. Anyone could have followed a direct line from Hodges' eyes to Rory. I put my arm around Rory to try to shield him. Thank goodness for Grady. He got up, pulled Lily to her feet and signaled me to follow. We all walked out of the church right in the middle of the preachin' with every single eye on us. I felt Preacher Hodges' eyes borin' holes in our backs."

She sipped her Diet Coke. "That's the last time I'll ever set foot in his church again as long as I live. If I ever find another church, it'll be where people are real Christians."

"What did Grady and Lily say?" Jane asked.

"Grady cussed and mumbled the whole way out of the church. When we got outside, he put his hands on Rory's shoulders and said, 'Son, that's no man of God in there. He's a devil, sure as I'm standin' here. And I only know one way to get the devil's dust off us. Let's wash it off with hotcakes and lots of syrup. What do ya say?' Before Lily could jump in with some remark about his diet, he turned to her. 'Lily, this is still the Lord's day, and the Lord just whispered in my ear that it won't kill me this once to have a stack of blueberry hotcakes with butter and syrup.'"

"Good for Grady," Jane commented. "What a sweetheart."

"So off we went to Ruby's for breakfast. While I was driving, I looked over at Rory and asked how he was doin'. Now, mind you, he'd never said he was gay. I thought maybe he'd say something to me, but he didn't."

"It's possible he still isn't ready, Ruth. Not all gay people know when they're young. I've even heard of some folks who come out in their sixties and seventies after being married for years. If he is, he'll know when it's the right time to tell people."

Not long after the conversation with Jane about the miserable experience in church, Ruth remembered the wrinkled piece of paper in her jewelry box. She went into her bedroom and pulled it out. The ink had faded a bit since she wrote on it years ago, but she could still read the name and phone number.

"Hello, Mary. This is Ruth Wilson. I'm sure you don't remember me. I typed a question on the PFLAG website and you emailed back and said to call. Well, it's taken me longer than I thought, but here I am."

"Ruth, I'm so happy you called. We all do things in our own good time and that's fine. How can I help you?"

Mary's voice was reassuring and Ruth told her about Rory's suicide attempt, the divorce, and their minister's reaction. Mary listened patiently and when Ruth had run out of words, she responded.

"Ruth, I know exactly how you're feeling. I went through a similar situation when my son Teddy came out. That's what we call it when they tell someone they're gay."

"I'm not even sure Rory is gay. He's never said he is."

"I know it's not been easy for you. Many parents have difficulty accepting this about their sons or daughters. You're not alone."

"I don't know anyone who has a gay child," Ruth replied.

"Well, now you do," Mary reassured her. "There are lots of us. That's why PFLAG was started, to give support to gay and lesbian youngsters. Sometimes I think it's more for the parents. Some of the kids have an easier time than we do."

Mary described how PFLAG members help each other. "We have a meeting coming up in two weeks that might interest you. A Methodist minister is speaking. His topic is 'There are No Abominations, Just Kids Who Need Our Love.'"

That struck an instant chord with Ruth. "I'd like to come to the meeting, Mary. I think I'm ready to take this step."

"Wonderful. You'll meet a lot of nice folks. Give me your email address and I'll send you directions. Want to meet for a cup of coffee before the meeting? I can take you and introduce you around."

"Yes, that would be great."

As they were about to hang up, Mary said, "Oh, one more thing, Ruth. Before my first meeting I must have changed my mind a hundred times, not sure if I had the nerve to go. I've been attending PFLAG meetings for over ten years now, and they've helped me have the kind of loving relationship with my son that we both want and need."

Chapter Seventeen

A few weeks into the new term, the eighth grade boys were changing in the locker room when Lyle Profitt slammed Rory's gym locker shut as he lumbered by.

"Quit it, Lyle."

"And who's gonna make me?"

Lyle strutted back to confront Rory. He was not as tall as Rory, but outweighed him by at least 20 pounds. His nose was crooked, and he had a large gap between his oversized front teeth. He snarled as he spoke.

Rory thought twice before answering the challenge. But then his father's mocking face flashed through his mind, and he shoved the bench that separated them, hitting Lyle in the shins.

"You freakin' faggot!" Lyle reached across the bench with a right hook and Rory ducked.

Rory took advantage of his height and longer reach and landed a tentative punch on the side of Lyle's head. The onlookers closed in to get a better look. One lone voice penetrated Rory's fear.

"Go, Rory. Kick ass!"

He stepped over the bench easily and without losing his balance continued punching in Lyle's direction. He was pretty sure he landed a couple in the boy's mid-section before he felt a strong hand on his shoulder.

"Knock it off, you two." The gym teacher pulled them apart.

"Okay, show's over," he said to the onlookers. "Get dressed and be on the floor in 30 seconds."

Mr. O'Donnell yanked Lyle and Rory into his office and shoved them toward a couple of chairs as he slammed the door. Rory felt pretty proud for standing up to Lyle. He didn't care if he was in trouble.

Lyle started to talk, but the teacher told him to shut up. Mr. O'Donnell appeared to be writing something at his desk while Rory and Lyle glared at each other behind his back. Rory sniffed and wiped blood from his nose.

Swiveling around on his chair, Mr. O'Donnell cautioned Lyle, "You'll get your turn in a minute, so cool your jets."

He nodded to Rory. "What's this all about, Wilson? You know fighting's against school rules."

Rory hadn't been in this situation before, but he knew Lyle had been thrown out of school for fighting before. Some of the kids had witnessed Lyle's father slamming him around in the parking lot after being suspended once. But Rory was angry and couldn't summon any pity for him.

He recounted how he'd been minding his own business, changing for class, when Lyle came along and slammed his locker shut. "I told him to quit it and he came back and asked who was gonna make him."

The events that followed were pretty blurred in Rory's mind, but he definitely recalled Lyle calling him a freakin' faggot. He hesitated before telling the teacher that part of it, but finally did. Mr. O'Donnell didn't react.

The teacher's chair squeaked as he swung around. "Well, Profitt, what's your story?"

As expected, his version was different. According to Lyle, he'd reached over and tapped Rory's locker as a way of saying hello. For no reason, Rory punched him. He hit back in self defense.

The teacher pointed his finger at both of them. "Don't either of you move a muscle while I'm gone."

Mr. O'Donnell left the office and addressed the students who were lined up on the gym floor, but Rory and Lyle couldn't hear what anyone said through the closed door. The class began a series of basketball drills, and the gym teacher returned.

"It seems you're not only a bully, Profitt. You're also a liar. Your classmates' stories are a lot closer to what Wilson said."

Rory felt smug, thinking he'd get off without punishment. His enjoyment of Lyle's discomfort was short-lived, however.

"And you left something out, Wilson. You forgot to mention that you shoved a bench into Profitt's legs before he threw a punch at you."

Rory looked at the floor.

"Go put on your street clothes, Wilson. Then, park your butt on the bench in front of my office. You're getting an F for the day."

"Profitt, you're going on vacation. I'm recommending a one-day suspension for you. This isn't the first time you've been fighting. Get dressed and report to the principal's office. Get going, both of you. And I'd better not hear a word coming out of the locker room. Got that?"

After the incident with Lyle, Rory resolved not to let the bullies go unchallenged. Word spread about how Rory had stood up to Lyle, and he hoped kids would find other targets to feed their insatiable lust for inflicting pain.

Rory didn't have to wonder long whose voice had called out encouragement that day in the locker room. A new boy had moved into the house down the street that had been up for sale. He'd spotted Jake but hadn't had any contact with him until he was assigned to Rory's homeroom and many of the same classes.

Jake had a shy smile that lit up his face when he was happy, but his dark brooding eyes told a different story. Rory studied that face for the first few days they were in class together.

One day after the scuffle with Lyle, they arrived at their seats a few minutes before the bell rang. Jake looked over at Rory and smiled.

"You put up a good fight in the locker room last week. I was hoping you'd beat the crap outta him."

"Were you the one who told me to kick his ass?"

"Yeah. You live down the street from me. I've seen you working in the garden."

Rory waited for a snide comment.

"The flowers are nice. Are they yours?"

"My mother started the garden, but she let me take it over a few years ago."

"Maybe I could come by and take a look some time." It sounded more like a question.

Rory wasn't used to kids reaching out this way. "Sure, if you want to," he replied. He thought about Jake for the rest of the day.

That afternoon Rory got off the bus and knew there'd be no gardening. The staccato pounding of rain on vinyl siding removed any chance Jake might walk down to look at his flowers.

For the next few days the weather was perfect, so Rory spent a couple of hours after school weeding and tending his flowers. So far, Jake hadn't ventured down the street. Rory wished he'd come by.

Eventually, Jake did visit and he and Rory began a relationship that would change both of their lives. Soon, they were sharing all of their free time. They ate lunch and walked home together, and, of course, the other students noticed.

Jake came to the house two or three times a week to help Rory weed during the warm months and rake leaves in the fall. On winter days they did what most kids in the mountains did: they stayed indoors and played video games unless there was an especially mild day. The boys rode the school bus during cold weather, but it was a toss-up which was worse, the taunting from the other kids on the bus or the freezing mile and a half walk in the cold and snow.

Despite the daily stress of being picked on by other students, Rory continued to earn good grades. He kept the problems he faced in school to himself except when he shared his feelings with Jake and Ashley.

After Jake's family moved in, Ruth had reached out to his parents a couple of times. She brought a lemon pound cake to the house to welcome them to the neighborhood. Jake's mother thanked her, but didn't invite her in. *Maybe I caught her at a bad time,* Ruth had thought. She'd yet to set eyes on Jake's father.

"Rory, what are Jake's parents like?" she asked one day.

"Why?"

"Oh, just curious. I've never seen his father, and his mother's kind of quiet. When I run into her in the supermarket or around town, she doesn't say much."

"Yeah, they're pretty quiet. When I'm there I'm usually in Jake's room, so I don't see much of them. Jake says his father drinks a lot. I told him I wouldn't tell anyone, so please, Mama, keep it to yourself."

"My lips are sealed," she said and reached out to push his hair out of his eyes. It was getting harder to do that because he was so much taller than she was. She had to stretch like a rubber band to reach the top of his head.

Ruth treasured the times she spent with Rory, more so because they were rare these days. If he wasn't at school, he was with Jake doing homework. Probably in remembrance of his father's belittling him for eating slowly, Rory had learned to inhale his supper in five minutes. He knew better than to bolt from the table while his mother was still eating, so she ate slowly and tried to squeeze as much conversation out of him as she could.

Chapter Eighteen

Once a year, each high school student had an appointment with a guidance counselor. Since Rory was a good student, the counselors were happy to cut his time short so they could devote their attention to the problem kids. He'd seen a counselor in April, so he was surprised in mid-May when he got a note in homeroom to come to the guidance office at 1:30. The note was from a different counselor.

Gym was scheduled for 1:30 and Rory didn't mind missing it a bit. He had the hardest time with bullies when testosterone surged during competitive sports, and he was never very good at athletics. He got a B in gym because he was always on time, had clean shorts and T-shirts, and kept his mouth shut. He was lucky they didn't grade him on his skills or lack thereof. Once, the gym teacher had talked to him about going out for the school basketball team because he towered over several of the other students. Rory said he'd think about it, but after the teacher saw that Rory couldn't get the ball in the basket to save his life, it became a dead issue.

"Come on in, Rory." The rich baritone voice came from Mr. Massey. He rose from behind the desk and Rory took in a tall, athletic-looking man with a pleasant smile. He extended his large hand and they shook.

"Sit down." Mr. Massey gestured to one of two chairs that faced his desk. As Rory sat, the counselor came around his desk. He pulled the other chair away from Rory's, sat down, and reached around to close the door.

"I'm sorry we haven't had a chance to meet before," he began. "I was supposed to talk with you in April, but I had to be out for a few days and Miss Harmon filled in for me. I thought it would be good if we got acquainted."

The muscles in Rory's jaw relaxed. At least I'm not in any trouble, he thought.

"So, tell me how things are going for you, Rory. I see from your records you're not having any problems in your classes. You've made honors every semester. That's great."

"There's not much to tell, I guess. I do okay."

"Do you have many friends?"

"A few."

"How about sports? You're taller than most of the boys. Do you play basketball?"

Rory looked at his feet, trying to hide his discomfort at talking to someone who was obviously an athlete. He answered, "No, sir." He hesitated and then added, "I'm kind of a klutz," and returned his gaze to the floor.

Mr. Massey realized the task at hand would not be easy. Rory was not used to opening up with strangers.

"Everything okay at home?"

"Yes, sir."

Taking a deep breath, Mr. Massey braced his hands on his knees and leaned toward the boy.

"Mr. Walters came to me a couple of days ago and told me he was concerned about your relationship with the other boys."

Rory squirmed in his chair and riveted his gaze on a focus spot on the floor. He wished he'd gone to gym class. A squeezing sensation gripped his throat and chest, and suddenly there wasn't enough air in that small office.

"He said the other boys call you names and make fun of you. Do you want to talk about it?"

Wait a minute, Rory thought. What's with this guy? He told me he talked to Mr. Walters, but before that he asked me about sports. If he talked with Walters, he knows I don't play sports. What's he after?

Rory continued to look at the floor.

"You know we don't condone bullying here, Rory. If you're being bullied, we should talk about it." Mr. Massey waited.

Finally Rory looked up. He gazed out the window, played with a snow globe on Mr. Massey's desk, and looked at the walls, everywhere but at the guidance counselor. The silence was strangling him.

"Son, look at me."

Rory obeyed. He felt relief when the bell rang signaling the end of class. He didn't want to miss his English class.

"Are you okay?" Mr. Massey seemed genuinely concerned.

"Yes, sir, I'm fine. I need to get to my English class. May I have a pass? I'm probably going to be late."

"Sure." Mr. Massey wrote out a late pass, but before handing it to Rory, who was standing in the doorway with his books, he hesitated. "If you ever decide you want to talk about anything, Rory, the door is always open."

Rory mumbled his thanks, took the pass, and escaped into the hall.

"Nobody likes a squealer," Ashley said when Rory asked her opinion. "If it was me, I wouldn't say anything. It seems the older those kids get, the meaner they are. It's only another month 'til school's out, and then we have the summer off. You can hang on."

"I s'pose I can. Maybe you're right. I want to talk to Jake about it and see what he thinks. You two are the only ones I trust."

The last days of school were mostly spent on what Rory called busy work. Teachers had collected books, and all the state tests were done. They tried to keep the students busy, but it was unusually hot and sticky for May, and nobody had energy to do anything. Even the gym teachers yielded to the heat. They told the boys to sit on the bleachers and amuse themselves.

Rory and Jake played hangman while the other boys took turns going to the bathroom to blow up condoms and float them in the stopped up water fountains on their way back to the gym. Each time a girl walked by the fountain nearest the gym door, they waited for a reaction. They were rarely disappointed. Sooner or later a teacher would put an end to their game, but for the time being it kept them occupied.

Jake shared Ashley's opinion. He, too, was a target of bullying and feared the consequences to his friend and himself if Rory opened up to the guidance counselor. Jake was a skilled athlete and had made the varsity soccer team. Regular practice and changing hormones had toned his body and given him a compact muscular appearance.

As his reputation on the soccer field spread, the bullying should have lessened, but hanging around with Rory kept a bulls-eye plastered on his back. Since both of his friends had advised him to keep his mouth shut, Rory decided to take their advice. School ended without a second visit to Mr. Massey's office.

Chapter Nineteen

"Are you up yet, boy?"

"I'll be out in a minute." Rory scrambled out of bed and after a quick trip to the bathroom, padded across the bare floor to the kitchen where Grady sat with a cup of coffee.

"Land sakes, I believe you've grown again since last month. I bet you're over six feet now."

Rory stepped over to the wall where his height had been marked since he could stand. "Come measure me, Papaw."

"I'll need a step stool to see the top of your head." Grady stood on tiptoe and put a pencil mark on the wall even with the top of Rory's head. "Now step away. Hmm. The date by the last mark is February, three months ago. You've grown another inch and a half, it looks like. You're the tallest person in our family now. Unless your daddy has grown, you're at least an inch taller than he is."

At the mention of his father, Rory grew silent. Darrell hadn't contacted Rory in nearly three years. Rory hadn't realized when his parents divorced that his father would eventually divorce him, too. It still hurt whenever he allowed himself to think about it.

Grady talked while Rory filled a bowl with corn flakes. "I've got a proposition for you. When school's out I could use help painting the barn and the house. If you think you can get up early, I'd pick you up at six and we could work for four or five hours before it gets too hot. I'll pay you. I was thinking maybe $3 an hour. I know that's below the minimum wage, but it's all I can afford. If you promise not to report me to the sheriff, you can make a few dollars and add it to your college fund. What do ya say?"

"Papaw, you don't have to pay me. I'll be happy to help you. Can we start an hour later, though? I don't think I can get up that early."

Grady ignored the last comment. "You'll be savin' me money. Of course, Meemaw will feed you lunch every day. That's probably worth more than what I'll pay you, knowin' how much you eat these days. Besides, I like to feel like we're helping you with college money." He held his hand out and they shook on it.

It would be the first time Rory was paid for work. He still earned money on weekends at the farmer's market, but nobody ever paid him to do actual work. He was excited at the prospect of adding to the $387 he already had in his college fund.

The painting lasted all summer and Rory still had time to tend his garden and sell produce on weekends. He missed spending time with Jake. Jake's parents had sent him to his uncle's home in Vermont. He had cousins there, and from the couple of post cards Rory had received, it sounded like he was having a good summer.

More and more, Rory thought about Jake. He was torn between wanting the summer to last forever and wishing it to be over quickly so Jake would come home. Jake continued to send postcards, and Rory wrote long letters. He'd debated with himself about whether he should sign his letters 'your friend' or 'love.' Safety won out.

He knew boys weren't supposed to love other boys, at least not the same way they loved girls. Many of the boys at school had girlfriends, and he'd often seen them kissing by the lockers in the hall. He had absolutely no interest in kissing girls. In fact, with the exception of Ashley, he didn't particularly want to spend time with them. Ashley was different; she wasn't like a lot of the other girls who wore heavy makeup and revealing clothes. They'd had a few conversations on the subject, since Ashley started hanging around one of the boys in Rory's class.

"I heard Jeffrey talking about you before school got out."

"What'd he say?"

"He said he thought you were hot. Is he your boyfriend?"

Rory felt no jealousy, just curiosity. He knew that he and Ashley would always be friends.

"Yeah, I guess you could say that. We went to the movies and made out a couple of times."

"What's it like to make out?"

"Haven't you ever done it?"

Rory shook his head.

"Well, you kiss a lot and if you're standing up, you rub against each other. That's about all there is to it."

Rory was trying to visualize the rubbing part.

"What do you rub?"

"Oh Lord, do I have to tell you everything? Stand up."

He did as she instructed.

"Put your arms around me like this." Ashley drew Rory's arms down around the small of her back and pulled him in close. She began to grind her hips against his. Rory quickly pushed her to arms' length. "Oh," he said.

"Have you ever kissed a girl, Rory?"

He shook his head and looked down to conceal his embarrassment. He was uncomfortable with the conversation, but curiosity pushed him to ask further, "Do you like kissing Jeffrey?"

"Well, at first I didn't, but then he showed me how. Now I like it. It feels good, and we get all excited when we do it. He even puts his tongue in my mouth. That's called French kissing."

"Did you ever hook up with him?"

Rory saw a flash of anger in her hazel eyes.

"What do you think I am, a whore?"

"I didn't mean anything by it, Ashley. I'm sorry," he added quickly. "Is it something bad?"

"It means screwing, you idiot. Honestly Rory, I can't believe you're so innocent. You have to get some experience."

Ashley paused for a moment as she worked on a scheme. "LuEllen is having a party Saturday night. I'm going with Jeffrey. I bet I could get her to invite you. Do you want to go?"

Rory was scared to death about going to a party with classmates. But he didn't want Ashley to think he wasn't grateful. Besides, he thought, maybe if he kissed a girl, the other boys might quit calling him a faggot.

"Do I have to bring a girl?"

"There must be someone you can ask. Let me call LuEllen, and I'll let you know what she says."

Rory hoped LuEllen would say no. His insides were tied in knots thinking of what he would say if he had to ask a girl to go to the party with him.

As he walked home, he thought about Jake and wondered if Jake had ever kissed a girl. They never talked about girls. There were more important things to discuss when they were together. They'd both reacted to open displays of affection at school. "That's so disgusting," Jake had said one day when they found themselves surrounded by love birds after school. Rory agreed, and the subject hadn't come up again.

"I want you home by 11, Rory," Ruth ordered.

"No problem."

Rory had changed his shirt twice in the last hour and a half. He was sweating like a glass of icy sweet tea on a July day.

"Nerves is all," Ruth had assured him. "It's natural this being your first date."

"It's not a date, Mama. We're just going to a party."

"Well, whatever it is, I hope you have a good time. You'd better get going if you're picking Emily up at 6:45."

Ruth's relief was indescribable when Rory told her he was asking a girl to a party. Maybe he's just a late bloomer, she thought. Other than Ashley, Rory had never shown any interest in girls. She hoped this might change everything.

Ruth had told Rory to introduce himself to Emily's parents and engage in some conversation before leaving for the party, so he'd practiced a couple of topics as he walked.

"Emily, your boyfriend's here," her younger brother yelled when he opened the door. The boy didn't invite him in, so Rory stood on the porch and waited.

"Harley, where are your manners?" A woman Rory presumed was Emily's mother came to the door. "You must be Rory. I'm Emily's aunt." Rory held out his hand and she took it. "Please come in. Emily will be ready in a minute." Rory stood awkwardly in the living room. "Have a seat. Would you like a CoCola?"

"No, thank you, ma'am. I'm fine." He sat on the sofa. Rory looked around the room at framed photos. He recognized Emily in a few of them and also the boy who'd answered the door. There was a large photo over the fireplace with Emily and the boy and a man and a woman. He'd ask her about it later.

"Sorry you had to wait," Emily said as she entered the room.

Recalling Ruth's coaching, he replied, "You look real nice, Emily."

"Aunt Becca, we're leaving."

Her aunt came to the door as they stepped onto the porch. "Have a good time."

Rory was happy that the party was only three blocks from Emily's house. That limited their time alone.

"Was that your brother?"

"Yeah, did he bother you?"

"Oh, no. He just opened the door and disappeared."

"That's what you think. He was standing around the corner watching you. He's a little sneak. Do you have any brothers or sisters?"

"No, it's just me and my mother. My parents are divorced." Rory brought up the subject of the large photo. "Are those your parents?"

He thought Emily seemed uncomfortable with the question. "You don't have to answer if you don't want to," he added quickly.

"I don't mind," she replied. "My parents live in Oregon. A few years ago they had a big fight, and to settle it my mama said she'd go live with Daddy on a farm with a bunch of other people. We live with my aunt now, Mama's sister. I used to think my parents would come back for us, but they haven't. My aunt's real nice, so we're probably better off with her anyway."

Rory empathized with Emily. After all, he believed his father had left because he couldn't stand him, so he had an idea how she must feel. They walked the last block to LuEllen's house in silence.

Rory felt all eyes were on him when they walked in. He searched frantically for Ashley; hers was one friendly face he could count on.

"Hey, Rory, Emily," one of the girls called. She was wrapped around another boy Rory recognized.

LuEllen greeted them. "Food's in here," she motioned to the dining room. They followed her. She pointed to a plastic cooler. "Drinks over there. Help yourselves." Then she was gone.

The music was so loud it would be hard to hear anything anyway. At least I won't have to talk much, Rory thought.

"Want a drink?" Rory shouted, mindful of his mother's instructions about seeing to it his date had a beverage and food.

"Sure. Thanks."

Rory was so focused on the kissing thing he hadn't given a thought to dancing. He'd danced a few times with his mother and grandmother when he was little but had since forgotten what they'd taught him.

It got quieter as a slow song began. Rory watched the other boys dance and figured he could probably do what they were doing.

"Wanna dance?" he asked Emily.

He held her the way his mother had taught him, but he observed other boys had their hands around the girls' waists or on their butts. He slid his arms around Emily's back, but he couldn't reach her waist since she was a full foot shorter than he was. He settled for a location near her shoulders and tried to keep from getting too close. He felt someone bumping his butt repeatedly and when he turned Emily around, his eyes met Ashley's. He was starting to get the hang of it when the song ended.

"Let's get some food," he urged. Emily returned to her seat with a slice of pizza while Rory piled his plate with pizza, lunch meat and a roll.

"Pizza's good, isn't it?" Emily asked in an effort to break the silence.

Rory had a mouthful and by the time he'd swallowed, Ashley had appeared.

"I see you managed to get Rory to dance."

"Yeah, he's a good dancer," Emily lied.

"I didn't know you could dance, Rory. Been holding out on me, huh?"

Emily was puzzled by that brief exchange. She wondered if they'd ever gone out. Another slow song began to play.

"Mind if I borrow him?" Ashley asked.

"No, go ahead."

Ashley pulled Rory off his chair and put her hands around his back. He did likewise.

"So, how's it going?"

Rory glanced around to see if anyone else had heard her. "Okay. She's real nice."

"Next time you dance with her, get closer and try to kiss her," Ashley urged.

"Don't you think it's too soon?" he asked, the pizza he'd just consumed rising in his throat.

"Nah, she'll probably let you. Try it. All she can do is say no."

"What if she slaps me?"

"Girls don't do that anymore."

By the time the music stopped, Rory had agreed. He tried but couldn't get up the nerve to kiss Emily in front of other kids. They danced and sat and Rory ate more pizza. A few kids left the party.

"What time do you have to be home, Emily?"

"By 11. How about you?"

"Me too. We'd better leave soon so I have time to walk home."

Rory walked Emily to the house and up the front steps. It's now or never, he thought.

"I had a nice time tonight, Emily. Thanks for going to the party with me."

Emily relaxed for the first time that night. "Thanks for asking me. This was my first date."

"It was mine too. I never asked a girl out before." The tension in his shoulders released as he smiled at Emily. He hadn't felt comfortable about kissing Emily in front of everybody, but now they were alone.

He faced Emily and leaned down. She didn't move away as he touched his lips to hers and lingered for a second or two. Emily leaned into him and opened her mouth slightly. He remembered what Ashley had said about French kissing and started to slide his tongue into her mouth when they heard, "Ooh gross. They're kissing!"

Emily pulled away and looked up. "Harley, I'm gonna kill you. Get away from that window." She and Rory laughed, and it was hard to tell which of them was more relieved.

"I better go now," Rory said and walked down the steps. He saw Emily's silhouette in the doorway as she waved. His head swam as he played back every moment of the evening during his 20-minute walk home.

Chapter Twenty

"Well, how was it?" Ruth asked even before Rory got his second foot in the door.

"It was okay."

"Just okay? Come on, tell me."

"Aw, Mama, I'm tired. I'll tell you tomorrow," Rory pleaded, playing for time.

Ruth tried to hide her disappointment.

Rory grabbed a Mountain Dew from the fridge and walked into his room, closing the door with his foot. He kicked his shoes off, stripped down to his shorts and T-shirt, and sat down at his computer.

Dear Jake, he typed. I sure wish you were here so I could talk to you. You won't believe what happened tonight. You know Emily Peterson? I took her to a party at LuEllen Washington's house tonight. Ashley talked me into it.

I was afraid Emily would see my knees shaking. The eats were good. It was OK, I guess, but I wish you'd been there.

I kissed Emily and she kissed me back. I tried this French kissing thing Ashley told me about. Did you ever do it? It's pretty disgusting. I hope I don't have to go to any more parties. All the kids do is eat and dance, and some of them were making out right in front of everybody. LuEllen's mama stayed in the kitchen.

Frank Skilling said he was surprised to see me there. He said Emily is a real nice girl, and he could see that she likes me. Frank's OK. He never picks on me. He asked me if Emily goes all the way. I told him I didn't know. Do you know what it means?

Well, that's all from hot Craggy Grove. I hope you'll get home soon.

Your friend,

Rory

Breakfast couldn't come soon enough for Ruth. "Well, tell me all about last night."

"They had great food and LuEllen made sure everybody ate a lot." He hesitated, wondering how much more to tell. "We danced a couple of times."

"Slow dances or fast?"

"Slow ones, Mama. You know I don't know how to dance."

He looked at his mother to gauge whether he had satisfied her curiosity. "And then," he continued, "I walked Emily home and came back here."

"Will you see Emily again?"

Rory knew exactly what his mother was asking. "Yeah, I'll see her in school."

He hardly had a chance to eat his Cheerios with all the questions. Ruth started to speak again and Rory stuffed a second spoonful into his mouth. He couldn't talk with a mouthful, so he let her go on. He'd put off swallowing as long as he could.

"Is she nice? What does she look like? Do you think she had a good time?"

"Mama, you sound like one of those TV detectives," shutting the door on further discussion.

Rory headed outside to tend his garden and get some space. He knew Ashley'd probably come by to see how the date had gone. He was on his knees weeding when he felt a hand on his shoulder.

"Shoot, Ashley. You about scared me to death."

"Sorry. Just wanted to get your attention."

"You sure did that," he said as he wiped dirt on his shorts. "You're late. You missed the interrogation."

"Oh good, then I get to ask all the questions myself." She punched him playfully on the arm.

"So, did you do it?" she asked.

"You mean kiss her?"

Ashley nodded and Rory swore her ears doubled in size before his eyes.

"Yeah, I did it on her porch. It was okay."

"Didn't you feel all excited when you kissed her?"

"No, I was too nervous, and I think she was too. She said it was her first date. I even tried the French kissing thing you told me about."

"You did? Way to go, Rory! Did she let you feel her up?"

Rory described how Emily's brother shouted out the window. "I don't know if I would have tried anything. She's a very nice girl."

He thought a minute. "Do you let Jeffrey touch you?"

Ashley looked embarrassed. "Only above the waist. Once he took my hand and tried to make me touch him down there," she said pointing to Rory's crotch, "but I wouldn't."

"I think Emily likes me," he continued, "but ...."

"But what? Aren't you going to ask her out again?"

"I don't think so."

"Why not? Didn't you have a good time last night?"

"It was okay, but it's a lot of work. I'd rather do something else, like watch TV or go to a movie."

"You're a hopeless case, I swear. Normal boys like to go out with girls. No wonder they call you names." She turned and walked away.

Rory reeled. How could his best friend be so cruel? He didn't see her for the next two weeks. She didn't come by the house, and he didn't call her. His hurt morphed into anger.

One evening a few weeks later, Ruth hollered, "Jake, for you." Rory galloped to the phone and Ruth saw something in his eyes she wanted to ignore. Rory had been anxious to hear from Jake, assuming his friend would return home from Vermont soon, since school was due to start in a couple of weeks. Rory was a bit disappointed to learn Jake had been home for a few days and hadn't called sooner. During their brief conversation, Rory told Jake about working at his grandfather's house in the mornings and suggested Jake come over the next afternoon.

During the two weeks before school started, Rory painted at his Papaw's house in the mornings and hung out with Jake in the afternoons. The first time Jake came to the house, Rory noticed he looked different. He'd firmed up a lot while he was away and grown taller. His hair was longer and lighter, and a head band moved his bangs to clear a view of his brown eyes. Jake was a really handsome dude, Rory realized.

"You seem different, Jake, like you're mad at me or somethin'. What's goin' on?"

"No, I'm not mad. I guess I'm surprised you wanted to hang out. I figured you'd be with your girlfriend."

"What girlfriend?"

"You wrote me about some girl you took to a party and said you were playing kissy face."

"Oh that. Nah, she's not my girlfriend. I haven't even talked to her."

"Oh," Jake said and smiled at Rory.

"I guess I'm just not that into girls. Ashley's the one who kept pushing me to kiss Emily." Then Rory recounted the wounding interaction with Ashley.

"I thought she was my friend," he said.

"Yeah, girls are funny that way. They turn on you," Jake replied. "Us guys have to stick together."

Chapter Twenty-One

On the first day of school Rory saw Ashley at the bus stop and she chattered away as if nothing had changed. Rory felt sick when he recalled their last conversation. At least she hadn't called him a faggot like the other kids.

Later that week, Jake came by after soccer practice.

"What'd ya think of the practice?" he asked. He'd seen Rory on the sidelines with other spectators.

"You looked pretty good. How'd you learn to play?"

"Before we moved here, there was a family from El Salvador down the street from us. I started to play with them and they taught me a lot. They said I was pretty good for a gringo.

"The coach got me a cup," he said as he took a plastic gadget out of his gym bag. "Do you have one?"

"What do ya do with that thing?"

"I'll show ya," Jake said and, in one swift movement, he tugged down his soccer shorts and briefs.

Rory had made it a practice never to look at other boys when they changed after gym. But here was Jake with his privates exposed, and Rory couldn't take his eyes off them.

Jake pulled the jock strap out of his gym bag, pulled the supporter on and then inserted the rigid cup in the slit. He worked to ensure a proper fit and then strutted in front of Rory. "It's to keep your balls from getting hurt. Wanna try it?"

"I don't have a jock strap or a cup," Rory replied.

"You can use these," Jake offered. Soon he was naked again.

Rory self-consciously sat on the bed to remove his jeans and shorts. He tried to put the jock strap on sitting down.

"Stand up, Rory. You'll never get it on that way."

Rory stood, and Jake took full measure of his genitals. Rory fumbled with the jock strap and was so anxious to step into it, he lost his footing. Jake reached out to steady him. Rory loved the feel of Jake's strong hands on his shoulder and arm.

"Make sure the straps aren't twisted over your butt," Jake coached.

Rory held his breath while Jake inserted the cup into the front slit, lingering longer than Rory thought necessary.

"Whoa, man. I'll never get this thing arranged if you get a boner."

Rory let out his breath with a gasp. Jake maneuvered the cup into place while Rory tried to will his body not to react.

"Okay, how does it feel?"

"Tight. I'm not sure I could walk with this on," Rory laughed and took a couple of mincing steps.

"Well, maybe you need a larger size. You're bigger than I am," Jake answered. "Do you think you can get them off by yourself?" he teased.

While Rory removed the cup and wiggled out of the jock strap, Jake watched him. "I learned some things this summer from my cousins in Vermont. Wanna see what they showed me?"

"Sure," Rory answered and reached for his briefs.

"Wait, don't put them on yet."

"Come here," Jake said, still naked from the waist down.

Rory was uncomfortable but went and stood facing his friend.

Jake reached for Rory's hand. At first Rory tried to pull away, but Jake held him firmly. "Don't worry. It's okay."

Jake reached over and took hold of Rory. Rory flinched and immediately felt the start of an erection.

"Slow down, man. Not so fast."

"I don't know if we should do this, Jake. It's not right."

"All the guys do it. It's fun."

Rory got so excited he let go of Jake and closed his eyes. Jake worked until Rory's breath came in short gasps and he groaned. Jake grinned. "Now, wasn't that better than a do-it-yourselfer?"

"Yeah," Rory admitted as his breathing slowed. He reached behind him and grabbed a handful of tissues from the dresser.

"Now, do me," Jake urged.

Rory returned the favor.

"It's better if you come together. Let's wait a little bit and try it, okay?"

"Do you do this with other guys?" Rory asked.

"Just my cousins. I'd never do it with guys at school. They'd call me a homo and probably beat the crap out of me."

Rory quickly lost his timidity and a short while later required no coaxing when Jake asked if he was ready to do it again. Following Jake's lead, Rory learned other ways of satisfying his sexual needs during the next couple of weeks.

Life took on new meaning for Rory, and Jake was at the center of it. Everything else moved to the back burner. He still gardened, but gladly left his flowers and vegetables whenever Jake came by. He and Ashley had patched things up, but their friendship wasn't the same. When he wasn't with Jake, Rory was thinking about him.

One day Jake confided to Rory, "A few weeks before school ended, Daddy was drunk one night, and he walked into my room without knocking while I was looking at some guy stuff on the computer. Pictures of guys having sex. He asked me if I was a homo, and he said he thought you seemed light in the sneakers. Said he bet we was suckin' each other off. He was shouting."

Wide-eyed, Rory asked, "What'd you say?"

"Nothin. Saying anything just makes it worse. Mama came in to see about the racket."

"Oh, Lord, did she see the pictures too?"

"No, I'd shut the computer down. She pulled him out of my room and steered him to their bedroom, motioning for me to close my door."

"Then what happened?"

"She does that when he gets on me sometimes. Then there's yelling and hitting. He calls her a whore and stuff, and after a while it gets quiet. Once when my uncle Travis, Mama's older brother, was visiting, he and Daddy got in a huge fight. He told Daddy he'd kill him if he ever raped Mama again. I didn't know what that was back then, but I reckon that's what goes on. The next morning I overheard my father on the phone with his brother in Vermont. He said he'd be obliged if my uncle would let me come up for the summer. He said I needed to be away from some little faggot I hang out with. The day after school ended, my father took me to Tri Cities Airport. When he left me at the security gate he said it would do me good to be at the farm with my cousins."

Rory couldn't help thinking about his own father. He could only imagine what Darrell might have done if he'd caught Rory looking at pictures like that.

Chapter Twenty-Two

School began with the usual details: new textbooks, learning new assigned seats in six classes, and for Rory, coping with the disappointment that he and Jake had only two classes together, Spanish and gym. Once, he would have been thrilled to discover Ashley in his English and science classes, but while they remained friendly, they'd clearly gone in different directions.

Mr. Shoun, Rory's English teacher, assigned the routine "What I Did on My Summer Vacation" essay on the first day of school. That night Rory and Jake compared notes.

"Why don't you write about what you learned from your boyfriend this summer? I bet nobody else will choose that topic," Jake teased.

Rory punched Jake on the arm, and Jake grabbed him around the neck and wrestled him to the floor. They landed a split second before the lamp from Rory's night stand crashed and shattered.

Ruth shot out of her chair in front of the TV when she heard breaking glass.

"What's goin' on in there? Sounds like you're breaking the place up."

Rory opened the door. "We had an accident," he said and pointed to the ceramic and glass shards on the carpet.

"Don't touch anything," she ordered. "I'll get the vacuum."

The boys tried to pick up the pieces and sure enough, Jake cut himself. Rory saw the blood at the same instant Jake did. "Come on," he said as he led the way across the hall to the bathroom. "You need a Band-Aid on that thing."

Jake let Rory clean his finger with peroxide and tried not to yell when the clear liquid burned the daylights out of the cut. He was sitting on the closed toilet seat when Ruth returned with the vacuum cleaner.

"I told you … You boys never listen, do you?"

Jake looked chastised, and Rory shrugged. Ruth picked up the larger pieces. She vacuumed the rest of the rug and cautioned, "Don't walk barefoot in here." Looking straight at Jake she said, "I don't want to send you home a mess of cuts. Your parents'll think you're not safe here."

"Yes ma'am. I'm sorry for the trouble. We'll be careful."

As Ruth carried off the broken lamp, Rory said, "Yeah, Jake, we don't want anyone to think you're not safe here," and grabbed at Jake's crotch.

"Quit it," he replied. After breaking Rory's lamp, Jake wasn't in the mood for games. He turned to look at the books on Rory's bookcase. His eyes lit on *Goodnight Moon*. "What's this?"

"Oh, that was a book my daddy read to me when I was little."

Jake flipped through the pages and began to read aloud as if he were reading to a little kid. Rory got up and grabbed the book. "Don't. It's one of the few nice memories I have from the days before he started to hate me."

"At least you can remember some good times with your father. Well, I'd better get home." As he walked toward the closed bedroom door, he pulled down his pants and stuck his butt out. "Say goodnight, moon," he said. Rory quickly turned and reciprocated.

They both pulled their pants on, and Rory walked Jake to the front door. Rory stood in the doorway watching Jake walk down the block, studying his movements. When Ruth entered the kitchen and saw him watching Jake, she cleared her throat. At the sound of his mother's voice, he closed the door.

Adolescent hormones were in full flow in Craggy Grove. Ruth wasn't the only parent wrestling with sensitive topics. She and Jane continued to talk regularly even though Rory and Ashley had drifted apart. After exchanging pleasantries on the phone one evening, Jane launched into a description of her latest confrontation with her daughter when she'd found what she thought was semen on Ashley's slacks.

"I think I'd put her on the pill just to be sure you don't become a young grandmother," Ruth offered. "Did you ask her about it?"

"No, I did exactly what I shouldn't have done. I flew into a panic and accosted her. I asked if she was having sex with that boy, and she got furious with me. I'm afraid I didn't handle it too well."

"What'd she say?"

"She cried and said she was no slut and that I should trust her. All of that was at the top of her lungs, of course. I'm surprised you didn't hear her."

Ruth tried to find a silver lining for her friend. "Well, at least it was on the outside of her slacks. Did she admit that's what it was?"

"Are you kidding? She gave me some crap about sitting in spilled ice cream."

"I'm glad I don't have a daughter. Thank the Lord boys don't get pregnant." They laughed.

"I'm so grateful I have you to talk to," Jane said. "I don't dare tell her father about things like this. He'd lock her in her room until she turned 21."

After one of the boys' sleepovers at Rory's grandparents, Lily told Ruth how pleased she was that Rory had such a nice friend. "Jake is so polite and well mannered," she said. "He always jumps up and helps with the dishes and empties the waste basket in the bathroom before they leave. He takes the sheets off the bed and even offered to wash them the last time they were here."

Ruth could think of only one reason Jake might want to wash the sheets, but she kept her thoughts to herself.

A few days into the new term, Ruth took Rory shopping for school supplies. Too many times she'd bought a notebook only to find out that it was the wrong kind, so now she waited. After picking through the bargain bins at Big Lots, Ruth swung the car in the direction of Walgreen's. She needed a few things and asked Rory if he wanted to wait in the car.

"I need some stuff, too." Rory said softly. He coughed. "Mama, I need some personal things, for gym. I want to go in alone."

"Oh, I see. Okay, here's my credit card. Just sign my name. I'll wait in the car. I can get my stuff another time."

Rory sighed. It would be so much easier if I had a father to talk to about this kind of stuff, he thought.

Rory came out of the store after about 10 minutes. Ruth handed him her purse.

"Put my credit card back in my wallet, please, and stick the receipt in the outside pocket."

That night after Rory'd gone to bed, Ruth was sorting through receipts from the day's shopping. She smiled when she saw the $23.99 charge for an athletic supporter, but her amusement faded when she noted $19.98 for condoms. She'd have reacted differently if Rory'd had a girlfriend, relieved to have confirmation he wasn't gay.

Ruth had acquired quite an education about gay sex from going to the PFLAG meetings. One speaker from the AIDS coalition had given some alarming statistics about the increased infection rate among young gay males in recent years. "These young bucks weren't around when the AIDS epidemic swept through the gay community, and they think they won't become infected." He went on to say he'd given his son a credit card for the express purpose of buying condoms. "No excuses about not having any money," he said. Mary had remarked that she jumped for joy each time she found condoms in her son's bedroom.

Ruth called Mary the next day to talk about the credit card charge for condoms. "It's unrealistic to expect Rory to be abstinent, Ruth. It's a new world out there. If he's in a monogamous relationship with Jake, and neither one is having sex with anyone else, they're trying to be responsible. You've heard some of the members talk about their kids' promiscuity. Be glad you don't have to worry about that."

"You're right, Mary. Sometimes I feel silly after we talk. You always see things so rationally."

"I didn't always. There were years when I'd fly off the handle whenever I was confronted with a reality I didn't want to accept. You're still pretty new at this, Ruth. Don't be hard on yourself. It takes time. One day you'll look back on all of this and laugh."

Ruth found it hard to imagine that day.

Chapter Twenty-Three

Besides Jake, the only thing that got Rory's full attention these days was his biology project. "I'm sure I can figure out a way to make tobacco less harmful," Rory told his biology teacher, Mr. Short. "So many folks around here smoke or chew it, and it's making them sick. If I could change that, I'd be able to save lives."

The gleam in Rory's eyes prompted Mr. Short to talk with a friend at East Tennessee State University who judged the high school science contests and told him to watch for Rory. "This kid's going places with his science," he told him.

On back-to-school night Mr. Short spoke with Ruth. "It's as if Rory can talk to the plants. He has an intuitive sense about what to do when he works with them. I hope you'll encourage his interest. It would be a shame for talent like Rory's to go to waste."

The rest of her meetings with Rory's teachers had gone well. There were good reports about what a conscientious student he was and how polite he was. So Ruth was shocked a few weeks later when she received a call at work from the high school principal asking her to come meet with him immediately.

"Is Rory okay?" she demanded.

"He'll be all right," Mr. Post replied, "but he's been assaulted."

"You mean he was fighting?"

"Well, not exactly. I'd really prefer to discuss this with you in person, Mrs. Wilson. Can you come by this afternoon?"

"I can be there in about an hour, less if I don't hit any traffic."

"That'll be fine. I'll see you then."

Ruth sat with her head in her hands and shook as she listened to Mr. Post's description of the horror that had taken place behind the school playing field.

"Where is my boy?" she choked. "I need to see him."

"Both of the youngsters are with Dr. Devlin, the school psychologist. We thought it best for them to have a chance to talk about the incident as soon as possible to try to head off further complications."

"And what about the boys who did this to them?"

"We've called their parents and sent them home for the remainder of the week. I want to consult with some of my staff before we decide on further action. You have the option of filing a complaint with the police, of course. That's entirely up to you. If I may make a suggestion, you might want to talk to an attorney before making any decision."

"Would I be able to talk to Dr. Devlin? I'm not sure how I should handle this."

"I'm sure we can arrange that. We want to do everything we can to help the boys and also assist you and the other boy's parents. Incidentally, we've not been able to reach Jake's family. Do you know them?"

"Not really. They keep pretty much to themselves."

"If I can't get hold of them after we finish talking, would you mind driving Jake home? I don't think he should ride the bus today."

"Of course."

The phone on Mr. Post's desk rang. "Thank you," he said. "I'll be right out." He turned to Ruth. "The boys are in the outer office. I'd like to bring them in here if that's okay."

He opened the door and waved the boys in. They shuffled in and Ruth saw they'd both been crying. She got up and grabbed Rory and hugged him as if the strength of her embrace could undo the hurt and humiliation he'd experienced. Jake stood quietly, and she walked over and hugged him, too. Mr. Post pulled a couple of chairs over and motioned for them to sit.

"Boys, I'm very sorry about what happened out there. I know it was not your fault. The students who did this will be punished severely. I'm sure Dr. Devlin told you he'll be available to talk with you any time."

They both nodded. Neither spoke.

"Jake, I've not been able to reach your folks. I'm going to give them another call in a few minutes. If I can't get hold of them, Mrs. Wilson will drive you home."

"They don't answer the phone unless I'm home," Jake replied, offering no explanation for the bizarre behavior.

"Do you think they'll talk with me?" Mr. Post asked.

"Prob'ly not," he said looking down at the carpet.

Mr. Post and Ruth exchanged quick looks. "Well then, maybe I should let y'all get along home now." He held his hand out to Ruth and she took it. "I'll be in touch, Mrs. Wilson. You take care now."

Ruth led the boys into the hall. "Do you need to get anything from your lockers?"

"Yes ma'am," Jake answered.

Rory said nothing but turned and walked with Jake down the corridor. They turned the corner and Ruth waited.

Once they were out of hearing range, Rory said, "I'm not coming back to this place, ever."

"Yeah, me neither. I'll never be able to show my face in this town again."

"If I had a shotgun, I'd come back here and kill every one of them. I bet they'll only get a few days' suspension," Rory hissed.

"I've got a shotgun, but I'm not willing to go to jail on account of them," Jake answered.

They reached their lockers and Rory took out his biology book and sneakers. He walked over to Jake's locker and saw his friend holding an armload of clothing. Rory recognized soccer shorts and a shirt as Jake tossed them into a trashcan.

"Won't need these anymore," he said and began to cry.

Rory looked around and seeing no one, he put his arm around Jake's shoulders. He knew the hurt Jake must be feeling. After all, it had been Jake's own teammates who had forced them to do that in front of everyone. The combination of betrayal and humiliation was more than Jake could bear.

The boys saw Ruth waiting at the door. In the car, Rory worried what would happen to Jake when his parents found out. As if she were reading his mind, Ruth asked, "Jake, would you like to come to our house for a while before going home?" She'd sensed from his comment in the principal's office that things in his home were even worse than Rory'd let on.

"Yes, ma'am, I would. Thanks." Rory pulled down the visor and looked in the mirror at Jake in the back seat.

Later that day, after a lengthy conversation with Jake and Rory, Ruth agreed that it would be better not to tell Jake's parents about what had happened. First thing the next morning she phoned Mr. Post.

She explained Jake's fear that his alcoholic father would beat him or worse and asked if it was possible not to tell his parents about the incident. Mr. Post hemmed and hawed and mumbled something about liability, but finally agreed, only if she would take responsibility for the decision. Ruth didn't hesitate.

Jake had called home the night before and told his mother he was staying overnight with one of his teammates because they had early morning practices for the rest of the week. He had told Rory she sounded relieved not to have him home. Later, Ruth informed Mr. Post she was keeping both boys with her for the next few days.

She'd called the professor and told him she had a family emergency and wouldn't be working on his manuscript for a couple of days. He understood. She knew her first duty to the boys was to provide a safe haven where they could stay away from other students and try to recover, but she was jarred when Rory told her there was no way he would return to school.

When the phone rang the next morning, Rory picked it up without a second thought.

"What're you doin' home, Rory? Are you sick?" Lily asked, surprised to hear her grandson's voice during a school day.

"Kinda, Meemaw. Here's Mama." He made a face as he handed the phone to Ruth.

"What was that all about?" Lily wanted to know. "Sounds like my grandson doesn't want to talk to me." Ruth spilled out the story of what had happened, relieved to have someone to confide in. There was silence on the other end of the phone. "Are you there?" she asked in a panic.

Lily's voice was hardly audible. "I'm here. I can hardly believe my ears, Ruth. Are they okay? I have to tell Grady. He'll want to know before he hears it in town."

"I don't want him to have a heart attack. Are you sure that's wise?"

"You know this town. It'll be all over in no time. Better for him to hear it from me."

Lily asked several questions and Ruth answered the best she could. Most of them concerned how the boys were holding up and what Ruth intended to do about it. "I don't know what's the best thing to do, Mama. I'm keeping them here with me today and tomorrow. Jake's parents don't even know about it. He's afraid of what his father might do."

Within minutes after hanging up with Lily, the phone rang again.

"Mrs. Wilson, it's Dr. Devlin from the high school. I'm just checking on the boys. Mr. Post told me they're both staying home for the rest of the week."

"It's nice of you to call," she replied. "They're still in shock, I think. We all are. I'm not really sure what we'll do from here on. Can you hold on a minute so I can change phones?" Ruth went into her bedroom and closed the door. "Dr. Devlin, I need some advice. Both of them say they're not going back to school. Should I force them? Rory said there were several ugly comments about the incident in emails. Isn't there any way to stop this?"

"I'm not at all surprised at their reaction. They've suffered severe humiliation in front of their peers, and they don't have the skills to cope. One of the reasons I'm calling is to see if you'd like me to come talk with them and you. I gather Jake's parents are a lost cause."

"Yes, he's terrified to go home. He's going to have to go home at some point, though to be honest, his mother didn't seem to care that he'd be away for a few days. I'd like very much to talk with you. I'm not sure if the boys will be willing to talk. So far, I haven't pressed them, but I'm sure they're talking to each other."

"That's good. They need to. When would be a good time?" he asked.

"We're not goin' anywhere today."

"Is it okay if I come by in about an hour?"

"Fine. I was about to give them some lunch, and we'll be done by then. Should I tell them you're coming?"

"If you're sure they won't take off," he answered. "It's probably best if they're not surprised."

"Oh no, neither of them seems to want to leave the house anyway. We'll see you shortly. Thank you so much."

Ruth made the old standby chicken noodle soup and tuna sandwiches on toast, comfort food, she hoped.

"Give me your hands," she said. She looked at the two of them and then bowed her head. "Lord, help us to heal from this tragedy. We thank you for the blessings of this food and ask for strength to overcome our hurt. In Jesus' name. Amen." Each boy murmured his own amen.

"Dr. Devlin said he would drop by this afternoon to see how you're doin'."

Rory spoke first. "He seems like an okay guy."

Jake nodded in agreement. "But I'm still not going back to school."

"Me neither." Rory chimed in.

Dr. Devlin brought two important pieces of information. First, he informed Rory and Jake that they had to attend school until they either graduated from high school or reached age 17. If they refused to attend school, their parents could be prosecuted. Both acknowledged they didn't want their parents fined and jailed. Given that Ruth had to work and Jake's parents would probably not qualify for home schooling him, the options were limited.

The second piece of information was equally important. Mr. Post had decided to expel the three boys who instigated the incident. They were reassigned to a school for incorrigible students. The other two participants were suspended for a month. Their parents were told if their sons got into any further trouble, they too would be sent to the special school. A letter had been sent to all parents informing them of the actions taken and reiterating the school's zero tolerance policy on bullying. Further, Dr. Devlin would be conducting a series of training sessions with all school staff on their responsibilities when they observed or suspected behavior that resulted in bullying.

"Are our names in the letter?" Jake asked.

"No, of course not. Your parents won't find out unless they hear it from somebody in town."

"They don't talk to anybody," he said, "and for once, I'm glad."

Ruth felt a bit of relief. The boys hadn't said they'd go back to school, but they hadn't repeated their intent not to. Dr. Devlin said he'd like to meet with Rory and Jake weekly once they were back in school. Ruth thought she saw Rory nod, a sign that he was thinking about attending school.

"If y'all don't mind, I'd like to talk to Mrs. Wilson," Dr. Devlin said. He watched the boys walk into the living room and waited until he heard them turn on the TV.

"I can't thank you enough," Ruth began, but Dr. Devlin waved it off.

"It's my job, Mrs. Wilson. Rory and Jake are going to have a tough time facing their classmates. The story has pretty much made the rounds of the building by now. I'm going to stay in close touch and run interference for them as best I can." Ruth reached over and touched his hand.

"What about you, Mrs. Wilson? How are you coping with this? If you don't mind my asking, what's your reaction to having a gay son?"

Ruth blanched. It was the first time anyone other than PFLAG people had actually said that to her.

"W-well," she stammered, "I don't know that he is for sure. Did he tell you he's gay?"

"No, but the other students believe he is. That's what started this whole mess."

He watched her carefully and waited, letting the uncomfortable silence lie there like dense ground fog.

"I've suspected it for some time," she said, "but I have no proof."

"If he is gay, do you think he feels you'd accept it? Gay kids often worry that their parents will reject them. Many do, I'm sorry to say."

"Of course I'd accept it. I might not like it, but he's my son and I'd have no choice."

"That doesn't sound too accepting, Mrs. Wilson, if you don't mind my saying so. Look, you need to do some soul-searching on this issue. If Rory thinks you won't accept him if he's gay, he may not want to risk losing your love by telling you." He handed her a slip of paper with PFLAG and a phone number on it. "If you want to talk to other parents about how they handle it, this is a good place to start.

Even if it turns out that Rory isn't gay, it might be useful for you to touch base with these folks."

Ruth didn't bother to tell him she already knew about PFLAG and had started to attend meetings. Dr. Devlin took the hand Ruth offered and patted it. "You'll be all right. Just give it some time and be there to listen if Rory wants to talk. You have my number if you need me."

As he was leaving, Dr. Devlin called to the boys, "See you guys next week."

Ruth distinctly heard Rory say, "Yes, sir," and she was so grateful she could have hugged Dr. Devlin. He winked and turned toward the door.

Chapter Twenty-Four

Later that day, Jane called to offer her support. Ashley had told her all about what had happened. She'd also read the letter from the principal that arrived a day ago.

Jane's call prompted Ruth to look at the pile of unopened mail she'd tossed on the kitchen counter. Sure enough, her copy was there. The letter did not go into details about the "unfortunate bullying incident" that occurred on school property, but it was likely most students had provided the details to their parents. The tone was sober and no one could mistake how serious the school administrators were about preventing future incidents.

Ashley came to the door on Saturday while Rory was at the kitchen table.

"Hey," she said. It was an awkward moment, and Ruth left the room.

"Hey," Rory answered and looked at the floor.

"I want you to know that I'm still your friend," she said. "Lots of kids are real upset about what happened."

"Yeah, I bet," he replied. "Are they all talking about it?"

"Not everybody, but some are. The ones who matter are upset. You have more friends than you know, Rory. I even heard some of the guys say they'd like to beat the crap out of those boys. Did you hear they got expelled?"

"I heard," he said. He was shocked that some of the kids were sympathetic.

"I thought maybe you'd want to go to a movie or something," she said. "Maybe you can get your mind off it for a couple of hours."

Despite the distance that had grown between them, her concern touched him. "Jake's here," he said, by way of explaining that he couldn't go to the movies.

"Oh," was all she said. "I guess I'll see you in school on Monday," and she turned to leave.

"Wait, Ashley." He hesitated. "It was real nice of you to come by. Thanks." He smiled at her.

She surprised him and walked over and gave him a bear hug. He half hugged her back.

"See ya, Rory." She slipped out the kitchen door.

"That was Ashley," Rory said as Jake entered the kitchen. "What'd she want?"

Rory explained. "It was nice of her to come over. Maybe she's sorry for what she said that time." Jake raised his eyebrows. "Yeah, until the next time she makes a crack."

"Ashley says some kids are mad at those guys. She said we have more friends than we know about."

"I'm not sure I believe that," Jake answered. "You goin' back on Monday?"

"I guess so. I sure don't want Mama to go to jail on my account. You?"

"I wouldn't mind seeing my old man in the slammer. It'd probably be my mama, though. He blames her for everything. Besides, I'd have to explain why I wasn't goin' to school, and I don't want to get into it with them."

***

"If I don't have a stroke before tomorrow, it'll be a miracle," Ruth told Lily when she called on Sunday to see how things were. "The tension is so thick around here I could chew it. I don't know who's more nervous, me or them."

Do you think it would help if Grady and me came over? You know he's good at distracting Rory."

"Maybe. I'm taking them out for pizza, and then I'm gonna drop Jake at his house. Why don't you come by at seven? I'll pick up some low-fat ice cream. That should help Grady's cholesterol and Rory's mood."

Ruth was reluctant to suggest going out, but she didn't feel like cooking and the boys' teenage appetites were recovering. She could tell they were skittish after being holed up in the house all weekend.

Rory and Jake were very slow to get out of the car at the pizza place. For a minute Ruth wondered if she'd be going in alone, but once they were out of the car they stuck to her like flies on flypaper.

There were several families at tables, and Ruth recognized a few of them. She nodded and said hey to a couple of the women. Seeing an empty table in the back, she took the seat facing the dining room and let the boys sit with their backs to the other diners. She noticed Rory's hands shaking as he read the menu.

The young girl who came to take their drink orders said hey to the boys. After she left, Jake said, "She's in some of my classes."

"Mine too," Rory said.

"What'll it be, boys?" Ruth asked. "I realize this is a dumb question, but how hungry are you?"

"I'm starved," Rory said.

"Me too," Jake echoed.

"If we order two large pies, will that hold you? I won't eat but one or two slices."

"That should fill us up, Mama."

"Tell our waitress we'll have two large pies with everything but pineapple and anchovies, please, and three Dr. Peppers. I'm going to wash my hands," she said.

The waitress saw her leave the table and took the opportunity to go over to the boys. "I'm real sorry about what happened. That was plain hateful. I hope you're okay." She smiled, and Jake and Rory muttered something that sounded like, "We're fine, thanks."

Alone again, Rory said, "Maybe it won't be so bad tomorrow."

"I'm not countin' on it," Jake replied.

Ruth hadn't mentioned taking Jake home until they were leaving the restaurant. "Jake, I'm going to drop you off at home. You'll need to get clothes for tomorrow and you should spend the night at home, I think."

"Yes ma'am," he answered. "Thanks for letting me stay over, Mrs. Wilson. I appreciate it."

"Will you be all right?" Rory asked as they pulled up to the curb at Jake's house. "Your folks got that letter."

"Yeah, if they ask what happened, I'll just say some kids got beat up. They won't care."

Ruth and Rory continued on home and pulled into the driveway as Lily and Grady inched up to the curb.

"Give your meemaw a big hug, Rory Calhoun." He did as he was asked. By the time he'd hugged his grandmother, Grady had walked around the car to where they stood. He grabbed Rory in a one-armed hug and kept his arm around the boy's shoulders as they walked into the house.

"Put this in the freezer before it turns to soup." Ruth handed Rory the tub of ice cream. Before he put it away, he held it out to Grady. "Look, Papaw, low-fat, just for you," he said.

Grady made a face, and Lily hit him playfully on his belly. "Ain't low enough to get rid o' this," she said and they all laughed.

Lily had been right. Grady knew how to distract his grandson. Between eating ice cream and listening to his grandfather's stories, Rory seemed more relaxed than he had in several days by the time his grandparents left.

Ruth hadn't had time to think about how tired she was. Now that Jake was gone and she and Rory were alone, a wave of fatigue swept over her. "Lord, I feel like I've been run over by a steam roller," she said. "Ready for bed?"

"Yeah, I'm pretty tired too. I could do with some extra sleep. To-morrow's gonna be rough."

They hugged and headed in different directions. Ruth turned to watch Rory walk into his room. As he swung around to close his door, he saw her looking at him.

"What is it, Mama?"

"Nothin', son. I was just thinking how much I love you. Sleep well."

"I love you too, Mama. Good night."

Chapter Twenty-Five

The next morning, Jake's homeroom teacher handed him a note. While the PA system bombarded the students with announcements, he slit the envelope open with his thumb and read, "*Jake, I'm sorry about what happened last week. Let's talk. Come on by the office during your fourth period study hall. I'll see you then.*
Coach Walters"

Jake's decision to quit the soccer team had been bitterly painful. It was tough acknowledging his own teammates had assaulted Rory and him. He hadn't socialized with the guys, but he considered them friends. On the soccer field they'd had his back, literally, so he was shocked that they suspected he was gay and, worse, attacked him for it. Jake had developed as a skilled soccer player, and his coach had hinted that there could be a college scholarship if the team won their division title. Jake knew it might be his only chance to go to college.

At the start of fourth period, Jake headed toward the gym. He knocked on the coach's door and saw him talking on the phone through the glass panel. The coach motioned for Jake to come in. "Sorry about that. It was a call from my wife." Reaching into the bottom drawer of the file cabinet, he retrieved a crumpled soccer uniform. Jake recognized his number, 12.

"The custodian found this in the trash on hallway C and brought it to me. He thought you might want it."

"I threw it there," Jake replied. "I'm done with the team." He expected a reprimand for trashing the uniform, which belonged to the school.

"Son, I know how hard this is for you right now. I can't imagine what it feels like, but you have to put this behind you. Otherwise, the bullies win."

Jake listened to this man he admired, but his resolution was firm.

"Come on, Jake. You're our best center forward. There's not another guy on the team who can do what you do on that field," he said. "I've already started talking to a couple of college coaches about you. Don't throw away a chance for a scholarship. Those morons aren't worth it."

Jake felt no need to say more, but the coach pressed. "You know Mitchell, Travis and Jeff are out of school for good, don't you?" he asked, referring to the three boys who'd been expelled.

"Yes, sir."

"Jake, I'm talking to you like I'd talk to my own son. I don't give a hoot if you like girls or boys or chimpanzees. What matters is that you're a first-rate soccer player, and I need you if I'm going to rebuild this team."

So that's what he really cares about, the team. He doesn't give a rat's behind about me, Jake thought. The crack about chimpanzees was a low blow, but Jake kept quiet.

"So, what do you say?" The coach held out Jake's uniform toward him. "Will you come back?"

Jake made no move to take the uniform. He thought briefly about what the coach had said about a scholarship, and while that was important to him, he couldn't bring himself to forgive what his teammates had done.

"No, sir, I'd never be able to trust my teammates again. If I play soccer again, it won't be for this school. Only reason I'm back at all is that the law says I have to be here. Otherwise, I'd shuck this place for good."

The coach was surprised at the vehemence of Jake's refusal. He'd always found Jake quiet and submissive except when he was on the soccer field.

"Well, think about it, boy. Don't throw your future away because of your pride. Will you at least do that?"

"Yes, sir, but I won't change my mind." Nodding to the uniform still in the coach's hands he said, "You might as well give that to someone else." As Jake walked across the gym he heard the unmistakable sound of a foot kicking a metal file cabinet, a strong, trained foot that had kicked many a soccer ball.

Rory's re-entry to school was less dramatic. A few classmates offered sympathetic comments. One girl even said she was embarrassed to tell people where she went to school.

"Yeah, me too," he said and walked away.

He and Jake had decided not to eat lunch together for a while. The less they were seen together, the better. Jake sat by himself and Rory accepted an invitation to sit with Ashley and a couple of girls she regularly ate with. Rory tried making eye contact with Jake as he ate alone, but he couldn't because Jake's head was practically in his plate.

That night Jake told Rory about the meeting with Coach Walters and Rory cautioned him not to be too hasty.

Jake snapped, "You of all people should know why I can't go back and play with those guys. Would you feel like spending time with them, showering in the locker room and all, after what they made us do? Where's your self-respect, man?"

"Geez, don't get mad at me. I was just saying maybe your chance for a scholarship was more important than the rest of it."

Jake backed off. "I'm sorry. I don't mean to yell at you. I'm startin' to get really pissed now. Don't you feel mad?"

"Yeah, and sad and ashamed. One minute I'm so mad I could kill somebody, and next minute I feel like I want to cry. It's weird. I talked to Dr. Devlin today. Did you?"

"Nah, I just tried to go to class and not talk to anybody except Walters. That was enough for me for one day."

"I'm so behind in biology I don't know if I'll ever catch up," Rory said. "I missed a test last Friday, but Mr. Short said I could make it up. At least the teachers are being nice. Some of the kids, too." He told Jake about a girl who said she felt like she was going to school with a bunch of Neanderthals, and they both laughed.

Ruth didn't know how much to push Rory to talk about school. Dr. Devlin advised her to let Rory set the agenda for conversations for a while, so that's what she did. He wasn't much of a talker, so conversation centered on what they were eating for supper, the weather, and if he wanted to spend some extra time at his grandparents'.

The incident, as the family began to refer to it, affected lots of people. Grady came home from the barber shop one day with steam pouring out of his ears, as Lily described him to Ruth. According to Lily, one of the men who regularly hung out there made a crack about two pansies putting on a sex show behind the athletic field. The only thing that kept Grady from jumping out of the chair during a shave was fear that the barber might slit his throat. Somebody must have shut the guy up because he didn't say anything else and nobody responded to his nasty comment.

"It took a bowl of ice cream and me rubbin' his shoulders for him to calm down," Lily told her daughter-in-law. "I fear he's goin' to have another heart attack over this thing." Ruth worried too. She knew the effects of stress on the body. She'd had every psychosomatic symptom in the book since the incident.

As the weeks went by, there were fewer and fewer references to the assault and Ruth hoped that meant Rory was starting to heal, if that was possible. She realized that wasn't the case when Rory brought home his report card.

He'd been a straight A student for as long as Ruth could recall, but a couple of his grades had slipped during the marking period. Not that it was a bad report. Most parents would have been thrilled with it.

For a few minutes she thought of what might have happened if she was still married to Darrell. He could never have contained himself if he'd heard about the incident. It was hard to fathom, but she was sure he'd have made both of their lives even more miserable.

She never asked Lily and Grady if they'd told Darrell about it. He seemed to have absolutely no interest in Rory, so she guessed they hadn't. The only contact Ruth had was when she received his monthly check. She rarely thought about him. Worry about Rory crowded out nearly everything else.

Jake often came to the house during the week, and the two boys stayed in Rory's room, supposedly doing school work. She tried not to think of what else they might be doing, and, of course, Rory still didn't have a girlfriend.

Ruth attended PFLAG meetings once a month in Virginia and

went to an occasional social function with some of the people from the group. She drove 50 minutes to meetings. There were none closer, not surprising as she couldn't imagine there were enough people who cared about gay kids to make up a group in her part of Tennessee. If her former preacher was typical, none of the churches around Craggy Grove were tolerant, let alone welcoming to gays.

Rory still hadn't told her he was gay. She thought he might have broached the subject with his grandparents, but when she asked about it, her mother-in-law said he'd never brought it up with them, either. Each year that Rory showed no interest in girls, she gave up a bit more hope that shyness was the reason.

Chapter Twenty-Six

Ruth heard the car crunch over the broken concrete in their driveway. Rory ambled in and kissed her. She was editing an article, one of several free-lance assignments she'd picked up at the university since the divorce. She waved him away.

"I'm on a tight deadline. You'll have to fix your own supper unless you want to wait a couple of hours to eat. This thing is due tomorrow morning."

"Aw, don't worry about me, Mama. I'll grab a bite in town. Then I'm goin' over to get Jake. We're going to the library to study."

Studying. That's what Rory had called it the night the call came about Grady's heart attack.

Lily'd been frantic on the phone. "They're puttin' Grady in the ambulance. Meet me at Watauga Medical Center."

Ruth ignored the closed door and burst into Rory's room. "Oh, Lord!" she screamed. That couldn't be her little boy underneath another naked boy on the bed. It just couldn't!

She slammed the door shut and yelled, "Put your damned clothes on. We have to go to the hospital. Grady's had a heart attack."

Lord help me, Ruth prayed. I feel like I've been stabbed. This can't be my Rory!

Then she spoke sternly to herself. Ruth, you've suspected this for years. It's the way he is. Don't drive him away. It's enough that you ended up divorcing Darrell over it. Don't lose Rory too.

Rory walked into the living room buttoning his shirt. "Mama, I'm ..."

She held her hand up. "Don't say a word, Rory. I can't deal with this right now. Grady needs us." She had managed to pick up her purse and keys, although she couldn't recall doing it. She pushed the keys at him. "You drive."

They got into the car and sat locked in their separate worlds of agony. Ruth remembered looking over at Rory while he drove and wondering how he could see to drive through his tears. She handed him a tissue without saying anything, and he wiped his eyes.

In a few minutes, she put her hand on his leg and said, "I'm sure he'll be all right."

When they arrived, they found Lily in the emergency waiting room. A woman was comforting her. Lily got up when she saw Rory and dissolved into tears. The stranger introduced herself as the hospital chaplain. "Mr. Wilson is waiting for you upstairs. I'll show you the way." Those words were a magnificent gift. Grady was alive.

As they got into the elevator, Lily told them the doctor said it was definitely a heart attack, but that he expected Grady to recover. That's when Ruth and Rory both lost it. Relief pried opened the floodgates, and they held one another and cried as the chaplain tended to Lily who had broken down again.

The elevator door opened and the chaplain steered them to the rest rooms. "I think it would be a good idea if y'all freshened up a bit before you see the patient." She had a warming smile.

When Ruth and Lily looked in the bathroom mirror, they saw what she meant. They splashed their faces with cold water, and Ruth found a comb in her purse.

Rory and the chaplain led the way down the hall. A sign on the door read Intensive Care. A nurse greeted them as soon as they opened the door. "Who are you here to see?"

"Grady Wilson," Lily said. "I'm his wife, and this is his grandson and daughter."

"Oh, yes, he's been askin' for you," she said as she looked up at Rory. "Come this way."

"I've brought your grandson," Mr. Wilson. "You didn't tell me he was so handsome."

Rory tried not to look startled by the oxygen in Grady's nose and the wires connected to his body.

"Hey, Papaw. We got here as fast as we could. How're ya doin?"

"Well, this ain't my idea of a good time, but the doc says I'll live.

They're poking me and taking my blood. How's a fella to get any rest in this place?"

Lily took his hand. "Some case of indigestion you've got."

She explained. "We were havin' supper when he grabbed his chest and said he had terrible indigestion. I knew nobody could have indigestion from eatin' my baked chicken and mashed potatoes. When he said his arm hurt, I knew for sure it was a heart attack. I called 9-1-1. This fool told me to cancel the call, insistin' it was heartburn, but I knew better."

Then she looked at Grady. "Most times you're right, but this time you weren't. I'm glad I didn't listen to you."

Ruth and Rory replied in unison, "Me too." Grady smiled.

The nurse came over and told them they had to let the patient get some rest.

"When can we see him again?" Rory asked.

"I can let you in again in an hour if you want to wait."

"We'll wait," Rory said and they headed toward the waiting room.

"If y'all are hungry, the food court is on the first floor," said the waiting room volunteer as they entered. "It's not great, but it probably won't kill you. If y'all want to talk with the chaplain, I can call her. There's a chapel right around the corner from the cafeteria." Then she left them alone.

Rory spoke as they sat down. "Meemaw, you saved Papaw's life," and he reached over and gave her a crushing one-armed hug.

"I saw on one of them *National Geographic* shows once that the Chinese people say if you save somebody's life, you're responsible for them forever. I don't reckon I'll ever hear the end of this."

They talked for a while until a man with a stethoscope around his neck stepped into the room. "Mrs. Wilson?"

"Yes," both women answered and then laughed.

He sat across from the three of them. "I'm Doctor Anderson, the resident cardiologist. I'll be taking care of Mr. Wilson while he's here." He reached out to Rory and they shook hands. "You must be Rory."

"Yes, sir."

"Your grandfather is mighty proud of you, young man. He talked non-stop about what a wonderful grandson you are. You're lucky to have someone who loves you as much as he does." The doctor went on to say that Grady's heart attack was not very severe, but he cautioned that it was a warning sign of heart disease.

"While we have him here, we want to run some tests to determine what we're dealing with. If all goes well, he should be able to go home in four or five days."

Lily spoke up. "Doctor, my husband doesn't care much for hospitals and doctors. He thinks he's 25 and doesn't need to take care of himself. I'd appreciate it if you'd tell him he has to go for regular checkups and take his blood pressure medicine."

The doctor smiled. "Mrs. Wilson, I'll try my best, but I suspect it might not go very far. He admitted to me, though, that if it hadn't been for you, he'd never have come to the hospital at all." The doctor walked over and put a hand on her shoulder. "I think you'll be able to keep him in line."

Ruth and Rory drove Lily home in the wee hours of the morning. Now that he was reassured Grady would survive, Rory's mind turned to what his mother had seen with Jake. He'd dreaded the day when he'd have to come out to his mother, but he hadn't imagined it happening this way.

Lily dozed on the ride home, and Ruth and Rory avoided conversation so they wouldn't wake her. Poor woman had been through the mill.

Rory walked his grandmother to the door and started to unlock it. "It's open," she said. "I figured if Grady was dyin' I didn't care if somebody broke into the house." She put her head on Rory's chest and began to cry. "Lord have mercy, Rory, I don't know what I'd a done if that'd happened. You know what I was thinkin' while I waited in the emergency room? I couldn't remember when was the last time I told your papaw that I love him. It's important to tell folks you love how you feel. You never know when it might be too late."

"You're right, Meemaw. Can I get you anything before I go?"

"Give me another hug, dear. You need to get you and your mama home."

Rory reached down and held her. "I love you, Meemaw," he said softly, testing the phrase he'd only said to his mother during his sixteen years, and not too often lately. "Get some sleep. Papaw will be all right."

Lily held on to her grandson a bit longer than usual but finally let go and watched him walk to the car.

"Is she okay?" Ruth asked.

"I think she'll be all right." He didn't plan to say what came out of his mouth next. He put the key in the ignition and then turned to his mother. "Mama, you know I love you, don't you?"

Ruth wasn't expecting that. She reached over and covered his big hand. She wasn't sure if he was trying to reassure her or attempting to figure out what her feelings for him were after what she witnessed. This had been a night of raw emotions for all of them.

"Son, I do know that. We'll talk tomorrow, but for now I want you to remember that I love you more than any living soul on this planet, and nothing will ever change that, nothing." She looked him in the eye and watched two large tears form and spill. Rory leaned over and hugged her tightly.

"Thanks, Mama," he croaked. "I needed to be sure."

They cried together for a few minutes.

"Let's go home." She handed him her last tissue. "Wipe your eyes before we end up as Papaw's roommates in the hospital."

Rory felt calmer than he had all night. What he'd feared most was that his mother might reject him. He'd heard horror stories about kids whose families threw them out of their homes when they found out they were gay. He'd always known that his father's disappointment in him was what led to the divorce, and he worried that his mother might resent him for it.

Chapter Twenty-Seven

"I think you might have something here," Mr. Short commented as Rory walked into the lab one afternoon. Rory had tried to change the genetic structure of a tobacco leaf so it would burn more cleanly, reducing the amount of tar residue. Each time he'd thought he made the right genetic alteration, the gummy black stuff in the beaker was as plentiful as in the previous test. He was starting to feel discouraged.

"Hope you don't mind, Rory. I had a friend of mine who teaches botany at the university take a look at your notebook last night. He specializes in the genetic engineering of broadleaf plants. He said he's never worked with tobacco, but the structure is similar to some plants he's worked on."

Rory was grateful that his teacher showed such strong interest in his experiment. They'd long passed the deadline for the regional science fair, but Rory's determination to succeed compelled Mr. Short to continue working with him.

"What'd he say? Does he think I'm crazy for trying to clean up tobacco?"

"No, to the contrary. He saw something in your notes that made him sit up and take notice. He wants to talk to you about it. Here's his phone number. He said you can give him a call any evening. His name is Dr. Ragatky."

"Thanks. I'll call him tonight. So, he thinks I might be able to do it, huh?" Rory was excited about the prospect of being able to talk to a real scientist about his work.

When Rory passed on dessert that night, Ruth asked, "Is something wrong?"

"No, I have an important phone call to make, and I don't want to call too late."

"Who're you callin'?"

Rory explained about the scientist at East Tennessee State University. Ruth had long since given up trying to understand what Rory was working on in the biology lab, but she knew it was very important to him.

When Rory came into the living room an hour later, his face was flushed with excitement. "Mama, you won't believe it," he started. "The professor knew about me. He knows the professor Miss Ebsen took me to see when I was in junior high school. He's going to be out of town for a couple of weeks, but he wants me to call him when he gets back.

Later that night, Ruth was watching a news story about a 22 percent increase in hate crimes against gay men in New York. When Rory came into the room, she waved her hand for him to wait and continued watching the report as he stood next to her chair.

He watched with her. At the conclusion of the story the reporter did a quick review of the 1998 Laramie, Wyoming murder of Matthew Shepard and showed a photo of the victim. Ruth was startled by Matthew's similarity to Rory. Except for the difference in their height, they could have passed for brothers. Rory heard the reporter say that the Matthew Shepard Act signed into law in 2009 included sexual orientation among categories of hate crimes.

Hearing it described on TV made him realize that he and Jake had been victims of a hate crime. Those kids who did that to Jake and me could go to jail, he thought. We could've ended up on the news. Jake and I could end up like Matthew Shepard.

"Rory, what did you want to tell me?" Ruth asked for the second time. Rory seemed to be in another place.

Snapping out of his thoughts, he answered, "Sorry, Mama. I didn't hear you."

Ruth looked at him strangely, but Rory related additional details about his phone conversation with Dr. Ragatky, excited about the scientist's desire to work with him on his tobacco project. He'd invited Rory to come to the university where they had better equipment.

"He thinks I might be on the cusp, that's the word he used, the cusp of a brilliant achievement. When he gets back, can I use the car to go to Johnson City?"

"It shouldn't be a problem."

Rory hurried into his room and hit the space bar to wake his computer. Usually, he logged off whenever he was out of his room so there was no chance Ruth might see any of the hateful email messages from kids at school. Since the time he'd forgotten to log off and arrived home to see 18 nasty messages, he tried to be more careful.

He typed M-a-t-h-e-w S-h-e-p-h-e-r-d. Google asked, "Did you mean Matthew Shepard?" Rory hit the enter key. For the next half hour he read with horror and viewed graphic photos of the gruesome murder of the 21-year-old gay man.

Though he no longer attended church, Rory still prayed to a God he believed loved him. Shaken by what he'd seen, he got off his chair and sank to his knees alongside his bed.

"Please Lord, don't let me be gay. I don't want to end up like that kid. I'll do anything. I won't do that stuff with Jake anymore, and I'll try to like girls." He leaned his head against the bed and beseeched God to undo what he feared might be irreversible.

Exhausted from prayer and overcome by fear, he went back to his computer and began a new email. He typed, "Dear Jake, I've been thinking and decided it's best if we're not friends any more. We could end up being killed. I'm sorry. Rory." As an afterthought he added, "P.S. Look up Matthew Shepard on the Internet, and you'll know why."

There was no response from Jake by the next morning, and Rory avoided him all the next day in school and tried not to think about him.

That evening while Rory and Ruth were finishing supper, they heard a siren and Ruth got up to see where it was coming from. "Looks like it's up the street," she called. She walked out the front door and yelled back to Rory, "Yeah, I think they're at Jake's house. I'm going over to see what's wrong. 'Coming?"

"Nah."

Ruth briefly wondered at this odd response as she walked up the street in time to see firefighters run into Jake's house. A few neighbors had gathered on the sidewalk, and Ruth went over to them.

An ambulance sped up the street followed quickly by another.

While the neighbors speculated about what was going on, a police officer walked briskly to where they gathered, told them there was a gas leak, and urged them to move further away.

"Is anyone hurt?" Ruth asked, but the officer turned and headed back to the house. The EMTs carried out two people on stretchers, their faces covered with oxygen masks. By this time, all the windows in the house were wide open, and the breeze carried gas fumes to where the neighbors stood.

Ruth's anxiety increased when she didn't see a third person removed from the house. A truck from the gas company had joined the assortment of emergency vehicles, and eventually the ambulances left with the two victims. Ruth had seen a woman sitting up inside the first ambulance just before it left. She strained to see if Jake was in the second one but her view was blocked.

Eventually, the police came out of the house and an officer came over to them. "Just wanted to let you folks know the EMTs said they're gonna be okay. They were overcome by gas. Somebody must've forgot to turn off the oven, but we got the call in time, thank the Lord. Which one of you called 9-1-1?"

They all looked at each other. Nobody spoke. "Well, whoever it was probably saved two lives tonight," he said.

Ruth asked, "Who'd they carry out?"

"A man and a woman. That's all that lived there, right?"

"No," Ruth said, panic rising. "There's a boy that lives there too, their son Jake."

"We didn't find anyone else," the officer replied. "There was a dog in an upstairs bedroom, and we let him out in the yard. He's still out there, but there wasn't anyone else."

Ruth was puzzled. Jake wasn't at her house, which was the only place he went at night as far as she knew. She headed home.

"Rory, do you know where Jake is?"

"No. Why?"

She described what had happened and that Jake wasn't home. "I'm going to write a note and put it on the door so he'll know what happened when he gets home. He'll wonder where his parents are."

Ruth quickly scribbled a note: Come to our house and I'll explain where your folks are. She handed Rory the note and a roll of tape.

"Go put this on their front door, okay?"

Rory didn't want to go near Jake's house, but he grabbed the note, ran to Jake's house, taped it to the front door and hurried home, where he busied himself in his room. He didn't want to see Jake when he came to the house.

He needn't have worried. Jake never came.

The next day Jake wasn't in school. Dr. Devlin appeared in Rory's algebra class. He whispered a couple of words to the teacher. She sent Rory out into the hall.

"Hey, Rory. How's it goin?" Dr. Devlin asked. He didn't want to alarm the boy.

"Jake's not been in school for a couple of days, and there's no answer at his house. Do you know where he is?"

"No, sir. I haven't seen him in three or four days." Rory told the psychologist about the gas leak and said he didn't know anything more.

"You two are pretty good friends, so I figured you might be able to help." It was more of a question than a statement.

Rory shook his head. "Sorry."

"Well, if you hear from him, please ask him to give me a call." He handed Rory a piece of paper with a phone number on it. "That's my home number. He can call me at school or there."

Chapter Twenty-Eight

That night a detective came to Ruth's door. "I'm Sergeant Haskell, ma'am." She invited him in.

"I hate to deliver bad news," he began. Ruth listened intently and was stunned by what he told her. She excused herself and went to Rory's room.

"A detective is here and wants to talk with you."

Rory followed her and shook hands with Detective Haskell.

"Sit down, son. I'm afraid I have some very bad news."

Ruth watched pain spread over Rory's face as the detective repeated what he'd told her. He sat silent.

Sergeant Haskell handed Rory an envelope addressed to him and Rory recognized Jake's handwriting. He took it and went to his room.

"Would you like a cup of coffee?" Ruth asked the detective.

"Yes, ma'am, if it's not any trouble. We do need to know what's in that note, but I understand your son wants privacy."

"I just can't believe Jake would do this," she said for the fourth or fifth time since the detective told her two hikers found his body hanging from a tree in a wooded area two miles from the high school. "Are you certain it was suicide?"

"We're pretty sure, ma'am. I expect we'll know more when we see what's in that note. We have questions, but I guess they can wait 'til tomorrow. I know this is a shock."

"What did his parents say?"

"Well, they were upset, of course, and when I asked if there was somebody I could call, like a preacher or somebody, the father said they'd call an undertaker. Struck me as strange. Do you know him?"

"No, they keep to themselves pretty much. Jake spent a lot of time over here, and I know he wasn't close with his parents." She lowered her voice. "There's domestic violence in the home."

Ruth wondered if she should say anything about what had happened to the boys at school recently, but decided against it. She was sure he'd speak with school officials. He'd find out then.

Rory had been in his room with the door closed for about twenty minutes, and Ruth was running out of things to say. The uncomfortable silent periods were too long, and she was getting anxious, so she went to his room and knocked on the door.

"Son, are you okay?"

An imperceptible grunt emanated from behind the door.

"The officer needs to talk to you about the note."

Silence.

Sergeant Haskell went to the door and motioned for her to let him talk. "Rory," he began, "I know you're upset about your friend. I'm real sorry about what happened, but I need you to show me his note."

"Yes, sir, be right out."

"More coffee?" Ruth offered.

"Thank you. It looks like it could be a while. I don't want to pressure the boy."

Ruth heard Rory's printer. After a few minutes, Rory's door opened, and he emerged red-eyed with the envelope in his hand.

"Here's the note."

Sergeant Haskell took the envelope and removed the typed note. He read, "Dear Rory, I just wanted to say goodbye. Your friend, Jake." He looked at Rory and Ruth.

"Well, this doesn't tell us anything, does it?"

"No, sir," Rory agreed.

"What did he say?" Ruth asked.

The sergeant handed her the note. She shook her head. "He had his whole life ahead of him. Why would he do it?" She directed the question to Rory.

Rory shrugged.

Sergeant Haskell knew this wasn't a good time to question Rory. "How 'bout if I stop by tomorrow evening?" He looked at Rory.

"Okay."

The detective thanked Ruth for the coffee and left.

"Rory, I'm so sorry about Jake." Ruth reached for him, but he shrugged off her attempt to comfort him.

"What were you printing in your room?"

"Nothing."

"I heard the printer going before you came out, Rory."

"The printer was cleaning the heads. That's all." He avoided looking at his mother.

Ruth knew Rory was hurting and figured he would eventually tell her what he'd been doing. Losing Jake had to be a devastating blow, and she sympathized with him.

"Do you have any idea why Jake would want to take his life?" she asked, hoping Rory would open up about his feelings. "Did he ever say anything to you about suicide? I know things were rough for him with his father. Did they have a blow-up recently?"

"No, he didn't say anything to me."

Ruth continued, "Do you think this has anything to do with what happened at school?"

Rory grew more upset as her questioning continued. He barely got the words out of his constricted throat, "Mama, I don't want to talk about it right now, okay?" He went back into his room, and Ruth heard lots of slamming and then music, loud music. She stepped close enough to his door to hear his sobs over the pounding bass.

Ruth's heart ached for her son. If he and Jake had been lovers, Jake's death was even more traumatic than if they'd just been friends. How could she support Rory if he wouldn't tell her the truth?

Chapter Twenty-Nine

Morning announcements were somber. The principal asked students to observe a moment of silence and then he requested anyone having information that might shed light on Jake's death to contact Sergeant Haskell.

A few minutes into first period, Dr. Devlin appeared and took Rory into the hall. "I'm so sorry about Jake," he began. "I know he was your buddy." He waited for a response.

"Yes, sir. Thanks."

"Do you want to talk about it?"

"Naw. I'm just tryin' to forget it for now."

Dr. Devlin knew that was impossible and cautioned Rory not to try to deny his grief. "How about coming by tomorrow? You have a study hall third period, I see. I'd really like us to talk."

Rory recognized this as more of a command than a suggestion and didn't want to arouse suspicion by arguing.

"Sure, I'll be by." Rory returned to class and retreated into a haze of grief and guilt.

***

Before leaving the school, Sergeant Haskell spoke with several of Jake's classmates and teachers. As expected, it didn't take long for information to emerge that made more sense of his suicide. When Haskell asked who Jake's friends were, all of them said the same thing. He seemed to have only one friend: Rory.

One conversation was particularly enlightening. When Coach Walters told the sergeant about the incident with the soccer team, more questions were raised in the sergeant's mind about what Rory was holding back. By the time the policeman approached Ruth's door that night, he had a fairly good idea that the solution to Jake's death lay with Rory. Haskell knew kids from the six years he'd worked the juvenile detail. He realized he had to tread lightly, or Rory would continue to clam up.

Students were pre-occupied with Jake's death all day, and details permeated conversation between classes and after school. As if by some plan, all but one cut a wide berth around Rory for the rest of the day. After school, Ashley waited in front of Rory's locker.

As Rory rounded the corner, he saw her. As soon as he got within two feet of her, she reached out and hugged him. She didn't say a word; she just stood there holding on to him. Several students witnessed their embrace and cleared the area around them.

"I'm so sorry, Rory." There was nothing more she could say that would make any sense. "Let's bag the bus and walk home."

"Good idea. I don't want any more people staring at me today," he answered.

"We don't have to talk if you don't want to," Ashley offered. "I just want you to know I'm here for you. We've been friends a long time."

Rory managed a slight smile of gratitude. "Yeah, we have," he replied. "Thanks."

They hadn't walked more than two blocks when Ashley's self-imposed silence gave way to curiosity. "Do you know why he did it?"

Rory didn't answer, just glanced at her sideways.

"Okay, I'll shut up. Sorry."

They walked the rest of the way home in silence until they reached Ashley's house.

"Wanna come in for a Coke?" she asked.

Rory's initial instinct was to refuse and go home where he could wallow in his guilt and grief alone, but he wanted to show appreciation for Ashley's support.

"Okay, but I can't stay long."

Ashley's mother was in the kitchen when they walked in. Jane was surprised to see Rory. Her maternal instinct overruled caution, and she reached out to him. He stiffened when she hugged him, but seemed to relax a bit before she released him. "We're all real sorry about Jake," she said.

Jane tried to continue some semblance of conversation with Rory, but Ashley's face told her she should let it be, so she walked out of the room and left the two of them at the table with their Cokes. Ashley smiled at Rory, conveying that she understood how uncomfortable he must be when people tried to talk to him about Jake.

Rory guzzled down his Coke and stood. Ashley took the empty can from his hand and let her fingers linger on his for a moment. "Don't be a stranger, Rory. If you feel like talking, I'm here." She watched him walk up the street to his house and felt immeasurably sad for her friend.

***

That night Sergeant Haskell knocked on the door. He was surprised when Rory opened it.

"Hey, Rory."

"Come on in. I guess you want to ask me some questions."

"Yes, son. I know this is tough, but we have to know why Jake took his life. You understand, don't you? It's my job."

Why can't you just let it alone? Jake's dead. Nothing you find out is gonna bring him back. It's just gonna stir up a lot of trouble, Rory thought. He noted the sergeant was almost apologetic, but that didn't make the prospect of answering his questions any easier. He gestured to a chair at the kitchen table.

"Tell me about the last time you saw Jake. Try not to leave anything out."

Rory thought back to the last evening he spent with Jake. No way was he going to tell the policeman everything. "Jake came over and we studied for a math test. We asked each other questions and worked on some problems. He left and said he'd see me in school the next day. That's about it."

"Did he say anything about feeling down or angry at his parents?"

"No. He didn't get along with his father, but he didn't mention it that night."

"Tell me about his relationship with his father."

Rory squirmed in his seat. He was uncomfortable talking about Jake's family. "His dad drinks a lot, and when he got drunk, he'd beat Jake up. He also beats Jake's mother up when he drinks. That's why we usually did homework here. He didn't like to stay home."

"Did you get along with Jake's dad?"

"I didn't go to their house much."

144

Haskell cleared his throat. "His father thought you two might have a homosexual relationship." He let the statement lie there and watched Rory's reaction.

Rory turned beet red but didn't respond.

Haskell continued, "I talked to Coach Walters at school today and he told me about a recent incident that happened after school. He told me Jake quit the soccer team after that." He thought his prompting was about to loosen Rory's tongue when Ruth entered the kitchen from the side door.

"Oh, Sergeant, I didn't know you were here." She sensed she'd interrupted something and made an excuse to leave the room.

Haskell repeated what the coach had said. He waited, hoping the uncomfortable silence would force Rory to talk. That was a technique that nearly always worked.

The ticking seconds on the wall clock echoed like gunshots in Rory's head. He alternately slid his hands under his bony butt and pulled them out. He looked around the kitchen but remained mute.

"Rory, I get the feeling there's somethin' you're not tellin' me. Did I embarrass you?" Again he let the question sit there while he studied Rory.

"Well, wouldn't you be embarrassed if people accused you of that?" Rory asked.

Haskell softened his voice as he spoke. "I'd guess it would be pretty rough to be gay. I have two teenage kids, and I know they can be pretty insensitive sometimes. Do you take a lot of crap from the other kids?" He looked at Rory's eyes. "Did Jake? He must have been pretty upset to quit the soccer team."

"Yeah, he felt like his own team had turned on him. He was mad more than anything."

Haskell noted Rory had not denied being gay, nor had he said Jake wasn't.

His suspicion about the note Rory showed him had grown. He wondered how to approach it without accusing Rory of tampering with evidence.

Haskell asked several more questions but Rory's answers were evasive at best. The detective was growing more impatient with each dodged question.

"The note you showed me last night, the one Jake wrote to you, was that the original note you got from him?" Haskell's eyes drilled into Rory's, and Rory looked down in an effort to avoid them.

Haskell reached over and placed his hand on Rory's shoulder. "Look at me, boy. Did you show me the note Jake wrote you?"

Rory stiffened, bracing for an assault. He squirmed until the detective let go of him.

"Yes, sir. You saw it." Rory blinked rapidly and rubbed his shoulder.

Haskell knew Rory was lying but didn't want to press him further. There'd be time later on for that.

Just as Rory thought he couldn't take any more grilling, Haskell got up from his chair. "Well, we'll talk some more, but for now I've got to be going. If you think of anything else, here's where you can reach me." He handed Rory his card.

The detective called to Ruth as he turned to leave. "See you, Mrs. Wilson. Sorry to hold up your supper."

"Oh, don't think anything of it," she responded.

Sergeant Haskell let himself out the front door, and Ruth joined Rory in the kitchen.

"Were you able to tell him anything?"

"There's nothing to tell."

Ruth knew guilt when she saw it.

"He thinks I didn't show him Jake's note. I bet he suspects me of hiding something."

"Well, are you?"

"Are you gonna interrogate me too?"

"As a matter of fact, son, I've wondered if you're holding back information about Jake. Last night when I asked you about hearing the printer, I had the feeling you weren't telling me the truth. That note that was supposedly from Jake just didn't look like a note he'd have written to his best friend or whatever you were to him."

Rory labored at cleaning his left fingernails with the fingers of his right hand. Whatever I was to him was a mistake, and it's nobody's business, he thought. Why does everybody have to be so damned nosy? I'm not really that way, and I'm not gonna do that stuff with anybody else.

"Rory, I'm your mother. Don't you trust me enough to be honest? It hurts me that you're afraid to tell me the truth. I'm not blind, son. I saw how you and Jake were with each other. I know you haven't had any interest in girls. Lord have mercy, Rory, get it out. You'll feel better if you do. Let me help you, boy." She took a couple of tentative steps toward her son and put her arms around his shoulders. As she held Rory close, she felt his body shake, releasing a torrent of sobs from deep within him.

Chapter Thirty

Ruth had been preparing for this moment for years. She held Rory for a long time. He was the size of a full-grown man, but he was still her little boy. His first words were like a knife in her heart. Obviously, she had underestimated his hurt.

"Oh, Mama, I'm such a horrible person," he began.

Ruth assumed he meant because he was gay. She listened while he poured out his feelings.

"Jake's dead because of me. I got so scared when I saw the pictures of that Shepard kid on TV that I told Jake we couldn't be friends anymore. That was the night the gas filled his house, and he must have left. I bet he wanted to kill his parents. His father's a monster. He was so mean to Jake and his mother. He was drunk all the time, and that's when he beat them up. Jake hated him. His mother doesn't have the guts to stand up to him. That's probably why Jake wanted her dead, so she would be out of her misery."

Ruth tried not to react, but she was shocked. Things had happened so quickly that she didn't have time to consider that there might be a link between the gas leak and Jake's disappearance and suicide.

Rory spoke as if someone had released a pressure valve. Words exploded out of him. "Me and Jake loved each other, Mama, but it wasn't natural. I couldn't help it. I knew it was wrong, but I was happy when I was with him. But I can change. I don't have to be that way if I pray really hard. I know I can get to like girls if I try. I want you to be proud of me."

He cried throughout this long explanation, and Ruth stayed very close to him. She reached over and pushed his hair out of his eyes a few times and picked his hands up in hers.

She searched her memory for the things she'd learned at PFLAG meetings and hoped she'd find the right words. She knew her handling of the situation could be literally a matter of life and death. She didn't have to look far to see what happens when a child isn't accepted by his parents. Poor Jake. Poor Rory.

"I hurt too when you're in such pain, Rory. It must be awful feeling the way you do. How did Jake react when you told him?"

"I didn't tell him to his face, Mama. I sent him an email. I never got to see him after that."

He put his hands over his face and cried some more, and Ruth reached up and put her hands on his shoulders. She hoped her touch would reassure him that she didn't think he was a bad person. She mentally sifted through the information she'd learned about homosexuality since she began to attend PFLAG meetings.

When he stopped sobbing, Ruth said softly, "Rory, you're not horrible. You're a good person who had feelings that some people think are unnatural. But son, humans aren't the only animals that are attracted to the same sex. You've spent enough time at Meemaw's and Papaw's to have seen the cows and goats. Haven't you ever seen two bulls or two billies trying to have sex?"

"Yeah, but I thought they were just playing. You think they're gay?"

"It's possible. There's homosexuality among lots of different animals, Rory. It's natural. Besides, if the Lord made you that way, do you think he made a mistake? There are a lot of gay people. I bet there are gay kids in your school that you don't know about. Do you know that out of every ten people, there's likely to be one gay one?"

Rory looked surprised. He wasn't quite ready to accept what his mother said.

"If being gay is natural, why do so many people hate gays? Why do the kids in school call me a faggot? Why did my own daddy call me one? Remember the kids who spray painted it on the house?"

Ruth remembered all too well. "I can't answer that except to say we humans have a lousy track record when it comes to tolerating people who are different."

She paused and decided to tell Rory about PFLAG. "I've been going to meetings in Virginia with parents of other gay kids, Rory. I didn't tell you about it before because you never seemed ready to tell me about yourself. I'd like you to come to a meeting with me. I think it would do you good to meet some of them.

"Why didn't you tell me you knew?"

"I had to wait until you were ready. I'm glad you finally decided to tell me."

"I was afraid, Mama. The last thing in the world I ever wanted was for you to be ashamed of me. I was pretty sure you'd still love me if I told you, but I worried you'd be ashamed."

"I'd never be ashamed of you. I love you and am so proud of you for lots of reasons. You're a good student, and you're doing that important work with the professor. Mostly, though, I'm proud of you because you're a good person, Rory. You don't need to change for anybody, least of all me. If you don't like girls, that's fine with me. Don't you let anyone tell you it's not okay to be the way you are. Hear me?"

Rory nodded, and a smile broke out on his tear-stained face. "Do Meemaw and Papaw know?"

"I think they have an idea, but they've never said it exactly. Do you remember the time that awful preacher started talking about gay people being an abomination? When we all walked out?"

"Yeah, I felt terrible that day."

"Well, if you recall, it was Papaw who got up and led us all out of the church. I suspect he thought the preacher might be talking about you, and he was so furious I thought he was gonna go up and punch him in the nose."

"Do you think I should tell them?"

"That's up to you, son. You have to decide if you want to."

"I think I do want to. I hate to have secrets from them. I'll have to find the right time to do it, though."

"We can talk more over supper. Go wash your face and let me fix somethin' to eat."

Ruth and Rory stood facing each other. "Mama, I should never have wondered about you. I'm sorry it took me so long." He reached down and hugged her before turning to walk into his room.

It's probably a good thing you waited, Ruth thought. I needed time to understand all of this. I might not have been so supportive if you'd told me earlier, but that's not something I need to share with you right now.

Rory reappeared in the kitchen in a few minutes. "Mama, is that why Daddy left us? Is it because of me?"

Ruth wasn't expecting that. She put down the can opener and the can of butter beans. "I'm not sure I'll ever know what happened to your father. What I do know is that he became an ugly person. The gentle man he was when I married him turned hard. He said he didn't want to be married anymore, but I always suspected there was more to it than that.

"Your grandparents have never told me anything about his life after he left, and I've never asked. I'm just grateful they still want to be part of our lives, and of course, they believe the sun rises and sets on you. Our divorce might have had something to do with you, but I doubt it. I think it had more to do with his own turmoil. That's one of the big mysteries in my life, but I can't spend a lot of time stewing about it. Neither should you. Now go wash up. Dinner will be ready in about 10 minutes."

As often is the case when floodgates open, the water rushes out for some time. They both had lots more questions. Ruth waited until they were eating dessert to broach the subject of Jake's note to Rory.

"Now that we're being honest with one another, how about Jake's note?"

Rory put his fork down and cleared his throat. "I think I'm in some trouble with the Sergeant." Rory spoke haltingly, thinking as he talked. "I lied about the note. It was too personal, so I quick typed up another one. I didn't want him to know about Jake and me."

"Do you still have the other one?"

More throat clearing, then "Yeah, I do, but I don't want to show it to him. Do I have to?"

"I think you do. It's evidence in a case involving a boy's death, Rory."

"Do you think they can send me to jail for lying?"

"Let's hope not. Sergeant Haskell seems like a decent sort. He's got kids of his own. Maybe he'll understand. It would certainly be better if you decided to tell him instead of making him search the house and find it, don't you think?"

"Yeah, I guess so. Will you call him?"

Ruth was about to agree but stopped. "I think it would be better if you call him."

Rory nodded.

Chapter Thirty-One

It's frustrating when one steels himself to say something painful and then doesn't get the chance to confront the person. However, Rory's disappointment mixed with relief as he heard Sergeant Haskell's answering machine ask him to leave his name and phone number.

"This is Rory Wilson and I've got some information for you. I'll be up 'til 11 or so if you want to call me back." He left his number.

"That was quick," Ruth remarked as she walked into Rory's room.

"I left a message." He sat down and picked up his homework.

Two minutes later, the phone rang. "Maybe that's him. Go ahead and get it," Ruth said.

Rory nodded as he heard Haskell's voice. Ruth mouthed, "Do you want me to stay?" Again, Rory nodded his head.

Ruth heard the quiver in Rory's voice as he tried to explain that he'd given the sergeant a bogus note and that he had the real one Jake had written.

Please go easy on him. He's been beating himself up, blaming himself for Jake's death, Ruth thought, smiling at his bravery.

"Yes, sir. Yes, sir. That'll be fine."

"He's coming over in about half an hour. He wants to see the note."

Ruth was curious about what the note said, but didn't want to ask. "I'm proud of you, son. That took a lot of courage. You did the right thing."

"Yeah, I hope I don't regret it. I hope he doesn't put what Jake wrote in the newspaper. I could never show my face around here if it gets out. The kids would call me a murderer, not just a faggot."

"Rory, I have a huge favor to ask."

"Sure, Mama, what do you want?"

"Instead of saying that awful word, can you just say 'the f-word'?"

Rory smiled. "There's another f-word, Mama. How would you know which one I meant?"

"Hmm, I hadn't thought of that. How about if you just say 'another f-word', and I'll know what you mean?"

"Okay, if you want me to." He didn't see why it was such a big deal; he'd heard faggot all his life.

Ruth finished the dishes and sat down to watch the evening news in the living room. She heard a car pull up. "Rory, I think he's here. Get the door." She decided to let Rory handle the conversation with Sergeant Haskell alone.

Haskell said his "How're y'all doins," and he and Rory sat at the kitchen table. Rory handed him the note.

Haskell read quietly, then looked over his reading glasses at Rory. "What did he mean by you turning on him? Did you two have a fight?"

Rory explained how upset he'd been when he watched the news story about the anniversary of Matthew Shepard's murder and how he'd sent the message to Jake about not being friends any more. Haskell listened and tried not to render judgment about their relationship.

"Well, this pretty much says it all, I guess. He obviously intended to take his life when he wrote this to you, like it says."

"Yes, sir," was all Rory could say.

"He didn't try to phone you or anything that night?"

"No, sir. I never heard a word from him." Then Rory added, "That's the whole truth. I'm sorry I lied to you about the note. I was afraid if I showed you what Jake wrote, it would end up in the paper or on TV."

The veneer of sympathy Haskell had used to establish rapport with Rory vanished. He'd gotten what he wanted and didn't have to pretend to be friendly any longer.

"You realize that withholding evidence is serious business, don't you?" His tone was angry.

"Yes, sir."

Ruth had been listening from the living room and jumped up when she heard the change of tone in the sergeant's voice. She walked into the kitchen.

"Sergeant, Rory was wrong to lie to you about the note, but surely you can see he was scared. Do you have any idea what he goes through? One boy is dead because of people's intolerance. His death will be a painful reminder to Rory every day of his life of what hatred can do." She glared at Haskell. "You're a parent. What if your son was gay?"

Haskell had not expected Ruth to attack him. She'd seemed like a gentle woman when he'd interviewed her. He'd never considered how he might feel if one of his kids turned out to be gay. He was pretty sure they weren't, but these days you couldn't be sure. After all, Jake was a star soccer player, plus the school staff said they didn't think he was gay. They'd all assumed the incident with the soccer team happened because Jake was friends with Rory, and most people thought Rory was gay. In fact, one of the teachers had praised Jake for hanging around with Rory when none of the other boys wanted anything to do with him.

Finally, Haskell answered Ruth's question. "That's an interesting question, Mrs. Wilson. I never considered it. I hope my wife and I would try to understand."

Ruth enjoyed watching the man squirm. He clearly wasn't used to having others question him.

Rory realized Haskell hadn't said whether the note would be shared with the media. Finally, the detective addressed that issue in a softer tone.

"There's nothing that requires me to tell the media what's in the note. We can simply say we found a suicide note and not mention where we found it or that it was addressed to anybody."

"Am I going to be in trouble?"

Haskell looked at Ruth as he spoke. "Well, I guess that will have to be up to your mama. She might want to punish you for lying. I'm happy to leave that up to her." He stood and tucked the note into his jacket pocket.

"If I need to ask you any more questions, I'll call," he said.

Ruth saw him to the door. "Have a good evening," Haskell said as he walked down the front steps. She hoped hers and Rory's would end better than it had begun.

Rory felt like a weight had been lifted from his shoulders.

In the weeks that followed, he continued to grieve, but he found it easier to come home after school because he no longer had to hide things from his mother.

People at school and in town talked about the suicide for several weeks, but soon they found other news to pass around. Rory watched Jake's house to see if the Vermont cousins or anyone came to pay their respects, but as far as he could tell, no one did. Rory felt like Jake had been deleted.

Within the year, Jake's mother died. Some of the neighbors said she just took to her bed and died, just like that, for no particular reason.

Not long afterwards, Jake's father moved out. Ruth heard he left all his furniture and belongings, just walked away one day and never came back. They had never talked to anybody, so everything about them remained a mystery.

Rory wished he'd kept a couple of pictures of Jake, but the night Jake died he'd deleted them from his hard drive. He worried that Sergeant Haskell might confiscate his PC, so he'd deleted every reference to Jake, all the emails, photos, everything. But he couldn't delete Jake from his memory and knew he probably never would.

Chapter Thirty-Two

Eventually, Rory's friendship with Ashley strengthened to the point where he felt comfortable with her again. One Saturday they went to a movie in Boone and walked across the parking lot for cheap Chinese food. They talked about the movie and classmates, and Rory brought up Jake.

"I was thinkin' about Jake this morning," he began. He looked at her for a reaction. Seeing none, he continued. "I can't believe it's a year since he died."

His remarks invited Ashley's question. "Why'd he do it, Rory?"

"Do you really wanna know?"

Ashley nodded. "If you wanna tell me."

Rory took a deep breath. Looking down at the chow mein on his plate he said, "You might not like me much if I tell you."

"I doubt that. We've known each other too long for that."

Rory related the sequence of actions that preceded Jake's suicide and Ashley listened. "So you think Jake wouldn't have committed suicide if you hadn't broken off the relationship?"

"Doesn't it sound that way to you?"

"There could have been lots of reasons, Rory. His father was a mean bastard, for one. He beat Jake up all the time. His so-called friends on the soccer team turned on him that day. That would have been enough for anybody to decide they didn't want to live."

Rory had been over all of those facts many times as he tried to convince himself that he wasn't the sole reason for Jake's suicide, but hearing Ashley's argument gave them greater weight. "You really think so?"

"It sounds like Jake had a really rotten life. I bet he would have killed himself even if you and he were never … friends." Ashley still hesitated to use the words gay or lovers to describe Rory's relationship with Jake.

The waitress came to clear their dishes and they stopped talking. It's a good point to end the discussion, Rory thought. He was grateful for Ashley's analysis. It was remarkably similar to his mother's.

All during that year, Ruth had wished Rory would get up the nerve to talk with his grandparents. She was certain they'd accept it well, but a couple of times when she'd asked if he'd spoken to them, he said he hadn't found the right opportunity. She couldn't push him; it had to be on his terms.

She'd invited Rory to accompany her to a PFLAG meeting, but he hadn't shown any interest. One evening, she mentioned that she'd heard there was a Gay Pride celebration coming up in Boone. She'd saved a copy of the *Mountain Times*.

Rory seemed surprised.

"Here, the schedule of events is in the paper." She handed it to him.

"I can't believe they put this in the papers," he exclaimed. "You'd think they'd be afraid to let people know where their events are happening."

"People in Boone are more open-minded than in Craggy Grove. I guess it's the university's influence," she offered.

Rory took the paper to his room after leaving the table. He's probably scared to death to go where there are other gay people, Ruth thought.

Going to a gay pride function by himself was out of the question, but Rory didn't know any other gay kids. He re-read the article to be sure he'd understood that the public was invited to a bingo event at a church. They called it drag bingo. It might be interesting, and maybe Ashley would go with him. If I walk in with a girl, nobody will know I'm gay, he thought. Just in case there's somebody there I know I'll be safe with her. He decided to make the phone call.

"Hey Ashley, it's Rory. I was thinkin' it might be fun to go to this drag bingo thing Friday night in North Carolina." He read her the description from the paper.

Ashley's reply was predictable. "But I'm not gay, Rory."

"No, it says the public is invited. I'm sure there'll be other straight folks there. I'll even buy your ticket. You get six bingo cards with the price of admission."

"Okay. If you really want to go, I'll go with you."

Several times Rory nearly called Ashley to cancel, but he was curious and wanted to go. He ate hardly anything at supper the night of the bingo party, and his mother could tell he was nervous about something. He'd said he and Ashley were going into Boone to mess around. She guessed they were going to a Pride event and felt confident he'd be safe with Ashley. Ashley didn't mind speaking her piece to anyone who got out of line, and besides, the event was being held in a church. There'd be plenty of adults around to make sure nothing happened.

Rory and Ashley drove into North Carolina and began looking for the church along Rte 421. They saw a bunch of multi-colored balloons tied to the mailbox on the road's edge and turned into the gravel parking lot. They walked into the church and were surprised to see a hundred people or more.

Rory paid for their tickets and handed the bingo cards to Ashley. The woman who took his money pointed out the refreshment window and told them they could sit anywhere they wanted inside.

"Come on," Ashley urged, sensing Rory's hesitance about entering the main area where the bingo games were going to be held. They looked around for seats toward the back of the hall.

"Oh, look." Ashley pointed to a group of drag queens. "One's taller than you."

She was right. A blonde-wigged man who wore a slinky red dress and 4-inch heels must have been well over six-feet tall.

"Me and my big ideas," Rory replied. He was embarrassed and regretted convincing Ashley to go with him. If he hadn't paid for the tickets, he'd have bolted for the door.

As if she'd been reading his body language, a gray-haired woman motioned to them to sit near her. Ashley grabbed Rory's hand and tugged him toward the seats the woman indicated. He followed reluctantly. The woman was in her 50s, he guessed.

"I'm Linda and this is my husband, Paul," she said. Then she pointed to the group of drag queens and said, "The one in the polka dot dress is my son, Greg. Isn't he lovely?"

Rory smiled and relaxed. This might be fun after all, he thought.

"You two looked a little lost," Linda remarked to Rory who sat next to her. "How'd you hear about this?"

"My mother told me about it. I've never seen a drag queen."

Rory knew not all drag queens were gay, and he was curious.

"Has your son been a drag queen long?" he asked. He figured it was okay to ask since she brought it up.

"Oh, Greg's loved to dress up in women's clothes since he was little. I used to get upset, but I got used to it." She signaled another young man to sit across from them. He caught her wave and smiled. As he inched his way to the saved seat, Linda introduced Rory and Ashley to Roger, Greg's partner.

Rory was amazed to see how casual Linda and Paul were about their son's having a partner. Rory wondered if it had always been so.

The Mistress of Ceremonies entered and after blowing kisses to everyone, she made several announcements. At first, Rory wasn't sure if it was a woman or a man. Ashley said it was definitely a man in drag, and Linda confirmed it.

With the preliminaries out of the way, the first game began. Each time somebody called "Bingo" they went up to the front and someone checked the card. Drag queens awarded the prizes and escorted the winners to and from their seats. Rory hoped he wouldn't win anything. He was sure he'd die if he had to go up and give his name and get his picture taken.

After the first four games, they took a break and people milled around visiting with one another. They all seemed to know each other, and there was lots of hugging. Linda and Paul got up to chat with some people on the other side of the room, and Roger spoke to Rory.

"Are you out to your parents yet?" he asked.

"How'd you know?" Rory asked.

"Gaydar," Roger answered. "It never fails."

"What's that?"

"Ooh, you really are new to the scene, aren't you? It's gay radar."

Rory blushed. "I've never gone to anything like this before."

Roger smiled. "Oh, honey, don't fret. We all have to come out some time. It can be exciting, but also scary as Hell. So, I take it you're not out to your folks?"

"It's just Mama and me. She knows, but nobody else in my family does," he answered.

"What about her?" Roger said pointing to Ashley who was making her way back to her seat.

"Oh, she's a good friend. She knows too. She's straight," he added quickly.

"How old are you, Rory?"

"I'm 17."

When Rory told him where he went to school, Roger rolled his eyes. "Oh, you poor boy. Are they wretched to you there?"

"It's pretty bad," Rory answered. He wanted to tell Roger more, but there were too many people around. By this time, Linda and Paul had returned, and it was hard to continue the conversation.

As the next game got underway, Roger reached across the table and handed Rory a slip of paper. It contained his email address and phone number. If you feel like talking, email or call me, he'd written. Rory smiled and tucked the paper into his jeans' pocket.

After all the prizes had been awarded, the drag queens paraded up the center aisle so everyone could get one last look at their finery. Everybody applauded and people started to leave. Rory and Ashley stood, and Roger called to them, "Wait a minute. I want you to meet somebody." He waved to Greg to approach the table where the three of them and Linda and Paul stood.

Greg kissed Roger on the lips and turned to Rory and Ashley.

"This is Greg. Meet Rory and his friend, Ashley," Roger said.

"It's Rory's first outing," Roger explained, knowing Greg would understand what he meant.

"So glad you could come out tonight," Greg replied, winking at Rory. "Wasn't it fun?"

"Yeah, it was," Rory replied, and he meant it. He was a lot more relaxed than he'd been when they arrived.

Rory said goodnight to the group, and he and Ashley headed for the parking lot.

Ashley was bursting with questions about the partial conversation she'd overheard between Roger and Rory. She couldn't wait to get him alone. Even before they got into the car she asked, "Was he hitting on you?"

"No, I think he was just trying to be nice."

"Yeah, right! You better watch out, Rory. I think he's interested in you."

"He's Greg's partner. You saw them kiss, and you heard Linda."

Ashley rolled her eyes and shook her head.

After school on Monday, Rory and Ashley took advantage of the nice weather and walked home together.

Rory bristled when Ashley asked, "So, did you contact Roger yet?"

She read his face and backed off quickly.

A few minutes later she said, "I'm worried about you." She knew she was invading sensitive territory. "I can't believe you didn't notice he was hitting on you."

Rory was usually pretty even-tempered, but Ashley's comment riled him.

"He was just trying to be nice, Ashley. I'm sure he noticed how uncomfortable I was. Don't try to make something out of it. He's got Greg, and it looked like they're pretty much into each other." He paused. "Besides, what business is it of yours, anyway?"

"Well, don't get all pissy about it, Rory. I was just saying, you know, he's older and he seemed more interested than just friendly. You don't know much about things like that, and I worry you're gonna be taken advantage of."

"Oh, and you're such a woman of the world!"

They walked for a few minutes longer without another word.

Finally, Rory broke the silence. "You must think I'm some kind of idiot. I don't need another mother. I want you to be my friend, but quit trying to mother me."

Ashley drew herself up to her full five feet three inches and tugged on Rory's arm to get him to stop walking. She faced him and looked at him long and hard.

"I guess you don't understand friendship much." Her tone softened. "Friends do look out for one another. You, above all, should know that. I'd expect you to have my back if you thought I was in danger. Wouldn't you?"

Rory was more contrite as he answered. "Well, of course I would, but I wouldn't act like you don't have a brain. I'd probably ask you if you wanted my help instead of butting in."

"Well, we're different. If I know you, Rory, you probably wouldn't ask me to help you in the first place. That's why I offered my advice. Anyway, let's not fight about this. It's stupid."

They walked a few minutes more without any conversation. Their strained words had nearly gobbled up the mile from the school to Ashley's house. She started to head up the front walk and then turned with a sly grin on her face.

"So, are ya gonna email him?" She put her hands up over her face as if to ward off a blow.

"You'll be the last to know if I do," Rory replied and laughed as he walked away.

After tossing the idea around for a week, Rory finally got up the nerve to email Roger, wondering if he'd even remember meeting him at the drag bingo. He'd deleted three different messages before he was satisfied with what he'd written. He wanted to let Roger know that he was eager to meet other gay boys, not insinuate himself into Roger and Greg's circle of friends. They were a lot older than Rory, and even though the guys had been very nice to him and Ashley, they intimidated him. Maybe he won't even answer me. I'm just a kid. Why would he want to bother with me, he wondered.

Since Jake's death, Rory had gone out of his way to find gay people. He'd Googled gay celebrities and was happy to learn there were so many. It was all part of his attempt to affirm that there were other gay people in the world and that some of them were liked and respected. He hoped one day he'd achieve that status.

Before going to bed that night, Rory turned on his computer to check email. Nothing from Roger. He shut it down and turned in. He lay on his bed thinking about Jake and cried softly until he fell asleep.

Chapter Thirty-Three

More and more, Rory found comfort by burying himself in his school work. He maintained his relationship with the ETSU professor who let him tinker in the botany lab a couple of times a week.

Rory was patient to a point, but when a string of experiments didn't work out, he grew disgusted.

"That's it," he muttered one day in the lab and slammed his pencil on the counter.

Dr. Ragatky turned to see what he meant and raised his eyebrows in a question.

"Nothing's going right. I'm ready to drop the whole project," Rory sputtered.

Dr. Ragatky knew this was just a temporary reaction; he'd seen it countless times with his students.

"Well, that's entirely up to you, Rory. Maybe you should take a breather and think about it. You've got talent, and I think you'd make a first-rate scientist, but if you don't have the heart for it, maybe you should just pursue a different kind of career."

That was the first time Dr. Ragatky had indicated he thought Rory was headed for a career in science. Rory wasn't sure what he wanted to study. He'd given some thought to being a teacher, figuring the education required was cheaper than other professions. He also felt he might be able to influence kids to quit bullying one another. Maybe he could make life easier for others who were different.

"I'm real grateful for all your help," Rory replied. "The lab has been the best place I've been for the past year and a half, but I'm not sure I'd want to be a scientist if it means getting disappointed with the results of experiments all the time. Don't you ever get sick of it?"

"Not really. When I was about your age, I started going to work with my father. He was a bench scientist for a pharmaceutical company. He'd take me with him on weekends when he had to go in to check on experiments. He'd let me do little chores in the lab, and I loved it. I never thought of doing anything but science, and then I ended up teaching it."

"You were lucky he did that with you." Once again he realized how much he missed having a father to take an interest in him. "Do you have kids?" he suddenly asked Dr. Ragatky.

The professor had never talked about his personal life, and Rory had only been in his office once or twice since they'd been working together. He recalled seeing some photos on the desk but none of children.

"My kids are all grown now, and they don't live around here."

Rory thought he detected uneasiness in the professor's answer, but he knew it wasn't proper for him to pry, so he dropped the subject.

"How old are you now, Rory?"

"Almost eighteen."

"You'll be making some decisions about college soon, I suppose. Have you considered where you'd like to go?"

"My mama doesn't have much money, so I'm not sure I'll be able to go to college. Maybe I'll work for a few years and save up and then go to a two-year school."

It galled Dr. Ragatky that college tuition had gotten so expensive that talented kids like Rory might not have a chance to learn. He'd seen promising youngsters drop out of the university because their families couldn't come up with the tuition.

"There might be something I can do to help if you decide you want to study botany."

Rory was shocked. He waited.

"We give scholarships to deserving students, and I might be able to get you one. I can't promise, and you'd have to do well on your SATs and keep up your grades, but it would let you pursue your dream of creating a strain of tobacco that wouldn't cause lung cancer. I'm fairly sure I could get funding for a full scholarship if that's what you decide to do."

Suddenly, Rory's frustration with the latest failure vanished.

"Really? You would do that for me?"

"I'd sure try, Rory. I think your talent for this work could make a difference in people's lives one day, but if you want to find some other kind of work that's not so frustrating, I'll understand."

"No," Rory almost shouted. "I do like this work. I was just mad because things didn't work out with this," he said and pointed to a sickly looking plant that had not responded the way he'd wanted it to.

"I'd like to come to the university. It's been my dream for the whole time you've been helping me. I'll work hard and keep my grades up, I promise. I don't know how I'll do on the SATs, but I'll study my butt off before I take them."

Dr. Ragatky suppressed a smile. He hadn't lost his ability to motivate talented kids.

Chapter Thirty-Four

While Rory sipped his coffee, he reminisced about that conversation with Dr. Ragatky two years ago. Now a sophomore botany major at the university, he had asked Ruth to invite the professor for Thanksgiving dinner. Rory had learned that Dr. Ragatky spent last Thanksgiving alone eating Chinese take-out food. His wife had died several years ago, and he was estranged from his two grown sons.

He laughed to himself as he recalled fantasizing about Dr. Ragatky as his father when he'd first met him. Ruth hadn't dated anyone since her divorce, though she spoke about how nice it would be to meet someone. Rory had invited the professor to his high school graduation to thank him for arranging the four-year scholarship, and Ruth met him then.

Rory mused about how certain people can change your life if you're open to change. For instance, his high school social life had taken a dramatic turn after he met the drag queen and his partner. He eventually heard back from Roger, who invited him to a meeting of a support group for gay teens he sponsored. Rory attended its meetings regularly for his remaining time in high school and enjoyed connecting with gay boys and girls from western North Carolina.

In fact, if he hadn't discovered the support of kindred souls from that group, he might not have made it through high school. Being able to meet and socialize with them every couple of weeks made life bearable. They had lots more in common than being gay; they were all persecuted in school and many had also experienced abuse at the hands of their families. For the first time, Rory was able to discuss his father's rejection with people who could relate and understand.

Two of the boys he'd known in the group were also studying at the university, and Rory hung out with them on weekends. Even though his home was close enough to commute to classes, he lived in a dorm because his scholarship paid for it. He also had a 15 hour per week work scholarship assisting in freshman biology labs. That provided pocket money.

When he was a Junior, Rory found out there was a gay bar in Johnson City, not far from the campus. He was still under age, but since he was tall and now had a full beard, he looked older and got away with buying alcohol. He wasn't much of a drinker. He'd grown up in a dry town and because his friends didn't drink in high school, he hadn't developed a real taste for it. That too was changing. He was beginning to like ale.

He learned that it was cool to have a preference, so he'd started ordering Fat Tire ale because he liked the name. The nutty taste began to grow on him, so that was what he ordered when he went to bars near campus. It beat the cheap stuff they drank at keg parties. After a couple of embarrassing waltzes with the hedges in front of the dormitory, he'd sworn off cheap beer.

Rory was nervous the first time the guys went to Pathways. He'd never been to a men's bar before and wasn't sure what to expect. His gay friends assured him there was nothing to worry about.

"Just be yourself," Sandy had coached as they pulled into the parking lot behind the alley entrance. "You might even get lucky tonight."

The three had agreed that they would all leave the bar together. There'd been too many stories in the gay press about straight guys cruising gay bars and picking up unsuspecting men who would later end up dead, and Matthew Shepard's murder was a constant reminder that one needed to be careful.

The first thing that hit Rory when they entered Pathways was the smell. There was a blue haze of cigarette smoke and you couldn't miss the tobacco smell, but there was another odor, not unlike the locker room at the gym, a male smell, a mixture of sweat, tobacco, cologne and sex. Men were standing three- and four-deep around the curved bar, some with bare arms that showed their sculpted biceps. Several of them turned to check out the new blood.

As Rory's eyes adjusted to the low light, he spotted some booths on the opposite side of the room and a few tables, mostly occupied.

Toward the back there were two pool tables where several men gathered around watching others play.

He passed some older guys and heard clucking noises. He soon realized it had something to do with him and his friends.

What seemed like a good idea when Sandy had proposed going to the men's bar was rapidly becoming less so. Wherever Rory's eyes stopped, somebody met them with a suggestive smile that unnerved him.

Rory and his friends edged in closer to the bar as two men headed toward them. One was tall with dirty blonde hair and electric blue eyes. His black T-shirt looked like it had been painted on. Rory couldn't take his eyes off the man's abs. He'd seen photos of washboard abs before, but this was his first close-up look, and he felt an urge to run his hands over them. The guy's pants were clingy, leaving nothing to the imagination. Definitely briefs, Rory thought, or maybe just a thong.

"You boys are new here," the guy with the abs said. He smiled as he spoke, his perfect physique enhanced by pearly whites. He held a bottle of beer in one hand and a pool cue in the other. "I'm Cliff," he said.

Rory hadn't breathed since this Adonis approached them. Never one to think of himself as particularly handsome, he assumed Cliff would be more interested in his buddies. He was shocked when Cliff addressed him.

"Do you shoot?" Hurriedly, he added, "pool, I mean." The guys around him laughed.

Rory couldn't control the blush that surged up his neck and reached his hairline. "I'm not too good. All I know is 8-Ball," he answered.

"You can't be any worse than my friend, here," Cliff said, nodding to the man who'd walked over with him. "He's the sorriest excuse of a pool player I ever saw."

His friend spoke. "Now that we've been properly introduced, I'm Rick." He shook hands all around. "Cliff's right. I'm not much of a pool player. Poker's my game. Any of y'all play?"

Sandy answered, "Me and Spud here are about as good at poker as you are at pool, I'd guess."

"That's music to my ears. Come on over to our table. I'm sure the boys will be happy to take your money."

Sandy and Spud followed him, leaving Rory with Cliff. Rory hopped onto one of two vacant stools.

"I take it you're not much interested in playing pool," Cliff said, but he didn't seem to care. "Save that seat for me. I'll be right back." Rory watched Cliff's rhythmic walk across to the pool table and saw him put the cue on the wall rack. As he returned to the bar, Cliff's eyes met Rory's in the mirror. He slid onto the bar stool and his knees brushed against Rory's thigh as he swung around to motion for the bartender.

"What'll ya have?" he asked Rory.

"Fat Tire."

Cliff held up two fingers and the bartender went to fetch their beers.

Rory wondered if he'd ever be as self-assured as Cliff obviously was. It had always amazed him how some people just had that swagger, that way of carrying themselves that said they were in full control. He envied that.

Rory took out money when the bartender placed the beers on cardboard coasters in front of them. Cliff was faster.

"Put your money away. This one's on me," he said leaving no room for discussion.

Rory's fascination with this man grew as Cliff began talking about himself. He was from Texas and had been working as a veterinarian's assistant until recently. He'd concluded that there was no future in that, so he'd decided to go back and get a degree in business administration.

"My goal is to make a million dollars by the time I hit fifty and then retire and take it easy," he told Rory. "I've met a lot of millionaires who weren't any smarter than me, so I figure I can do it."

Rory didn't doubt it. He was that sort of guy. Rory tossed out a question now and again, and Cliff kept talking about himself. It was easy to keep the conversation going. Cliff loved to hear himself talk. All Rory had to do was try to look more interested in the man's words than his tight jeans.

Cliff asked Rory a couple of questions, but as soon as Rory started to answer, he interrupted and brought the conversation back to himself. They were on their second round of beers when Cliff jumped on the fast track.

"So, Rory, do you have a boyfriend?"

"No."

"I share a place with Rick, but we're just friends. What do ya say we go over to my place for a while?" He waved his hands around as if trying to part the smoke. "It's just five minutes from here."

Rory knew exactly what Cliff had in mind, and he was definitely interested. He was a little apprehensive. He knew nothing about this guy. Much as he wanted to go with Cliff, he was wary. But he didn't want to pass up this opportunity.

"Let me give Sandy and Spud your number. They can holler when they're ready to leave. I rode in with them."

Cliff hesitated and Rory sensed something wasn't right.

"Rick has the number. They can get it from him," Cliff replied.

Rory's sixth sense told him to persist. He took out his phone. "What is it?" His finger was poised over the tiny keypad.

For the first time that evening, Cliff looked nonplussed.

"I never call myself. I don't know the number." He looked embarrassed, but there was more to his expression than that. He seemed angry.

"Hang on a minute," he said and walked over to the table where Rick was playing cards with Sandy, Spud and a fourth guy. Cliff bent over and spoke to Rick who laughed. Rick tossed his cards down on the table, and got up. He walked toward the door with Cliff, and they left the bar.

Rory swallowed the last of his beer and waited for Cliff to come back. One minute turned into five.

He sauntered over to the table where Sandy and Spud sat watching the door. "What's happenin', man?"

"That's what we're wonderin'. This Rick dude just got up and said 'I'm done, boys.' We thought he meant for that hand, but he went out with his buddy and hasn't come back."

Rory stuck his hand out to the stranger at the table. "I'm Rory."

"Jake. Pleased to meet ya."

Rory flinched at the name. He hadn't met anyone named Jake

since his first lover.

Jake laughed, "You boys are too new to know these characters." He looked at Rory. "I bet Cliff was gonna take you to his place, right?"

Rory was ashamed to admit he'd been dumped. "Yeah, somethin' like that."

"Everybody around here knows Cliff's the horniest guy in town. He's a cherry picker. He probably figured you was ripe for the pickin', son. His game's pretty rough, from what I hear. Be glad he bolted."

Rory felt like a prize fool. He was disappointed, but also grateful that Cliff had decided to leave without him.

Sandy announced he'd had enough excitement for one night. Rick had won 10 dollars from him and he was down to his last two dollars.

"I'll be right back," Rory said and headed for the bathroom. The narrow hallway leading to the rest room was darker than the rest of the bar, and Rory had to squeeze by a couple of guys who were getting acquainted.

"OK, I'm ready when you are," he said to Sandy and Spud when he got back to the table.

The three of them started for the door. As they approached the doorway they stepped back to let two men enter, and Rory was startled. He recognized one of them.

"Hey, Doc," he called out, and the professor turned to see who had addressed him that way.

Ragatky was clearly surprised to see Rory, or more to the point, to be seen by him.

"Rory," he said. "How's it goin?"

"Oh, okay. We were just leaving."

"Right. See ya."

"Holy crap. Do you guys know who that was?"

"No, should we?" asked Spud.

"That's Dr. Ragatky, my advisor. He got me the scholarship. I can't believe I just saw him here."

Sandy and Spud spent the next several minutes making lewd comments about why the professor was so interested in Rory's work, and Rory recalled a reaction he'd had when Dr. Ragatky got close to him one day as they worked.

They debriefed on the drive back to campus, comparing notes on their impressions of various men they'd met.

"What was that clucking stuff while we were walking in?"

"Rory, where you been all your life, man?" Sandy laughed.

Spud answered, "Ain't you never heard of chicken, country boy?"

Rory knew better than to assume Spud was referring to poultry. "Un uh. What is it?"

"It's you, honey." Spud and Sandy laughed at Rory's reaction.

Spud stopped laughing long enough to explain that a chicken is an inexperienced, young guy, usually under the legal age for consensual sex.

"I don't know if they were warning everybody that we might be jail bait or advertising that they were looking for trainable young uns like us. I'm guessin' that Cliff guy thought you were a virgin."

"Good thing I didn't go to his place then."

Sandy looked at Rory in the rear view mirror. "You mean he would have been disappointed?"

"That, too. From the look on his face when I asked for the phone number, I'm not sure I would have made it back alive. He's a strange dude."

"He wasn't the only one eyeing you at the bar. Did you see the two older guys, the ones wearing Harley jackets at the other end of the bar?"

Rory didn't recall them.

"One of them, I'd guess maybe in his late 40s or so, a little paunchy, came over to our table while we were playin' cards. He stood there for about five minutes, not sayin' anything. After the hand was done, he asked if we were with you. It was plain to see you and Cliff were hittin' it off. We just said, "Yeah" and he went back to the bar."

"I didn't see him," Rory said.

Sandy mentioned, "That Jake seems like a nice guy. He was tellin' us about a men's ranch not far from here. Said we should check it out some weekend. I think he said it's called Tall Trees or somethin' like that. They have a website."

Sandy looked at Rory. "You know him? You seemed to react when he introduced himself, or am I imagining things?"

"No, it's the name is all. I used to have a friend named Jake."

"A friend or more?"

"More." Rory's silence begged for questions.

"Come on, man, tell us."

Rory began talking and didn't finish until 25 minutes later when Sandy turned onto University Parkway.

"Bummer, man," was all Spud could say.

"Yeah, big bummer," echoed Sandy.

Sandy pulled up to Dossett Hall, and Rory got out. "See ya guys. Thanks for the ride."

Rory heard Spud clucking as the car pulled away from the curb. He turned quickly and flipped him off, laughing as he opened the front door to the dorm.

Chapter Thirty-Five

Rory kicked off his shoes as he entered his dorm room. He had a dull headache that he attributed to the smoke in the bar. He tugged his shirt over his head and tossed it on a chair. Living semi-nude in this overheated room sure saved money on clothes. He rarely wore more than shorts. Anything else felt like an overcoat. Several times he'd put suggestions about turning down the heat to save energy and money in the box near the desk downstairs, but nobody paid any attention.

He stooped, and pulled the last Coke from the half refrigerator in the corner and reviewed the events of the evening. He smiled as he recalled seeing Dr. Ragatky.

His mood grew somber as he thought about what he'd told Sandy and Spud about Jake. Over the last four years, he'd reached a point where he could go weeks without thinking about Jake, but tonight his presence was huge and raw.

Rory tossed the crumpled Coke can into the wastebasket and let his mind focus on the "what ifs" of his life. What if his father hadn't been such a homophobe? What if his mother and grandparents hadn't been so supportive?

He knew he was luckier than many gay boys whose parents had thrown them out of the house when they found out about them. He knew two boys and a girl from the youth group in North Carolina who lived in homeless shelters while social services tried to find them foster families. Nobody wanted to take in gay kids.

He remembered the night when Gussie announced to the group that she was set to move in with a family in Greensboro in a couple of days. "I met them, and they seem real nice," she told the group at the meeting. She'd fixed her hair and looked better than Rory'd ever seen her. She had hoped this was the break she'd been waiting for since being abandoned eight or nine months earlier, but when Rory arrived at the next meeting two weeks later, Gussie told the group through tears, "When they found out I was a lesbian, they called it off. Said they were afraid I'd give their two young girls ideas. The social worker tried to change their minds, but they started spouting scripture, and that was that. They even told her I probably had AIDS and would infect the whole family."

Rory had been angry, but he could tell the fight had gone out of Gussie. Much as the group facilitator tried, nobody could offer her hope of finding a home. Rory had been so moved by her experiences that he'd even talked to his mother about taking her in to live with them. Ruth had been sympathetic, but their financial situation made it impossible. Besides, Gussie was a North Carolina ward of the court, and they lived in Tennessee.

Gussie eventually got her GED and a job at a supermarket as a cashier. When she turned 18, she got a furnished room and the last anyone heard, she was managing to hold it together. He wondered about her and some of the other kids he'd known then. He knew that but for the grace of God and his mama, that could have been his fate.

What if Jake had not taken his life? Would they still be lovers?

But Rory knew that Jake's death might actually have saved him. He felt guilty each time the thought crossed his mind. Some of the kids who tormented Rory had left him alone after Jake died and Ashley had heard from some of her friends that the school psychologist had met with several students and laid it on the line about the responsibility those who had bullied Jake had to accept for his suicide.

And finally, what if he'd not met Dr. Ragatky? He might be collecting carts in the Wal-Mart parking lot instead of going to college. On that upbeat note, he drifted off to sleep.

Chapter Thirty-Six

After a gut-wrenching conversation, Grady and Lily listened to Darrell ride off on his motorcycle.

"If I hadn't a heard it for myself, I'd a never believed it," Grady sighed. "Do ya ever feel like maybe you've lived too long, like you'd a been better off not being around to see some things?"

Lily reached over and put her hand on Grady's arm. "I'm not all that surprised, to tell you the truth. This makes all that mess with Rory years ago understandable. I knew there had to be an explanation. A father doesn't walk away from his son like that for no good reason."

Grady looked at his wife in disbelief. "Did you have an inklin' about this?"

"I didn't at first, but as time went on and Darrell never had any girlfriends after the divorce, the thought did cross my mind. It ain't natural for a man that age not to have a woman. Then when he went on those vacations with different men, I thought that was kinda strange for a grown man."

"Wish I had some o' that women's intuition," Grady replied. "I just figured he soured on women after the divorce. Never gave it a thought."

They sat quietly at the kitchen table for a few minutes trying to take in all Darrell had said.

"I'm worried about Darrell. It's clear he's havin' a hard time with this. Do you remember what he said when he started talkin'?"

Grady scrunched up his face. "What'd he say?"

"I have something awful to tell you about myself."

"You're right, Lily. I'm glad one of us can remember stuff. That is what he said. I thought he was gonna tell us he'd killed somebody or

176

robbed a bank."

"Does that sound like a man who's at peace with who he is? The only other time I saw him so upset was when he told us Ruth threw him out of the house and they were gettin' a divorce. He hasn't talked much about his feelins' all these years."

"Remember the time I suggested he might want to see Rory after Rory started workin' with that professor? I was pretty shocked when he said Rory was probably better off not seein' him. I never had the nerve to bring it up again."

"Yeah, maybe we should have pressed him more. Maybe it would have been better if he'd a told us sooner. I sure wish he could bring himself to see Rory. That boy has blamed himself all these years for his father turning on him. That's a heavy load for anybody."

"Maybe I'll ask him if he plans to contact Rory. I was too shocked to say much tonight. I'm glad your brain was workin' quicker 'n' mine, Lily. You said the right thing to him when you told him we love him no matter what. It got to him; I could see that. I don't think I've seen Darrell cry since he was a boy. I could tell he was fightin' it, but when you told him we loved him, he just couldn't keep it in."

Lily smiled. "A mother just knows. It's instinct."

Grady pushed his chair back from the worn wooden table, taking care not to pull off the plastic tablecloth as his belly brushed the edge of the table. The dessert dishes were still where they'd left them when Darrell started the conversation.

"I think this is the first time you didn't jump up to clear the table, Lily. It's like you knew we should stay put once Darrell started to talk."

"Well, when your son says he has somethin' awful to tell you, washin' dishes doesn't seem important."

"I know what you mean. I was thinkin' I needed to go to the bathroom after dessert, but I forgot about that too. I better get there right quick. My plumbin' ain't what it used to be."

Without words, they agreed to set aside their reactions to Darrell's news until they'd both had time to digest it. Lily washed dishes, and Grady turned on the 10 o'clock news. For the next 30 minutes each one processed the conversation alone. Lily ran over the whole thing as she washed and dried dishes and stacked them neatly in the cabinet. Grady tried to focus on the newscast, mumbling about each story as if the anchor required his reaction.

At 10:30 Grady turned off the TV and went into their bedroom. Lily came in as he was slipping under the covers. Grady propped his head up with one arm and turned to face her.

"What?" she asked.

"I been thinkin'. You know Darrell was always into sports. Still is. Nothin' keeps him from his Monday night football games and that March craziness with basketball. He knows more about those Nascar drivers than anyone I know. Nobody'd ever know he was gay to look at him or to hear him talk. He's not girly-like or anything."

Lily nodded and wondered if Grady was questioning what Darrell had told them.

"And then there's Rory. He's the exact opposite. Never did take to sports. Always was gentle and didn't rough-house with the other boys. He's still involved with plants just like he was when he was little. I guess you could tell Rory's gay when you look at him."

Lily waited while Grady gathered his thoughts. She was used to his way of thinking out loud, testing his theories as he spoke.

"It makes me wonder how many other gay people there are around that we don't know about. They're sure not all the same. Darrell never had trouble in school gettin' picked on like Rory did. It must be easier for the ones who look and act normal. I wonder if Darrell knew about himself when he was a boy. That's somethin' else I'd like to ask him."

"Maybe he suspected it and that's what made him angry when he saw it in Rory," Lily offered. "I never could understand why he got so furious when Rory didn't do what the other boys did. I wish there was a way we could bring them together. It might help Rory feel better about himself."

"That's not likely to happen, at least not any time soon. You heard Darrell say he didn't want Ruth to know about him, so that means Rory can't find out. What Rory knows, he tells his mother."

"Well, one thing I know is that we're not going to solve these problems tonight, Grady. We both need to get some sleep." As she'd done for 56 years, Lily leaned over and kissed her husband good-night. "Sleep tight," she whispered. "You too," he replied and turned over. Lily smiled as she heard his first reassuring snores. "Lord," Lily implored as she said her prayers quietly, "let me figure out a way to help my son and grandson. This family has been torn apart too long. I want those two to get back together. I need your help. Amen."

Chapter Thirty-Seven

"I'd love to join you and your family for dinner, Mrs. Wilson. How nice of you to ask. No, I eat everything, but thanks for checking. Okay, I'll be there at two. Oh, is it all right if I bring a bottle of wine? Good, I'll see you then. No, I have a GPS. I'll find the house. If you'll email me the address, I should be able to locate it without any trouble. Thanks again."

Ruth didn't understand why her palms were sweaty. Instead of hanging up the phone, she punched the speed dial number for Lily. It rang several times until the answering machine picked up. Ruth always got a kick out of Grady's automatic message.

"We're not here, but you probly already figured that out. Tell us who ya are and we'll holler back at ya."

"Hey Mama and Daddy. It's Ruth. I guess y'all are out and about. Just callin' to say Rory's professor is joining us for Thanksgiving dinner. Wanted to give you time to get spruced up for the occasion, is all. You can call me later. Bye."

Next she called Rory's cell phone. She never could keep his schedule straight, but knew he wouldn't pick up if he was in class. Normally it wasn't an issue. She rarely had time to call him during the week when she was working, but today she was on personal leave.

"Hey, Mama. How's it goin'?"

"Remember when we talked about my inviting your professor to dinner for Thanksgiving? Well, I called him, and he's coming."

"Great, Mama. Listen, I'm on my way to class, so I can't stay on. You gonna be home tonight?"

"No, I have a date with the Prince of England. Of course, I'll be home. Where else would I be? Talk to you later. I love you."

Rory thought his mother sounded pretty excited about Dr. Ragatky's accepting the invitation. It really wasn't a big deal as far as Rory was concerned. Maybe it was to her, though.

Two days later Rory was in the lab updating his notes when Dr. Ragatky turned on the light in his office. The professor waved and walked out of the glass enclosure and over to where Rory was working.

"Your mother invited me to Thanksgiving dinner."

"She told me. She's all excited about it. You'll get to meet my grandparents. They've heard a lot about you, and it'll be nice for them to put a face with the name. My papaw is even getting a haircut for the occasion." Rory laughed. "I don't think he's cut his hair for a couple of years."

Dr. Ragatky felt the fringe at the back of his neck. "Maybe I ought to get a trim too. I'm way overdue for my three-month haircut," he joked.

"Speakin' of haircuts, I better get over to the barber myself. Mama hasn't seen me in a couple of months. She'll have a fit with this long hair. Last time she saw me she said I looked like a hippie."

"What're you working on?" Dr. Ragatky peered over Rory's shoulder at his notes. His physical closeness made Rory uncomfortable. Rory slid the notes over to him.

There'd been a couple of other times when Rory sensed Dr. Ragatky was closer than men usually got to each other, but he had dismissed it as his own imagination. After all, the professor was widowed and had children. There had been no reason to question his sexuality until their chance meeting at Pathways.

Dr. Ragatky slid the notes back to Rory without saying anything and walked back to his office. Rory resumed working.

A few minutes later the professor returned. "About the other night, Rory."

Rory waved his hand in the air. "No big deal. I won't say anything to the other kids."

"No, it's not a big deal, but I do want to talk about it. I wondered if you might be gay too, but it wouldn't have been appropriate for me to bring it up. Besides, they're so damned homophobic around here. I've always been extremely careful not to give anyone an excuse to hassle me."

Rory nodded. "I'm not out to anyone here except the two guys who were with me that night. I've known them since high school, and we hang together a lot. They're okay. You don't have to worry about them either."

"Why'd you choose to come to school here, knowing how it would be? If I'd been in your shoes, I think I would have picked a school in New York or California, somewhere else, anywhere where people are more tolerant."

"Well, for one thing, this is where I could get a full scholarship, thanks to you. Otherwise, I could never have afforded to go to college. For another thing, my mother is alone, and I didn't want to be too far from home. My grandparents are close by, but they're getting up there, and if anything should happen to either of them, I'd want to be close enough to be able to drive home on weekends to help out."

"You're a good kid, Rory. But someday you might want to live somewhere else where you don't have to look over your shoulder and watch everything you say and do. But there's lots of time for that after you graduate."

"I hate to feel like I have to leave my home to be who I am. You know what I mean? I was born and raised here, and I want to believe that someday it will be different. Do you think it will ever change?"

"I've been at the university for 12 years, and I've seen a few changes for the better. Among my colleagues, it's not as bad as it once was. When I first came here, it wasn't unusual for people to use gay slurs openly. That's stopped. We've all had diversity training, and the administration at least goes through the motions about making the campus safe for all students."

"I've heard that the local hospitals no longer freak when somebody gets admitted with HIV or AIDS," Rory said. "A friend of mine who knows someone who teaches in the medical school told me horror stories about the way it used to be here with doctors and nurses not wanting to treat gays. Of course, it helps that most of the new cases are heterosexual folks. Maybe that's what changed their attitudes."

"All true, but until the day that you and I can be open about our sexual orientation, we still have lots of work to do. One of the reasons Dr. Robbins and I go to the bar from time to time is so that gay students will know that they have a couple of faculty members they can feel safe with if they need to talk. He's the guy I was with the other night." Dr. Ragatky cleared his throat and then said, "I just want you to know that I'm here for you, Rory, if it ever gets bad and you need someone to talk to."

Rory smiled and extended his hand to his mentor. "Thanks, Doc. Same here." They shook hands and laughed.

Chapter Thirty-Eight

Ruth cleared dishes from the table, and Grady groaned as he loosened his belt. "That's the best Thanksgiving meal I've ever had, Ruth. Where'd you learn to cook like that?"

Everyone joined in the chorus of praise.

"Judging from the amount of leftovers, I thought y'all didn't like the food. I'm glad it was okay."

"It was considerably better than okay, Mrs. Wilson. I don't know when I've had a better meal. This sure beats what I had last Thanksgiving," Dr. Ragatky said.

"Ya musta ate your own cookin' last year," Lily commented and drew laughs from everyone.

"No, it was worse than that. I went to the local Chinese take-out place and got Kung Pao chicken, a dish I usually like a lot. There must have been something wrong with it because I was sick for two days. As if I wasn't feeling guilty enough eating foreign food on the most American holiday of the year."

Throughout the meal Rory noticed his mother looking at Dr. Ragatky, and unless he was badly mistaken, her looks were more than friendly. When she spoke to him, her voice had that flirty lilt to it.

Lily and Ruth worked side by side cleaning the dishes. "So ask him if he wants to see a movie. I've heard women don't wait around for men to do the asking anymore. He seems nice enough."

The conversation came to an abrupt halt when Rory carried the turkey platter into the kitchen, but not before he heard enough to realize this could be a dicey situation. He was sure Lily was talking about the professor. As he left the kitchen he thought about how to handle it. Now what do I do, he wondered. I don't want to out

Dr. Ragatky, but I don't want Mama to get hurt, either. Should I say something to her?

Lily was pleased that Ruth was showing interest in such a nice man, and she encouraged her. As far as she and Grady knew, Ruth had not dated anyone since the divorce. They'd been discussing it a week or so before Thanksgiving when Lily speculated.

"This professor sounds like a right nice fella. Ruth says he's divorced, too."

"Are you fixin to do some matchmakin'?"

Lily looked at him with a sly smile. "Who me?"

"Ruth's a grown woman. I'm sure she can arrange her own matches, Lily. Nobody likes a meddler."

"It's not meddlin' to want to see our daughter-in-law find some companionship."

Grady knew after all his years with Lily that nothing he said would dissuade her once she set her mind to something, so he had walked away.

Ruth was disappointed when Dr. Ragatky didn't say anything about seeing her again when he left that evening. She knew what Lily said was true, but she was raised the old-fashioned way, and asking a man for a date was not something she thought she could do.

Later that evening when Rory had dried the last of the dishes and Ruth had put them away, she sat at the kitchen table to rest.

"Come have a cup of coffee with me, Rory. I've hardly had a chance to talk to you since you came home Wednesday night. With all the cooking and cleaning and then dinner today, I felt like I just had to keep pushing. It's so good to have you home, even if you have to go back Sunday. I wish you had more time."

Ruth parked the sugar bowl in front of Rory. He dug in and put two heaping teaspoonfuls into his cup and stirred absentmindedly, as if he was trying to hypnotize himself with the swirling motion in his cup.

"What's the matter, Rory? You look like you're a million miles away."

"Oh, nothin' Mama. I'm just tired. Turkey always makes me sleepy. You must be exhausted. It was a great dinner." He hesitated before mentioning the professor and then plunged in.

"It was nice of you to invite Dr. Ragatky. I think he was happy not to spend the holiday alone."

"He's got two sons, doesn't he? Does he ever see them?"

"No, but I have no idea why." It occurred to Rory that Dr. Ragatky's sons might avoid him because he's gay. He'd never told the professor about his own father's staying away from him for that reason. Over the years, Rory had become convinced that his parents divorced and his father abandoned him because of his sexual orientation.

"Does he have a girlfriend?" Ruth didn't see any reason to beat around the bush, and Rory was the only one who might know.

Oh man, I have to do something, he thought.

"I don't know about any girlfriend, but he's pretty much of a loner. I guess you could say his work is his mistress."

"He's a nice-looking man and he's cultured. I'm sure lots of women would like to go out with him."

"Yeah, well, I think he might have gotten divorced because he doesn't have time or energy for anything but his work. Some people are like that."

"If I didn't know better, I'd think you're trying to discourage me from having any interest in this man, Rory."

"Well, I guess I am in a way, Mama. It would be kind of awkward for me if you were dating my professor.

"Really? I hadn't thought about it like that. I guess I can see why it might make you uncomfortable. I'm glad you told me. I was trying to screw up my courage to ask him for a date."

"You were gonna ask him?"

"Yes, Lily says that's the way it's done today. Women don't wait around to be asked."

"Oh, like she'd know about such things. Was that what you two were talking about when I came into the kitchen before?"

"Yeah, I think she's trying to get me to start dating again. I've been pretty gun shy since my divorce. I like my life just fine the way it is, but with you away at school, I do get kind of lonely sometimes."

This was not the kind of conversation Rory wanted to have with his mother. He was working on a graceful exit strategy when the phone rang.

"I'll get it." Rory jumped up so quickly he turned his chair over. Ruth got up and righted it, checking to see if it was broken. The chairs had belonged to her mother, and she took special care to make them last.

"Oh, hey, Meemaw. We were just talkin' about you. Mama was tellin' me how you're trying to play matchmaker." He grimaced at his mother. "Aw, I'm just pullin' your leg. Here, I'll let you talk to her." He reached out the phone and Ruth took it.

"Oh, you're welcome, Mama. I enjoy cooking. You know that. Really, you want to do Christmas dinner this year?" Ruth caught Rory's eye and he gave her a thumbs up. We can talk about who's bringin' what. We've got four weeks."

Chapter Thirty-Nine

Rory checked his cell phone out of habit; he didn't expect to hear from anyone. Most of his friends had left campus to go home for the holiday. He was surprised to see a cryptic text message from Sandy: "Pathways gone. Poof. News at 10."

Pathways, of course, was the gay bar in Johnson City. That much Rory could figure out. He glanced at his watch, saw it was 10:15, walked into the living room, and clicked on the TV. The CBS local station was replaying highlights of the various Thanksgiving parades around the country. He watched to see if they'd mention anything that might relate to Sandy's message about Pathways.

One of the problems with living in Craggy Grove was there was no local TV news. The Johnson City channels reported news from Craggy Grove occasionally, but short of a tornado whipping through town or a major crime spree, which happened maybe once every hundred years, you had to get local news from *The Mountaineer*, and it only came out on Tuesdays and Thursdays.

The commentator recapped football scores and then the weather guy showed spots around the country where events were a lot more interesting than in eastern Tennessee. Rory sometimes thought Craggy Grove was the perfect place to put people in the federal witness protection program. Once you entered the town, you pretty much ceased to exist to the outside world.

Rory was about to turn off the TV when he heard the announcer say, "Recapping the day's news ..." and Rory recognized the front of Pathways. "Fire officials are investigating a suspicious fire at a notorious men's bar, Pathways, a known magnet for homosexuals." So that's what Sandy's message meant.

Rory remembered there was a meeting scheduled for Thanksgiving night at the bar. It was closed for regular business, but community members were urged to attend a discussion about the latest developments in the treatment of AIDS and HIV. A doctor who had pioneered treatment of AIDS patients at the university medical center was presenting the latest research.

Rory recalled thinking that was a weird time to schedule a meeting with most of the students gone, but he overheard the bar owner telling someone the presenter hoped the older guys would attend since they were more likely to be needing treatment.

The announcer went on to say there had been two fatalities and several injuries resulting from the fire. Rory hoped he didn't know any of them.

He texted back to Sandy. "Saw on TV. Bummer."

Rory might have forgotten about the fire except for recalling that before he left, Dr. Ragatky had said to him he had a meeting that evening. Nobody has meetings on Thanksgiving, Rory had thought and dismissed it at the time. Now he worried that the meeting at Pathways was the one Dr. Ragatky meant. He hoped not.

How can I find out if he's OK? I've got his cell phone number, but I hate to call. He'll think I'm being intrusive. He gave me the number in case I had a work-related question when he's away from campus, he recalled.

Ruth joined Rory in the living room. "Anything good on tonight?"

"I don't know. I didn't look. I was just watching the news."

"Are we at war with anybody new? I haven't paid much attention to news for a few days. The way things are going, you don't dare blink."

"I don't think so. They just covered the Thanksgiving turkey's getting a presidential pardon and showed clips of the parades all over the country. Oh, and they showed the winner of the big dog show."

Ruth noticed Rory kept looking at his phone. He seemed distracted, but so did most people his age these days. If they weren't using two or three electronic gadgets at a time, they feared they'd miss something. Ruth had a cell phone that she used for old-fashioned calls. It had all sorts of other features, but she didn't know how to use them and had little interest in learning.

"Oh, crap," Rory exclaimed as he looked at his phone. He got up and headed toward his room.

"What's that about?" Ruth asked. "Is something wrong?" Rory usually didn't use language like that around her.

"Nothing," he replied and shut his door.

The TV remained on and Ruth glanced at the screen one time to see a crawler message about a fire in a bar in Johnson City. Officials had raised the number of fatalities to five. At that moment, Rory burst out of his room carrying his jacket. He had a worried look on his face.

"Mama, I have to go back to campus. Something happened to a friend of mine, and he's in the medical center."

"Oh, Rory, I'm sorry. What happened? Will you be back tonight?" Ruth knew how long it would take Rory to drive there and back.

"I'll fill you in later. I need to go. If it's too late, I'll spend the night in the dorm. I'll call and let you know. How late can I call?"

"I'm sure I'll be up 'til 11:30 or so. I hope your friend will be okay." She walked him to the side door. "Be careful. I'll talk to you later."

Rory bent down, kissed her cheek, and blew out the door.

Ruth read until the 11 o'clock news came on. The lead story was about the fire. Again the commentator described Pathways as a magnet for area homosexuals.

Oh, I bet that's how Rory's friend was hurt, Ruth thought. Thank the Lord, Rory was here. For all I know, he could have been at that place too.

The reporter made no attempt to conceal his personal feelings about Pathways. He remarked about the neighbors' considering the bar a nuisance. He said multiple incidents had occurred there over the 12 years it had existed, but the police had no success shutting it down.

Ruth made a mental note to ask Rory about the bar when he returned. It sounded like an unsafe place, and she worried about him. She turned off the TV and called it a night.

Chapter Forty

Sandy jumped up and waved to get Rory's attention. "Over here," he called. The hospital lobby was unusually crowded for a holiday.

Rory had torn up the road driving from Craggy Grove, taking some of the mountain curves a lot faster than he should have and stopping only for three red lights.

Rory sat down and noticed dark circles under Sandy's eyes. "How's Spud? Is he gonna make it? What do the doctors say?"

Sandy put his head in his hands and studied his shoes.

"Oh, man, is he dead?"

Sandy looked up. "No, but he's a mess. He's got burns over at least half of his body. They gave him something for pain, but he's still moaning."

"I'm glad you called me. Did you reach his parents?"

"No, they don't give a crap about him. Remember? He had to live with his aunt for his junior and senior years of high school. I called her. She doesn't have any way to get here."

"Yeah, I forgot," Rory said. "Can we go see him?"

"I had a hard time convincing the nurses to let me see him. Only kin are allowed in. I hope you don't mind, Rory, but I told the nurse you were his brother and you were on your way. At least that way they'll let you in."

"Nah, good idea. Let's go up."

"Before we go, I have to tell you something weird. There's an older guy in the bed next to Spud's. He got burned pretty bad too, not as bad as Spud, but he's pretty out of it. Nobody was with him, so I walked over and asked if I could call somebody for him. I noticed the name on the chart was Wilson, so I figured he must have kin around here. He was half delirious and mumbled something about

191

his son. I had trouble understanding him, but it sounded like he said the kid's name was Rory. I wasn't even thinking about his last name, but when I asked where his son lived, I was pretty sure he said something grove. Don't you live in Craggy Grove?"

There wasn't a drop of blood left in Rory's face. He nodded in answer to Sandy's question.

"Are you okay, man?" Sandy reached over and touched Rory's arm. "You look like you're gonna be sick. Want some water or anything?"

As they spoke, an older man in a motorcycle jacket approached them. He was soft- spoken and apologized for interrupting.

"Are you guys here about somebody from Pathways?" he asked.

Sandy answered. "Yeah, our buddy is burned up pretty bad. He's upstairs. What about you?"

"My name is Paul Manos. Sorry, I forgot my manners." Sandy and Rory stood and shook his hand. "My boyfriend's upstairs, but they won't let me in to see him. I told them I have medical power of attorney for him, but they don't care. They told me I'm not family, and only family can see him."

"What's his name? Maybe we can tell him you're here," Sandy offered.

"His name is Darrell Wilson." Then, as if it had just registered, he looked at Rory. "Did you say your name is Rory Wilson? Darrell's got a son by that name."

Nobody moved fast enough to catch Rory as he slumped to the sofa. Sandy bent to help his friend up.

"I'm all right," Rory said weakly after a few seconds. "Maybe I just need some water." Paul went in search of a vending machine or water fountain.

"Are you one of those guys who gets weird when you're in a hospital?" Sandy asked Rory. "You just passed out. Should I get a doctor?"

"No, I'll be fine. I just need a few minutes to get my head around this." Rory spoke softly. "I think Paul's partner is my father, Sandy. Remember the night we were in Pathways and you said some older guy came over and asked if you were with me? I bet that was Paul. When you asked me about it, I didn't remember, but now I recall seeing two older guys in motorcycle jackets watching me that night. I didn't recognize them, but I haven't seen my father in seven or eight years."

"Holy crap! Do you really think it's him?"

"It could be. I might know if I see him. Since my name's Wilson I can always tell the nurses I'm his son. If it's not him, no harm done. We can still tell him Paul is down here. How many Darrell Wilsons can there be with sons named Rory? Hell, I only ever met one other Rory in my life."

Paul returned with a bottle of Dr. Pepper. "Sorry, it's all I could find. The machine was out of water."

"Thanks. It's fine."

Sandy and Rory told Paul they were going upstairs. "We'll tell him you're here," Sandy said.

"Thanks very much, boys. I appreciate it. Tell him I love him, please."

Rory and Sandy noticed tears forming in Paul's eyes. Sandy reached out and touched the man's shoulder. "No problem. We're glad to do it."

"If they wouldn't let Paul in, how'd you get in to see Spud?" Rory asked as he and Sandy left the lobby.

"I sort of conned my way in. When they asked if I was Spud's family, I just told them to take a good look at my face. They assumed I was his brother. When I said our brother was coming over, they probably thought I meant blood brother. You gotta think fast with these people. Always stay one step ahead of 'em."

The elevator ride seemed longer than it should have. When the door opened, Rory caught a whiff of antiseptic he always associated with hospitals.

"Now, don't faint on me here. They'll slap you in a bed."

Rory smiled sheepishly. "I won't. I'm fine now. Let's get this over with."

Sandy led him to Spud's bedside. Spud was sleeping, but Rory saw him wince every few seconds and guessed it was from pain. They stood for a few minutes, and Sandy nodded toward the next bed.

Slowly, Rory approached the man in the bed. As he stood there, the man opened his eyes and stared directly at him. Rory quickly turned his head and looked at Sandy. He nodded. Yes, this was his father.

A nurse approached the bed. "Are you his son? He's been asking for you. Is it Rory?"

Rory didn't recognize the voice that squeezed out of his throat. It sounded so childish. "Yes, I'm his son."

"I nearly forgot," Rory said to his father. "Paul is downstairs. They won't let him in." He hesitated and then delivered the rest of the message. "He said to tell you he loves you."

Darrell smiled enough to let Rory know he'd understood. He tried to speak, but all he could get out was "Rory."

Rory turned and walked back to Spud's bed, relieved to be away from the person who'd hurt him worse than all the school bullies he'd encountered.

Chapter Forty-One

Rory talked to himself aloud as he drove to the campus, practicing how he would tell his mother. There was no easy way. His thoughts lurched in a thousand directions. Lord, how do you tell someone she was married to a guy who turns out to be gay? Maybe she won't know about the bar fire. I can just make up something about what a coincidence it was to run into him when I visited my friend in the hospital.

But why should I try to protect him, he wondered. What did he ever do to help me out? Mama's gonna be shocked enough that I ran into him without me having to tell her he's gay.

Of all the damned messes. I thought I was done with him, and here he shows up again causing more trouble. Oh Lord, I have to tell Papaw and Meemaw. This'll kill Papaw for sure.

By the time Rory got to his room, he'd pretty much settled on what he would say to Ruth. Before he called, he washed his hands at the sink and looked at himself in the mirror. Without warning, he started to laugh. He laughed like a lunatic as waves of hysteria forced their way up from his gut. He shouted at the mirror, "My father's a faggot just like me. Oh, Lord."

Rory tried to be serious, but the more he attempted to stop, the funnier things seemed. He tried unsuccessfully to control himself. This is no laughing matter, he thought. My father is in the hospital, and I have to tell my mother that the man she used to be married to is seriously injured and gay.

He continued talking to the mirror. "He was in a freakin' gay bar when it caught fire. He and all the other faggots got burned up." He remembered the dictionary definition of faggot the first time he looked it up.

One sobering thought helped him rein in his hysteria. The meet-

195

ing at the bar was about AIDS. He wondered if his father had AIDS.

It took a few minutes, but he finally regained enough control to punch in his mother's number. It was 11:15, an unusually late hour for phoning her, but she'd said to call.

Ruth picked up the phone on the first ring. She was relieved to hear his voice.

"I need to stay here for a couple of days, Mama."

"But that's the rest of the weekend, Rory. You just got here a day and a half ago."

"I know, but things are pretty bad with my friend, and he doesn't have anybody else near here."

"Was he in that bar fire?"

"How'd you know about that?"

"It's all over TV."

"Yeah, he was, Mama. That's not all. I have some shocking news to give you."

"What is it?"

"The guy in the bed next to ..." Rory's voice faltered, and he stopped for a few seconds.

He began again. "The guy in the next bed to Spud's is my father. He was burned pretty badly on his hands and arms and chest. They have him sedated."

No sound came from Ruth's end of the phone.

"Mama, are you okay?"

"No, I'm not. I'm not okay at all. What in the world are you talking about? Are you telling me your father was in a gay bar? Lord have mercy, I cannot believe this!"

"I'm sorry to shock you like this, Mama, but I thought you'd want to know." He waited for her to say something. When she didn't, he said, "It's complicated."

"You can say that again. Are you okay?"

"Right now, I'm having trouble keeping my eyes open. I promise I'll call first thing tomorrow morning."

"Do you want me to come over there? I can bring Grady and Lily."

"The nurse said he's in critical condition, but that's standard with third-degree burns. She said it's not life-threatening. I suppose you can tell them he's here, but I'm not sure if you should mention the bar and, you know."

"Maybe I should wait 'til I hear more from you in the morning. What do you think?"

"That's probably a good idea. It's too late for them to go over there, anyway. Let's all sleep on it. This night has wrung me out like a dish rag."

"All right, son. Call me as soon as you're up in the morning."

"I promise, first thing. We can figure out what to do about Papaw and Meemaw. Get some sleep. G'night."

Ruth tried to piece together the events of the evening, but no matter how she tried, there were too many gaps in her information to make much sense out of what Rory had said. She'd long since stopped wishing Darrell any harm, and truthfully, she felt little more concern for him than she would for a stranger. She'd nearly succeeded in wiping him out of her life. Sure, she was sorry he was burned, but she'd feel that way about anybody.

She reflected, I was married to that man. How could I not know he was gay? Maybe he's not gay. Maybe he was there with a friend who is. Just because somebody was in a gay bar doesn't make him gay, does it?

She ran through the years they'd spent together to see if there was anything that might suggest that he was gay. He played sports in high school and college. He hung out with guys. He hunted, and he loved NASCAR. He never lost interest in sex. If he was faking, he sure convinced her he enjoyed their lovemaking. He hated Rory's effeminate characteristics. She knew that was what drove a wedge between him and his son and eventually led to the divorce. How could someone who was so homophobic turn out to be gay?

Chapter Forty-Two

"What're your plans for the day?" Lily asked and handed Grady a cup of steaming coffee. He reached for the sugar and she playfully slapped his hand. "Here, use this. It might keep ya around for another couple o' months." She handed him a yellow packet of Splenda. Grady grimaced, but took it from her as the phone rang.

"Wonder who that is callin' so early," Lily said. "Wilson residence," she answered. "Yes, I'm his mother. Is something wrong?"

Grady's worried expression mirrored Lily's.

"Let me get that address. I'm not sure I know where it's at." She scrounged around on the counter for a piece of paper and a pencil.

"Say that one more time, please. I can't write so fast."

"Please tell him we're on our way. We'll be there directly. Yes. Thank you." She turned to Grady. "Darrell's been in a fire. He's in the Johnson City Medical Center. He's got burns over half of his body, but the lady said they expect him to recover."

"Did his apartment burn down?"

"She didn't say, but what does it matter? Come on, Grady. Let's get in the car." Lily picked up her purse from the kitchen chair.

"Give me a minute. I've got to use the bathroom." He looked at her strangely.

"What is it?" she asked impatiently.

"Are you goin' like that?"

"Oh, shoot. I forgot." She began pulling the curlers out of her hair and finger combed the gray swirls they left behind. "I can comb it while you drive. Come on."

"I hate these durn things," Grady mumbled as they got into the hospital elevator. Lily knew he was scared they'd crash, but he was in no shape to climb three flights of stairs. She was relieved when someone got in with them. Grady wouldn't whine with another man around.

They approached the nurse's station. "We're Darrell Wilson's parents. Can you show us where he is, please?"

A young woman whose name tag identified her as a doctor smiled and led them down the hall. "He'll be so pleased that you're here. His son was here last night. It always helps when family members are around."

Grady and Lily exchanged shocked looks.

"He didn't get a whole lot of sleep. The pain from his burns is pretty intense," the doctor continued, "but a visit from Mama and Daddy might be the best medicine." They turned a corner. "Here he is," she said.

Darrell opened his eyes. "Mama, Daddy, how'd you get here?"

"We'd a flown if we could've," Grady answered. "We came as soon as they called us." Darrell was groggy, whether from drugs or his pain and lack of sleep, they couldn't tell.

"Are you in a lot of pain?" Lily asked.

"My skin feels like it's still on fire."

"How'd this happen?"

"I was at a bar, Mama, and it caught fire. The fire spread really fast. We had to run through it to get out the door."

"Lord have mercy."

Lily remembered yesterday was Thanksgiving. "Did you have dinner there?"

"No, there was a meeting. The bar was closed to the public. I had dinner earlier with friends, like I told you."

"Did they say when you'll be able to get outta here?" Grady asked.

"No, I feel too rotten to ask. It'll be a while, I'm sure."

"I didn't know you and Rory were in touch. We were surprised to hear he came to see you." Lily didn't ask any questions. She just put those thoughts out there hoping Darrell would respond.

"I wasn't sure he actually was here. I thought I was hallucinating. So, he was really here? I'm surprised I recognized him. He's so big."

"The doctor said he was here. I don't think she's on drugs."

"Let's hope not," Grady chimed in.

"Son, can we get you anything? Do you need something to read or eat?"

"There's somebody I'd like you to meet," Darrell began. "I'm sure he's downstairs in the lobby. His name is Paul Manos. He's my partner. Paul and I have been together for four and a half years. He's a really nice guy."

"Why isn't he up here?" Grady asked.

"Only family members can visit patients in this unit."

Grady shook his head and looked at his wife.

"Well, that's ridiculous," Lily declared. "We'll see about that."

Grady rolled his eyes, something he often did when Lily made pronouncements like that.

"Have ya got a taste for anything?" she asked Darrell.

"I'd love to have some ice cream. I heard somebody say there's a cafeteria downstairs. If they have some, that would be great."

Grady took advantage of the opportunity to escape. Even another elevator ride was worth it. He hated being around sick people, and while he loved his son, he'd already had more than enough time in the place. "I'll see what I can find."

"Before you go," Lily said, "see if you can find a chair for me. I can't stand for too long. My arthur in my knees acts up."

Grady delivered a chair to his wife and left the room. He searched the lobby and saw a man stretched out on a sofa with his eyes closed. He matched the description Darrell had given of Paul. Grady stood over the man wondering if he should wake him. While he was deliberating, the man opened his eyes and said in a startled voice, "May I help you?" He sat up quickly.

"You can if your name is Paul."

"Yes, I'm Paul Manos. Is there news about Darrell?"

"He's no worse than he was when they brought him here. I'm Grady Wilson, his father." Paul stood and reached out his hand. Grady took it.

"Darrell told us they won't let you up to see him."

"That's right. You have to be family."

"Well, son, you just got adopted. I'm on my way to get Darrell some ice cream. I'll stop on my way back, and we can go up together."

"Yes, sir. Thank you. You have no idea what this means to us."

He dug his fingernails into his palm, trying to keep from crying. "His favorite flavor is chocolate, by the way. Didn't know if that had changed since he lived at home."

Ten minutes later, Grady and Paul passed the nurse's station. A woman looked at Paul suspiciously. He knew she recognized him from the previous night. She was the one who wouldn't let him see Darrell.

"Only family members are allowed to visit ICU patients," she said in an officious tone.

"I'm Darrell Wilson's father and this is my other son," Grady said, his chin jutting out as he pulled himself up to his full five feet ten inches.

Her face told him she knew he was lying. He was glad she chose not to challenge him.

"Around that corner," she snarled.

"Thank you so much for your kind assistance," Grady said and offered a Cheshire Cat smile to go with it. As they walked away, he distinctly heard her mutter, "Son, my ass." He glanced at Paul to see if he'd heard it too. Paul's smile confirmed that he had.

Grady and Paul stood at the foot of Darrell's bed. His eyes were closed again. Lily put her finger up to her lips to indicate silence, so the two men stood and looked at Darrell. Lily knew who Paul was before he walked over to her and whispered his name. She smiled at him, but her warmest smile was for Grady. She was so proud of him.

They didn't have to wait long. Darrell opened his eyes and looked at Paul. Darrell reached for him with his good hand, and Paul stepped around to the side of the bed to take it. Lily noticed they had matching rings.

"How'd you get him in here?" Darrell asked.

In a voice much louder than was necessary Grady said, "I found your brother waiting in the lobby, so I brought him up." Then, for emphasis, he added, "A man needs all the love he can get to heal."

Lily put her hand to her mouth to conceal a smile.

Ruth punched in Lily and Grady's number for the second time. It was only half past eight, too early for them to have gone anywhere.

She fussed with her hair as she listened to the endless ringing. She knew it was too cool for them to be having breakfast on the porch. Damn, where can they be? I don't want to leave this kind of message, she thought.

She tried several more times and considered driving over there, but Rory still hadn't called, and she didn't want to miss his call.

She thought about Darrell. It had been years since she'd seen or talked to him. She wasn't sure she'd recognize him if she passed him on the street. The mirror told her she'd aged considerably since the divorce, and there was no reason to think time had been any kinder to him.

Again, questions nagged at her. She'd long since accepted the fact that she had a gay son, but this was different. Darrell had been her husband; surely she would have noticed something.

Ruth was so deep in thought that she almost didn't hear the phone ring. As she pushed the talk button, she glanced at her watch. It was nearly ten o'clock.

"Rory, I'm so glad you called. I've been on pins and needles since I got up at 5:30 ... No, I couldn't sleep. How'd you sleep? ... Good. I've been calling and calling. Nobody answers over there. ... I can't imagine where they could be. ... Yeah, I'll keep trying to reach them. ... Can you keep your phone on? ... Oh, right. How stupid of me. ... Why don't you call me when you can use your phone? They have to come home sometime. You know how your Papaw is about having his meals regularly. I bet Lily will be getting home any time now so she can fix his lunch. ... Sure, talk to ya later."

Ruth threw in a load of laundry and sat down to pay bills. She'd only written two checks when the phone rang. Rory again.

"Hey. ... When did they get there? No wonder I couldn't reach them. ... Have you seen Darrell?"

Ruth was glad to know where Grady and Lily were. At least she could quit worrying about them. She was relieved not to be the one to break the news to them. When Rory told her they were at Darrell's bedside with his partner, Paul, she wondered how they were dealing with this latest news. Grady's heart wasn't the strongest.

"How's your friend doin? What's his name again? ... Right, Spud. That's not his real name, is it? Give me his last name in case I want to call and see how he's doing." She scribbled the information on a piece of scrap paper.

"Oh, good. Yeah, I realized after you flew outta here last night you forgot your books and things. Will you get here in time for supper? … If you're gonna be delayed, let me know. Bye."

Why do I have this nagging feeling that I should be at the hospital, Ruth wondered. Darrell was nothing to her anymore. Maybe she'd send him a card. She thought of how she'd sign it. Maybe "your ex-wife and mother of the son you abandoned" or "the woman you slept with before you turned gay."

She was puzzled by her anger. What business was it of hers what Darrell does? One thought kept running through her mind: I wonder if people call him that word. Wouldn't that be justice? He's turned into what he hated in his son.

Chapter Forty-Three

"Good Lord, Grady. Look what time it is!" Lily turned the clock with large luminous letters so he could see it. Neither could recall when they last slept until 7:30. They were usually up an hour earlier.

Grady pulled himself up so he was resting on one elbow. "Whyn't you wake me?"

"Cause I was sleepin'," Lily answered. She dangled her legs over the side of the bed and fished around for her slippers.

Lily shuffled into the kitchen and realized the coffee maker held a couple of cups of coffee from the day before. In her haste to get to the hospital, she'd unplugged it, but didn't take time to wash it. She rinsed it quickly and put in a new filter.

"Durn," she muttered to herself. She'd intended to do the weekly grocery shopping when they rushed off to see Darrell the day before, and they were out of coffee. Well, nearly out. Maybe she could coax two cups of weak coffee. It was better than nothing.

As usual, Grady dressed and walked outside to fetch a couple of small logs. He came in and offered his weather report for the day. "It's a tad colder 'n yesterday." He put the logs into the wood stove in the corner and lit the crumpled piece of newspaper before shoving it between the logs.

"Want some eggs?"

"We got any of that wretched turkey bacon to go with them?"

"Nope, we're clean out of bacon, wretched or otherwise," Lily replied. "I never did the grocery shoppin' yesterday. I'll scramble you some eggs and fix toast. Here's your coffee."

Grady had weaned himself off cream after his heart attack. Lily used skim milk in hers, but Grady said he'd rather have nothing than that gray dishwater. He'd gotten used to Splenda at Lily's insistence, so he emptied a packet into his coffee, stirred it, and took a sip.

Lily watched for a reaction. He walked over to the sink and spit it out.

"Better not pour the rest of it out," she warned. "It's all we have. I stretched one tablespoon of coffee into two cups."

Grady could tolerate a lot as long as he had his morning coffee. "How come you let us run out?" he asked.

"I told you. I didn't get to grocery shop yesterday. That's how come."

"Seems to me we should keep extra on hand just in case—"

"When they start givin' it away, we'll get extra. 'Til that happens, I have to buy what I can. Your Social Security check didn't clear 'til yesterday."

Grady backed off. He knew Lily did the best she could on a tight budget. "I'll get some at the hospital later," he said and poured out the rest of the diluted coffee.

He sat down at the table to eat his breakfast as Lily hopped up and went to the refrigerator. "Have some orange juice. You need something to wash that down."

"That Paul seems like a right nice feller, don't you think?"

"He's fond of Darrell, that's for sure. Did you notice they have the same ring?"

"No, I didn't catch that. I can't believe Darrell didn't tell us he had a …" She hesitated. "What do ya call it when a man has another man?"

"Darrell called him his partner."

"Yeah, partner. Well, we always wanted another son. I guess we got one. If Darrell's happy with Paul, that's all that matters. I'm sure he's not gonna march around in a parade on TV like some of 'em do. I don't think I'd want to see that. It would be hard to explain."

"Explain to who? Whose business is it 'cept ours?"

"Well, friends, neighbors, people who know us. I just wouldn't want to have to get into it with 'em." She remembered something she'd meant to share with him. "I don't think you were around when Darrell told me Paul's family disowned him when they found out he was gay. Imagine throwin' your own child out? What gets into some people?"

"Religion. They listen to preachers like that Reverend Hodges, the one who says homosexuals are an abomination. Remember?"

"I don't understand how people who call themselves good Christians can hate anybody. Do they think God made mistakes when he made gay people? Honestly. I'm goin' to pick up a few things before we head for Johnson City or you'll have another morning without your precious coffee. Do you think we'll be home for supper tonight?"

Grady shrugged. "If nothing happens, we should be able to leave in the afternoon. Now that Paul can be with Darrell, we don't need to stay so long."

The phone rang and Lily answered. "Yes, we're still alive. I was just fixin' to call you. We got home too late last night. ... Yeah, it was quite a day. ... The doctor says he'll be all right. The main thing is to keep infection from starting. ... No, Rory didn't come over to him while we were there. He was visitin' his friend in the next bed. He hugged us when he saw us, but then he walked back to his friend's bed. ... I'm sure it was hard for him."

Ruth filled Lily in on Rory's impressions from the limited conversation they'd had. Rory had said he had no further desire to see his father. "Well, it was mighty nice of him to talk to Darrell. He's so sweet. But I understand his feelings. You can't expect to fix a relationship that busted up years ago. I'm sure Darrell knows that. Can I ask you something? I don't mean to pry, but I'm curious, Ruth. Did you ever suspect Darrell was gay?"

"You could have knocked me over. I never had a clue. What about you? Were you as shocked as I was?" Ruth asked.

"He told us some time ago, but never mentioned it after that one time. ... No, we didn't know he was seeing someone. Me and Grady were just talking about it. Darrell called him his partner, so that's the word we'll use. ... Well, I don't care what they say on TV. Partner sounds better than lover to me.

"I'm fixin' to pick up a few things from the Food Lion and then we're goin' back to the hospital ... Oh, you don't have to do that ... Well, if you're goin' anyways, I need coffee, a package of hamburger, a can of red kidney beans, and a green pepper. I'm makin' chili for supper. ... Just keep it in your refrigerator. I'll call ya when we get back and we can pick it up. ... Thanks, dear. We'll talk later."

Chapter Forty-Four

Darrell recovered from his burns over the next several weeks. Six months after the fire, Ruth learned from Lily that he'd returned to work. After that, Lily resumed her practice of not mentioning Darrell to either Ruth or Rory, except to suggest to Ruth from time to time that she might not want to drop by because Darrell would be at the house. Life settled back into the usual routine with Rory away most of the time at school and Ruth's trying to turn a part-time job into a full-time escape from loneliness.

Grady had given everyone a scare when he complained of chest pains one night. Lily had driven him to the emergency room. He now wore a container of nitroglycerin around his neck and was told to put one under his tongue whenever he felt chest pain. Within a few days, he joked about the TNT he carried and warned people not to mess with him or he'd blow the place up.

***

One day Ruth opened the kitchen door and dumped the mail on the counter. She tossed her jacket and purse on a chair and made a beeline for the bathroom. When she returned, she noticed an envelope addressed to her in a familiar handwriting. Sure enough, the chicken scratch in the upper left corner read D. Wilson at a Johnson City address.

What's he want, she wondered.

She opened the envelope and began to read the letter, stopping to insert editorial comments as she read.

"Dear Ruth, my foot. How dear am I after he never bothered to call all this time to see if we were alive or dead?" She read on. "Hmph, if he wants to know how Rory is, he should try calling him." She turned to the second page. "Oh, you want to talk, do you? I doubt you want to hear what I'd have to say or Rory either, for that matter."

After re-reading Darrell's letter, Ruth reached for the phone. "Damn these message machines," she huffed. "Hi Rory, it's Mama. Everything's fine. Give me a call when you get this message. I have something I want to talk to you about. Talk to ya later. I love you."

Ruth was happy to see Rory's number on the caller ID that night and returned his call immediately.

"Hey, Rory. How are you?"

"Good. Yeah, I told you everything's fine. Why do you always think something's wrong when I call? You're such a worry wart."

"I got a letter from your father today. ... Let me read it to you."

When she finished reading she asked, "What do you think?" She listened intently to Rory's reply. "Umm yeah, that's exactly what I said. At least he recognizes there's no way he can make up for what he did to us. I'll give him that much. ... No, I haven't exchanged a word with him in years. Lily and Grady almost never mention him. Have you run into him again?"

As they were talking, Ruth heard a beep indicating someone was trying to call. "Hold on a second, Rory." She pressed the flash button on the phone to see who it was.

"Speak of the devil. ... Yeah, it's him. I don't know another D. Wilson and he did say he'd call to see if we could get together for a cup of coffee. I'm not sure I want to talk to him. I have to think about it." They chatted for a couple of minutes and Ruth ended the call the way she always did. "I miss you, darling. When do you think you'll get home?" She frowned, even though there was nobody there to see it. "I know. Well, study hard. I love you. Bye."

Ruth needed to talk to somebody about Darrell's letter. She called the only person she felt comfortable asking for advice, her sister, Rebecca. Even though Ruth was the oldest, Rebecca seemed to get the lion's share of wisdom among the four sisters. They weren't close. They talked on the phone two or three times a year, mostly so they could swap information about each other's kids. But for some reason, Rebecca had always been the one whose opinions mattered to Ruth.

Rebecca was as surprised as Ruth to learn about Darrell's letter. She listened as Ruth read it and wished Ruth wouldn't ask her opinion, though she knew that was impossible.

"Well, what do you think I should do? ... I know it's my decision, but I need your opinion. ... I promise I won't argue. Tell me."

Rebecca said she didn't see anything wrong with meeting Darrell and hearing what he had to say. "People can change, you know," she said and then laughed when Ruth reminded her how Darrell had switched from women to men since she'd last seen him.

"I didn't mean that. You know what I mean. Maybe now that he's figured out he's gay, he's not so angry. Maybe he understands his behavior better now. I'd meet with him. What have you got to lose?"

"Well, I'll think about it. It would be awkward after all these years. It's not like we parted on good terms. I wouldn't want my meeting him to sound like I've forgiven him. I haven't."

"You don't have to decide tonight. Sleep on it. That's what you always told me when we were little." Rebecca laughed again.

"What's so funny?"

"I don't think I ever told you this. Once when I was upset about something and went to you for help, I must have been about seven or eight at the time, that's what you told me to do. I took it literally and wrote down the thing I was upset about and put it under my pillow that night. It worked. Whatever it was resolved itself by morning, and I thought you were the wisest person in the world."

"Maybe I should put this letter under my pillow and see if it still works."

They laughed, and Rebecca said she had to check on the boys to see if they were doing their homework.

Ruth drew a hot bath and planned to relax and think about what she wanted to do. While she soaked, the phone rang. She heard a man's voice leaving a message.

She towel-dried her hair and put on her favorite pajamas before going to the answering machine and pushing the blinking button. It was odd hearing Darrell's voice in the house after such a long absence. She thought he sounded older and tired.

"Hey, Ruth. It's Darrell. If you haven't already received it, you'll be getting a letter from me. I'm just calling to follow up on it. I'll call another time."

Isn't that just like him? He didn't ask how I was or Rory was, she thought. Just got right down to business. Some people never change.

Chapter Forty-Five

Rory finished his third year with a 3.98 grade point average, earning him fourth place in his class, and Dr. Ragatky had received a new grant that allowed Rory to continue to work on his project during the summer. The professor thought Rory was on to something with his genetic modification of tobacco. He hoped by the time Rory was out of school, the tobacco companies would show some interest in his work.

There were two weeks between the end of the spring semester and the start of summer session. At Dr. Ragatky's urging, Rory planned to take time off from lab work to have some fun.

"Hey, Rory, this year we have to do something spectacular," Sandy said as he sprawled on the bed vacated by Rory's roommate at semester's end. "I'll be legal, man. We never did anything much to celebrate your 21st except study for exams. What should we do?"

"I've always wanted to go to Provincetown," Rory said, "but I don't have enough money for that."

"Yeah, I wish there was someplace like that in Tennessee," Sandy replied. "Can't you just see it? They'd have to have an army of security agents to keep us from getting killed." They laughed at the thought of a gay-friendly resort in conservative Tennessee.

"Remember that guy Spud and I played poker with in the bar? He mentioned a men's ranch in Tennessee."

"I should ask Ragatky. He and some of his friends go to a men's ranch not too far from here. I wonder if it's the same one. I don't think he'd mind if I asked."

"Yeah, ask him. I could afford to drive someplace within a few hours if I don't need snooty clothes."

"Okay, I'll ask him later. I held on to my paycheck from last semester's work scholarship."

They wished Spud were there to join the celebration, but he'd had to drop out for the remainder of the year to undergo two surgeries and lots of physical therapy. He was recuperating at his aunt's home in North Carolina.

Later that day Rory called Sandy. "Tall Trees is the name of the place Ragatky goes to. He says it's not too expensive, and they always have a big party on Memorial Day weekend. That would be perfect, three days after your birthday. Wanna check it out?"

"Hang on a minute. Here's the site."

"Hold on. Let me come over and we can look at it together. Be right there."

They spent half an hour exploring the Tall Trees website. After agreeing that they could spend the $155 per night for a three-night weekend, Sandy volunteered to call to get a reservation.

A friendly voice on the other end of the phone replied, "We'll put you in Manly Meadows. Cabin 3A's got your name on it. It should take about 30 minutes for you to get here from campus. Oh, and bring your IDs. Yes, breakfast and dinners are included." Sandy gave him a credit card number to hold the reservation.

Once the deposit was placed on the room the days seemed to drag. Until now, the only place they'd been where there were more than a few gay men was the bar, and the fire had wiped out that venue as a playground. They weren't even sure if it would reopen. There were rumors that it was going to be rebuilt, but several neighbors were organizing to protest.

One afternoon Rory and Sandy were planning the trip using the Tall Trees site. "Hey look. It says clothing is optional," Sandy said. "I'm gonna travel light. Speedo, sandals, maybe shirts and shorts for meals and night time. The cabin has one double bed and a couch. The guy told me they make up the couch as a bed, and the double is upstairs. We can toss for the bed or take turns, whatever."

Since Rory and Sandy had never been sexually involved, Rory was happy to have separate beds, although from what Sandy said about the partying at Tall Trees, anything could happen.

Rory had never been on a real vacation. Money had been too tight, and Ruth always had work to do. Ashley's family was the only one Rory knew that went away. Her parents often rented a house at Wrightsville Beach for a week each summer.

When he thought about spending over $250 on a three-day spree, Rory experienced twinges of guilt, but Sandy convinced him they deserved a fling to celebrate turning twenty-one. After all, Sandy argued, next year this time they'd both be job- hunting, and there'd be no time for vacations. Just this once, they were entitled to be wild for a few days. Rory agreed and since he'd been careful with his money, he had it to spend.

Friday afternoon finally arrived. They tossed their small bags into the trunk. Sandy drove and Rory held the directions. He preferred being the navigator since Sandy had some directional challenges. This way, he knew they'd get there without a bunch of wrong turns. He guided Sandy to Interstate 81 North and watched for their exit.

"This one's it. Bear right at the top of the ramp," he directed.

In five minutes they turned into a gravel driveway and saw the gate. A discreet sign welcomed them to Tall Trees. Sandy pushed the call button and a voice asked their names.

"Welcome, y'all. Drive up the hill and park anywhere and come into the main lodge to register."

As they drove to the lodge, they saw men everywhere, and Rory gazed out the side window as they passed the pool. He provided Sandy a running commentary on the buff bodies in and around the pool. Most of them wore swim trunks, but a few were nude. Sandy leaned over to look.

"Keep your eyes on the road. If you want, I'll drive down so you can sight see," Rory offered.

They passed men walking in the road and heard several comments about fresh meat. Most of the men were older than they were. Several smiled, and some called out "Hey, boys." This promised to be a weekend to remember.

At the reception desk they got keys and a map and a few quick instructions how to find Manly Meadows.

Once they unpacked, Sandy wasted no time getting into his Speedo. He stood at the cabin door waiting for Rory to come downstairs so they could head for the pool.

"Hey, Rory. Lookin' good, man." Sandy gave his friend an approving look.

"Not bad, yourself," Rory replied. "If we don't get lucky, we might have to settle for each other."

Sandy looked surprised. "From what I saw out there, there'll be no problem. We're gonna be busy bees this weekend."

That turned out to be an understatement.

Wherever Rory went around the resort, he felt like he'd won Most Popular in his class. It didn't take long to figure out that if you were reasonably good looking and new to Tall Trees, you'd get plenty of attention. His inexperience prior to his Tall Trees party weekend promised to become history.

Rory and Sandy quickly found men to talk to and separated after the first few minutes at the pool. After dark, Rory caught a few glimpses of his friend at the poolside Tiki bar. Later, there was an awkward moment when Rory brought a guest into the cabin and couldn't find an empty bed, but it was a warm night and the grass was soft.

Rory wasn't much of a dancer, but with enough Jack Daniels to shore up his courage, he enjoyed bumping to the D. J.'s rhythmic music in The Tavern with a variety of eager men. He was having the time of his life until he followed an older guy, Ray, to the bath house. As they walked down the hill from The Tavern, Ray described the action and promised to introduce Rory to some new and different activities.

Rory was quite drunk by this time and a willing apprentice. As they entered the bath house, Rory heard the sound of flesh being slapped. He knew some guys were into spanking, but when they rounded the corner, Rory stopped short. He recognized a man who stood naked, his hand raised over a crouching figure. In his alcoholic haze he tried to sort out where he'd met him. It came into focus slowly. It was Paul, his father's lover, whom he'd met at the hospital the weekend of the Pathways fire.

Paul's eyes met Rory's and he stopped his arm as it began a downward arc toward the buttocks of the crouching man. Ray tugged Rory's arm. "Come on, man. It's too crowded in here. Let's go outside." Rory didn't move.

Despite the chaos around him, Rory stood and stared at Paul and then slowly cast his eyes down. The two remained motionless for what seemed like several seconds while Rory observed burn scars along the side of the crouching man's torso.

Ray sensed Rory was upset and assumed he was reacting to the spanking. "Hey man, I didn't mean to freak you out. Let's go outside," he urged again. He didn't want to let this cute young trick get away. This time Rory followed him.

Once outside Ray asked, "Do you know that guy? You looked like you knew each other."

"You might say that," Rory answered, suddenly feeling quite sober. For him, the party was over for that night. "Sorry," he said to Ray and turned to walk back to his cabin. He wished Sandy would be there. He wanted to talk, but Sandy didn't get back until Rory had fallen asleep alone.

Rory slept well past breakfast and was hung over and hungry when he turned over and saw it was half past noon. He threw on his swimsuit and walked downstairs where Sandy was munching on ham biscuits.

"Where'd you get those?"

"I drove over to the truck stop. Here, I brought you a couple and coffee. Figured you could use it."

They swapped stories about what they could recall from the night before, which wasn't much. Rory ate while Sandy recounted his conquests.

"Didn't know you could dance. You were a regular disco queen last night," Sandy commented.

"Yeah, I should have stayed at The Tavern. Did you make it to the bath house?" Rory asked.

"No. You?"

Rory told Sandy what he'd seen there. "I can't seem to get away from him. He's like a bad penny that just keeps showing up. The only good thing about it was seeing him get his ass beat. I wouldn't have minded taking a switch to him myself."

"Not if it made him happy," Sandy offered with a slight smirk.

"Yeah, you're right. I hope I don't run into him again. I didn't see them at the pool or the tavern, so maybe I'll limit myself to those places."

"Did he see you?"

"I don't think so, but Paul recognized me, and I'm sure he told him."

"Well, maybe he'll crawl back under whatever rock he came from and stay away. Let's go to the pool." They joined the other young guys who were eager to show off their firm nude bodies.

When Rory walked into the lodge for dinner that night, he looked around the darkened sitting room and breathed a sigh of relief when neither his father nor Paul was anywhere in sight. He ate enough to make up for the missed breakfast. The food was surprisingly good. He hadn't expected much, since food didn't seem to be the focus of most of the guests, but it was obvious there was a real chef in the kitchen.

Rory buddied up with a group of young men at dinner. Stick to guys your own age, he reasoned, and you're less likely to run into Daddy. He planned to spend the evening with them.

The weather was perfect, another warm night, not too humid, with a spectacular night sky that seems visible only in the country. Rory had resolved to drink less that night. He hoped to remain coherent so he could take home some memories that weren't blurred by alcohol. Besides, he was tired. Not sure if he'd slept or passed out the night before, he could have used a long nap to renew his energy, but that didn't happen. He'd have plenty of time to sleep when they got back to campus. He came here to party.

Rory's plan worked. He ended up spending the night in one of the plush RVs in Manly Meadows. He didn't give a second thought to the fact that the room he was paying for was going unused. He figured Sandy would put it to good use. Besides, it was Sandy's turn to have the bed, and the couch wouldn't have been as comfortable as the queen-sized bed in the RV. And the company wasn't bad, either.

Breakfast on Sunday was quiet. Only a handful of guys managed to make it up to the lodge. For somebody who was used to coffee and maybe a piece of toast or bagel, this was a feast. Rory stuffed himself with biscuits, cheese grits, eggs, sausage, waffles with real maple syrup and fresh fruit. He quit drinking coffee after three cups and thought he'd have to roll down the hill to the pool.

He stood talking to some men outside the lodge when he recognized two figures approaching on a golf cart. He shifted so he was partly concealed by someone nearly as tall as he was, but he was too late. Darrell got out of the cart and started toward him. His companions were too busy talking to notice Rory stiffen as his father approached.

"Mornin', Rory."

"Mornin."

"How're you doing?"

"Fine, thank you." Rory was polite but signaled disinterest.

"Can we talk?" Darrell motioned to a bench near the lodge.

The men he'd been talking with began to move away, and Rory wanted to go with them. "Gotta go," he said and started to walk away.

Darrell reached out and grabbed Rory's arm. "I really want to talk to you," he pleaded. Rory didn't understand why he hesitated or didn't pull away, but those few seconds gave his father the advantage. "Come on, Rory. I have some things I need to say to you." Reluctantly he followed Darrell to the bench and sat down.

"I rehearsed this so many times," Darrell began, "but now I don't know where to start."

"Well, if you don't know what to say, I have better things to do," Rory said and stood to leave.

"Wait, please sit down." Darrell looked so pathetic Rory almost felt sorry for him.

Rory sat, and Darrell found his tongue. "Rory, I know I wasn't a good father to you." Rory had trouble containing himself but remained silent. Darrell went on about how he regretted not having a better relationship with his son, and Rory saw it was still all about his father's needs.

After a few minutes Rory tired of listening and stood. "My life is just fine without you. I have a mother who loves me for who I am and grandparents who couldn't care less that I'm gay. I have good friends and a promising career ahead of me. My life is very full, and I don't need you. The best thing you did for me was to show me I can stand on my own two feet. I don't need you in my life." As Rory began to walk away, he turned and said, "Oh, and one more thing. I hope every time someone calls you a faggot, you think of me." He turned and walked off.

As Rory walked down the gravel road to the pool a cleansing sweat poured off his forehead and down his chest. He'd never wanted to have a confrontation with his father, but he was glad it had happened. Their brief conversation showed him that his father was damaged goods, not capable of caring about anyone but himself. He didn't need anyone like that in his life.

Chapter Forty-Six

Ruth took the cup of reheated coffee out of the microwave and grabbed some pretzels. It was amazing what passed for supper these days. After a long day with a trip to the university in Boone and a two-hour meeting with her boss, she was too tired to cook, and fixing a meal for one person wasn't much fun. The only time she enjoyed cooking now was when Grady and Lily came over or when Rory was home. She settled into the most comfortable chair in the living room and tackled the stack of magazines that grew weekly.

She leafed through a couple of issues and put them aside. I'll just shut my eyes for a few minutes and rest them, she thought. When the phone jarred her out of a sound sleep, she jumped. She was groggy when she got to the phone.

At first, the voice on the other end didn't register. "Hey, Mrs. Wilson. This is Sandy Hodges." She grew more alert when she heard, "I'm a friend of Rory's. Now, I don't want you to worry ..." words no parent ever wants to hear. Fully alert now, she waited for him to deliver bad news.

"Rory and I had a wreck on our way back from vacation. Rory's banged up some, but he's okay. He asked me to call you 'cause he can't talk too well. His front teeth got broken and one of them split his lip. It's pretty swollen. We're at the hospital in Bristol. They're stitchin' him up."

"Oh, Lord," was all Ruth could get out at first. She hadn't known Rory was going on vacation. He usually told her if he was going out of town, but he hadn't said a word.

"Do you think I should come get him?" she asked.

"Well," Sandy hesitated, "my car is totaled, and we have no way to get out of here." He sounded embarrassed to ask.

"Tell me where you are."

Sandy gave her directions to the Bristol Regional Medical Center. She jotted down the exit number from I-81.

"It'll take me about an hour and a half to get there. Meet me in the emergency waiting room." She gave him her cell number.

Ruth talked to herself the whole way out to the car. "I sure hope alcohol wasn't involved. If it was, I'll give those boys a piece of my mind."

She fumed at the 25 mile per hour speed limit as she drove through Damascus, Virginia on the way to I-81. She knew too many people who'd gotten speeding tickets there. She didn't want to be one of them.

Ruth was not prepared for what she saw when she entered the emergency waiting room at the hospital. Rory's mouth was at least four times its normal size. No wonder he couldn't talk.

"You're Sandy, I suppose. I'm Ruth Wilson, Rory's mother." She stuck out her hand to shake Sandy's but pulled it back when she realized his right arm was in a splint. "You look like you went a few rounds with Mohammed Ali," she said as she gingerly hugged Rory. He mumbled something she couldn't understand and handed her the discharge instructions.

"This says you'll need to have the stitches removed in a week to 10 days and then you'll need to see a dentist." She turned to Sandy. "Did all of his front teeth break?"

"I'm not sure. There was so much blood it was hard to tell. He reached into his shorts pocket and pulled out a small plastic bag. "Here are his teeth."

Ruth recoiled at the sight of the bloody mess in the bag. She put it in her purse. "Where's your car?"

"They towed it with a wrecker. The state trooper said he was sure it was totaled."

"Do you have insurance?"

Sandy's red face was enough of an answer.

"Who was at fault?"

"Oh, the other driver, for sure. When we were pulling onto the exit ramp, the guy behind us didn't slow down. He plowed right into us. Good thing nobody was in the back seat. Rory's face hit the dash-board, and my arm banged into the steering wheel. The back end of the car looked like an accordion. My old junker didn't have airbags."

"Did the other driver have insurance?" Ruth was thinking of what it would cost to replace Rory's teeth. They didn't have dental insurance.

"Yes, ma'am. He said he's fully insured." Ruth sensed there was something Sandy wasn't saying, and her mother's intuition revved up.

"Was there drinking involved?" She asked it indirectly so he wouldn't think she was accusing him.

"Not as far as I know. We weren't drinking. I know that for sure."

"Did you get the other driver's information?"

"Yes, ma'am." At that point, Rory reached for the instruction sheet and wrote something on it. He pushed it toward Sandy.

"'You sure?" Sandy asked.

Rory nodded.

"W-well, Rory wants me to tell you who hit us."

"Who was it? Somebody important and rich, I hope."

"No, ma'am. It was his father."

"What? You can't be serious."

"Yes, ma'am. That's who hit us. We think he must have followed us."

"Followed you from where? What's going on?"

Ruth sat down. She wasn't taking them anywhere until she got some answers. "I suggest you start from the beginning, young man."

Sandy told her where they'd been over the weekend and that Rory had bumped into his father there. They'd had a few words and Rory told him off. Darrell tried to collar Rory a couple more times during the weekend, but Rory told him he wanted no part of him. "We think he might have followed us so he could talk to Rory."

Ruth could hardly contain her anger. She'd heard enough. "He'll talk to Rory's lawyer if I have anything to say about it," she fumed. "What an ass! Pardon my French, but he is."

"Let's get you back to campus," she said to Sandy. "Rory, I want to bring you home. You need some lookin' after for a few days." Rory mumbled again but he didn't seem to disagree.

Sandy reached into his pocket and retrieved a prescription bottle.

"Pain pills. The doctor said he'll need them for a few days 'til the swelling goes down." Ruth put them in her purse next to the bag with Rory's teeth.

As they walked toward the exit, the sliding doors opened and two men started to walk in. "Ruth," one of them said. It took a few seconds for Ruth to recognize Darrell. He'd lost much of his hair since she'd last seen him.

"You haven't done enough to ruin our lives," she screamed. "Now you're trying to kill my son? Are you crazy? Never mind; I already know the answer to that."

He had to shout to be heard. Darrell looked at Rory. "Are you all right?"

"No, he's not all right. Look at him. Does that look like all right to you?"

Rory and Sandy stepped off the sensor pad that kept opening and closing the doors. Sandy wondered if he'd have to call the police. Ruth's angry enough to cause some real damage if she attacks Darrell, he thought.

"I'll see to it he gets the best medical care," Darrell said and tried to keep his voice steady. "I'll call you in a couple of days after you've calmed down," he said.

"You're damned right, you'll pay for this. I'll see your sorry butt in jail for what you did." To everyone's relief, she proceeded through the next set of doors onto the driveway. "Come on, boys," she said motioning to them to follow her.

The adrenaline rush made Ruth dizzy. When she got to the car she leaned against the door.

"Are you okay, Mrs. Wilson?" Sandy asked nervously, worried that in her agitated state they'd have another wreck.

"I'll be fine in a minute," she answered and she seemed calmer. "You boys get in the back seat. I don't want anything else to happen to you tonight."

Chapter Forty-Seven

"Land sakes! You poor thing," Lily said as she stepped into Ruth's kitchen and saw Rory sitting at the table holding an ice pack against his mouth.

"You think that's bad?" Ruth asked. "You should have seen him day before yesterday. I could have walked past him and not known him."

Rory lifted the ice pack off his face. "Hey Meemaw, Papaw." It came out garbled.

"Hush, you don't need to say anything. Your mama told us all about the wreck."

Lily didn't mention that Darrell had called two or three times since the accident to find out how Rory was. She also didn't mention that she'd lambasted her son. The conversation was still vivid in her memory.

"You sure have an interesting way of trying to get back in Rory's good graces," Lily had said when Darrell called.

Darrell repeated Ruth's threats.

"Well, can you blame her? I'm sure she's worried silly about how she's gonna get his teeth fixed. They don't have dental insurance."

Darrell had been quick to say he'd pay for everything.

"I don't know that this will make Rory any more likely to want to talk with you. I know you don't want to hear that, son, but it's the truth."

After she'd hung up, Lily had tried to ease gently into the conversation with Grady. "Now don't get your pressure up. This sounds worse than it is." She related Darrell's conversation including Ruth's threat to prosecute him.

"Sometimes I think Darrell doesn't use the brains the good Lord gave him," Grady said. "All those years we tried to get him to talk with Rory! Now when the boy has lived without his father for so long, Darrell decides to try to make amends. If I was Rory, I'd have punched him in the nose. I always said Darrell doesn't know when to leave well enough alone."

"We can't be takin' sides in this, Grady. Darrell's our son, and it's not right to go against him. I'm sure he knows it was stupid to follow their car. He felt right bad about it."

"Let me see your teeth," Grady said to Rory.

Rory gently moved his lips so his grandfather could see the damage.

"Shoot, boy. You're gonna need dentures, I 'spect."

Ruth walked into the kitchen holding a plastic bag. "Did you say you wanted to see Rory's teeth?" She held the bag up for Grady's inspection.

"Have we got any Krazy Glue?"

Lily swatted Grady on the arm. "Ain't funny. Can't you see he's in pain?"

Grady believed humor would improve any situation and Lily's warning didn't stop him. "I've got an old set of dentures I can't wear anymore," he continued. "Maybe we can get Dr. Emory to redo 'em to fit Rory."

Rory rolled his eyes. That was easier than trying to talk. The swelling had gone down quite a bit, but the stitches in his lip made talking difficult and painful. Grady put an arm around his shoulders and they headed for the living room.

Lily heard chicken sizzling in the skillet and saw Ruth cutting greens and onions. "Smells good, dear," Lily said as she took her sweater off and put it on the back of the chair she knew would be hers. She went to the silverware drawer and counted out utensils.

Once the table was set, Lily hung around the kitchen. She knew better than to hover over the chicken; years of respecting each other's cooking styles had set the rules for what was acceptable when in the other woman's kitchen.

Lily took the opportunity to poke the chicken when Ruth went to the phone. She noted a scowl on Ruth's face. She understood what caused it when she heard Ruth say, "We don't need to discuss anything. Just give me your address, and I'll tell the dentist to send you the bill. … No, there's nothing we need to talk about." She reached for a pen and wrote on the back of an envelope. "I've got it." She hung up the phone and turned to Lily, "Your son."

"Do you think Rory will ever be willin' to talk with his father?" Lily asked.

"That's up to him. You know I wanted him to have a relationship with Darrell, but Darrell didn't want to be bothered. Rory's gotten used to having just one parent. It's a shame, but that's the way Darrell wanted it."

"I thought maybe after Darrell and Rory found out they had something in common, bein' gay and all, that might change things, but maybe not," Lily continued.

Ruth announced supper would be ready in five minutes. She knew Lily was dying to do something with the food. "See if that chicken is ready, Mama. I'm sure it is, but check it, please."

Lily poked a couple of larger pieces. She removed the chicken from the pan and put it on a platter lined with paper towels. "Perfect," she said. "Want me to cover it?"

"Sure, you do that while I mash the potatoes and put the greens and onions in a serving dish."

Grady reached for Rory's and Ruth's hands and bowed his head. "Lord, thank you for the blessings of this fine meal with our family and let me live long enough to see some healing, not only of Rory's injuries, but of the wounds that this family has suffered these many years. In Jesus' name. Amen.

The issues raised by Grady's blessing went unanswered as wisdom trumped curiosity, at least during supper.

Rory managed to eat mashed potatoes with gravy and drink sweet tea with a straw. Grady tried to give him cornbread soaked in gravy, but opening his mouth that wide was too painful, and he waved it away. Nothing that required serious chewing would enter his mouth for a couple more weeks.

Rory ate enough ice cream to keep the meal from being a total loss. Ruth had stocked up on as much ice cream as would fit in the freezer, knowing it might be the only food Rory could eat and he needed the calories to keep him from losing any more weight. He didn't have much to spare.

Lily and Grady said their goodbyes, and Lily's behind had hardly touched the car seat when she lit into Grady. "What was that all about?"

"What are you talkin' about?" he answered, though he knew full well what she meant.

"The blessin'. Why'd you have to bring that up? I thought we agreed we weren't buttin' in."

"I'm not interferin'. I just said what I hoped might happen. You know, we're not getting' any younger. I'd sure like to see Rory and Darrell patch things up before I meet my maker. Wouldn't you?"

"Course I would, but it's not for us to mix in. That's between them. The only way we've stayed on good terms with Ruth all these years is by keepin' our mouths shut about Darrell. What's gotten into you?"

"Darrell really wants to try to make it up to Rory. He told me so. I just thought I'd plant the idea is all. Nothin wrong with that, Lily. You're too sensitive when it comes to this stuff."

"Well, one of us has to be." She folded her arms across her chest and stayed quiet for the rest of the drive home.

Chapter Forty-Eight

"Not bad, compared to what I bet you must have looked like before," Dr. Ragatky said when Rory reappeared in the botany lab. "I heard you got pretty banged up. What happened?" Rory told his mentor about the accident, leaving out the part about who hit Sandy's car.

"I'm getting a bridge to replace the missing teeth," Rory remarked. "It'll be ready next week. I'll be glad to be able to eat normally."

"That's great timing," Ragatky said. "We have a dinner invitation."

Rory raised his eyebrows. "We do? Who from?"

I got a call yesterday from a guy named Carlo Petri. I met him at a botany conference a few months ago and happened to mention your work to him. He's over at the medical school at Duke. He was very interested in your project and said he'd like to meet you. I told him if he was ever in this neck of the woods, to give me a call and I'd set something up. I never thought he'd follow through. People often say stuff like that at conferences and then forget about it."

Rory's attention ratcheted up a notch at the mention of Duke. "What does he do there?"

"He's in charge of research. Anyway, he said he's going to be out this way for a few days and wanted to know if you and I could have dinner with him next week. When do you get your new choppers?"

"The dentist said they'll probably be in by Monday. I have a Tuesday morning appointment unless something gets held up."

"That should work out okay. He said he could do it either Thursday or Friday evening. That gives you a day or two to get used to your new teeth." Ragatky smiled then turned serious. "This could be a big break for you, Rory. Senior vice presidents from Duke don't invite undergraduates to dinner every day, you know. This guy didn't waste time letting me think he was interested in seeing me. It's you he wants to meet."

"What do you think I should bring with me? Do you think I should invite him over to the lab to see the plants?"

"My guess is he's going to try to size you up, get a feel for how smart you are and how much promise you show. He might ask specific questions about methodology to see if you know what you're doing. I would expect him to question you about your results and how you've modified the strains to try for different outcomes over the last two years."

"Gosh, I'm nervous already. Should I wear a coat and tie?"

"Probably not a bad idea. He might think we're all a bunch of hayseeds out here. It never hurts to look professional. I guess I should dress up too." They laughed. Dr. Ragatky was not known for his fashion sense.

"Wear what you had on when you came to dinner at my house. It certainly impressed my mother and grandparents." More laughter. Although Rory never spelled it out, he had hinted at his mother's interest in the professor after that Thanksgiving.

"What do ya think? Clip-on or regular?" Rory asked Sandy as he dressed for his dinner with Dr. Petri.

"The bow tie makes you look too Ivy. He's Duke, not Princeton. I'd go for the regular tie."

Rory finished dressing and checked his new front teeth in the mirror. He tucked some notes into his jacket pocket and turned to Sandy for a final review.

"Well?"

"You look fine. Just remember not to pick your teeth at the table and no peas on the knife."

"Funny man. Nobody's ever gonna put a toothpick near these teeth. Did I tell you what they cost?"

"Yeah, you did, seven thousand and change. Good thing your old man was payin' for 'em. Your teeth cost more than my car."

"Least he could do," Rory muttered as he left the room and headed for the stairs.

"Wake me when you get back if I'm asleep. Good luck," Sandy called.

Rory got into Dr. Ragatky's waiting car.

"Smile," the professor ordered. "Let me see 'em."

Rory complied.

"Very nice. Nobody'd ever know they weren't yours."

Rory wondered why they had to leave so early. The drive to Abingdon took no more than half an hour. He'd heard of The Tavern Restaurant but had never eaten there.

"I made a 7 o'clock reservation, but I want to get there early so we're sure to get a good table. I haven't been there before."

It hadn't occurred to Rory to ask who was paying for the dinner. He'd assumed Dr. Petri was and when he took his first look at the menu, he sure hoped it wasn't him. This was the most expensive restaurant Rory had ever been in.

At two minutes past seven the maitre'd led a distinguished-looking man to their table. Dr. Ragatky stood, and Rory followed suit. Introductions were made and they sat. Rory detected a slight foreign accent when Petri spoke, Italian he guessed. He was the picture of self-assurance, and Rory suddenly felt smaller than his six feet three inches. The wine steward approached the table and offered them a wine list.

Without looking at the list, Dr. Petri asked if they had a wine Rory had never heard of. He probably couldn't have pronounced it anyway; it was French. The steward apologized and said they didn't have it but suggested another that he said was an admirable replacement. Petri nodded.

Well, that settles it, thought Rory. He didn't even ask if we wanted that wine, so that must mean he's picking up the tab.

After Petri tasted the wine and gave an approving nod, the steward poured a glass for each of them. Rory wasn't used to wine and tried not to show his dislike for the dry taste. He felt obligated to like it since hearing the steward say it cost $80.

"What do you recommend?" Petri asked Dr. Ragatky as he perused the menu. Rory was amused since he knew his mentor had not been to the restaurant before. He watched to see how Dr. Ragatky would handle Petri's question.

"To start, I'd recommend the escargot if you like them," he said. No hint that he'd never eaten there. "Of course, the salads are nice, and they serve a fine filet."

Rory assumed he was referring to the filet mignon. This was going to be an adventure. Rory'd never eaten most of the items on the menu.

The waiter came and described two daily specials, but neither sounded like they'd beat the signature medallions of filet mignon. He'd never ordered filet mignon before, but this was his big chance. He worried momentarily about whether his new teeth could handle steak, but the waiter had said it was so tender one could cut it with a fork.

"Escargot all around?" Petri asked and placed an order. Each man ordered in turn, and Rory was glad he was last. He knew ahead of time what questions he'd have to answer.

"And how would you like that prepared?" the waiter asked. Rory'd heard that it was considered unsophisticated to order good beef well done, but that's the way he preferred it. At the last minute, he decided to take a chance. "Medium well, he replied." He thought the waiter winced but hoped it was his imagination.

They engaged in small talk about the weather and the beautiful surrounding area. Finally a server brought the appetizer. Rory looked at the plate of snails in front of him and wondered what Papaw and Meemaw would say if they could see him now.

He watched carefully and copied what the men did. He took his napkin in hand, picked up a shell, and with the small fork that came with the plate, picked out the snail. He dipped it into the butter sauce and wished Ragatky had not suggested snails.

Well, here goes, he thought as he slipped the snail into his mouth and began to chew. It was not at all slimy as he'd imagined it would be. Not bad, he thought. By the time he'd come to the last one, he was beginning to like the taste. He'd always liked garlic, and the snails were smothered in it.

Entrees were served and still Rory hadn't been called on to say much. The two professors discussed the future of higher education funding and other topics he knew nothing about, so he ate. Petri had ordered a second bottle of wine and the two men were drinking it like water. Rory was still working on his first glass.

After the plates had been cleared and dessert ordered, Dr. Petri addressed Rory.

"Dr. Ragatky told me about your work with tobacco. I'm quite interested in what you're trying to do. What attracted you to this work?"

Rory explained how so many of his neighbors and relatives had suffered with pulmonary diseases, namely emphysema and lung cancer, as a result of smoking. Several others had mouth cancers from chewing tobacco. He'd always been interested in working with plants, and a couple of his school science projects had won notice. He'd been raised not to brag, but thought it a good idea to mention that a competition judge had referred to him as a "budding scientist."

Dr. Ragatky chimed in. "That's how Rory came to our attention. His science teacher thought he showed remarkable promise and told me about his projects. I convinced Rory to consider the university and the rest is history, as they say."

Rory began to describe in minute detail the genetic mutations he'd introduced to his tobacco plants and paused only when a server brought dessert to the table. He'd never had creme brulee before and hoped he would get a moment to eat it before continuing to talk about his work.

Dr. Petri was absorbed in what Rory was saying and motioned him to continue as he spooned the dessert into his mouth. Rory couldn't talk and eat, so he opted to talk. Mercifully, Dr. Ragatky came to his rescue and suggested they give Rory a few minutes to eat his dessert.

"Of course, yes, eat this wonderful creme brulee. It's quite remarkable," Dr. Petri replied.

"Good choice, Dr. Ragatky. Do you come here often?"

Rory smiled as he ate, not only because he liked the dessert but also because he knew Ragatky didn't want to admit he'd never been there. He watched the professor squirm a bit.

"When I'm not eating at my desk in the lab," he said, "it's a welcome change from my own cooking."

Clever, Rory thought. He didn't exactly lie.

While they finished their coffee, Dr. Petri asked Rory several questions about his future plans. Rory told him he'd love to go to graduate school, but financially that didn't appear to be likely.

"I'd like to talk more with you about your work and your future, young man. When is your next break? What's the best way to reach you? Email, I suppose?"

"Yes, sir, or by phone. This is my cell phone number and my home number. He handed Petri a card that he'd written out earlier.

"I don't get out here too often. Would you be willing to come to Durham?"

"Yes. I'm sure my mother would lend me her car," Rory answered.

"Oh, I'd send you a plane ticket. You could fly from Tri Cities to Raleigh-Durham, and I'd have someone pick you up."

"That would be great," Rory replied and before he could stop himself, he blurted out, "I've never flown before." He mentally kicked himself as soon as the words were out of his mouth.

Dr. Petri smiled. He signaled for the check and placed an American Express card on the table. Rory couldn't believe he didn't even look at the check before giving the waiter his credit card.

Rory thanked Dr. Petri for dinner and said he'd look forward to hearing from him and visiting Duke. The men shook hands all around, and Dr. Petri left to go to the men's room.

Rory grinned like a little boy who'd hit the Christmas jackpot. "Well, that went well. Ready to leave?" Dr. Ragatky asked.

"I need to stop in the men's room, but I didn't want to go when he was in there," Rory said.

"It'll look strange if we go in after he comes out. There's a fast food joint down the street. We can stop there." As they left the restaurant, Rory hardly felt his feet touch the ground.

Chapter Forty-Nine

Rory sat in his room in his mother's house and thought about all that had happened since that night a year ago when he met Dr. Petri. Once again, it reinforced his belief that life could change if you were open to people who wanted to help you.

"Come on, Rory, time to go." Ruth called. It was a crisp mountain morning and mist still clung to the surrounding mountains as Rory and his mother drove up the familiar gravel driveway next to the Wilson's farm house.

A couple of months earlier, Grady had suffered another mild heart attack and this one had aged him badly. Rory helped his grandfather into the car.

Once in the car they tackled the decision of where to go for breakfast.

"You know what my choice is," Grady said. "If your meemaw will let me go off this doggone diet, I'd sure like some of Ruby's hot cakes."

Rory turned to look at Lily who had replaced Ruth in the front passenger seat.

"Oh, all right," she grumbled. "I guess it's not every day we get to celebrate a Wilson goin' off to Duke Medical School."

"Ruby's it is," Rory answered as he backed the car down the driveway.

"Did you have to wear that Blue Devil shirt?" Grady asked. "Bad enough you're turnin' traitor and goin' to Duke instead of Vanderbilt."

Rory knew from Grady's smile that his teasing hid enormous pride at Rory's full scholarship to Duke. Recalling his grandparents' insecure reactions when he'd described how Dr. Petri wined and dined him on his three trips to Durham during his senior year, Rory raised his coffee cup and proposed a toast.

"To the most important people in my life, Mama, Papaw and Meemaw. If it wasn't for the love and support you've shown me all my life, I'd never have made it this far. I'll do my best to make you proud of me, and I'll never forget where I came from. No matter what, my heart will always be here with y'all."

"I hope your body will show up from time to time too, darlin'," Ruth said. "Aren't any of us getting any younger, you know." She had to remind Rory, as if he wasn't conscious enough of his grandfather's fragile health.

They all wiped their eyes, including Rory. Each knew he wouldn't be around Craggy Grove much for the next several years. Medical school would be more demanding than anything Rory had tackled as an undergraduate, and he'd be putting in long hours studying and doing research.

Rory smiled as the waitress brought stacks of steaming hot cakes and poured more coffee. "Dig in, y'all. This breakfast's on me," he said.

"Oh, in that case, I think I'll have a steak with mine," Grady said.

"You most certainly will not," Lily replied. "Rory's gonna be a doctor, but he's going into research, not cardiology, so no steak for you, mister."

Grady shrugged, knowing that case was closed tighter than a tick.

It seemed as if half of Craggy Grove had driven to the airport to see Rory off the next morning. The Wilsons turned out in force, including some cousins Rory hadn't seen since he was in elementary school. They'd read about Rory's scholarship in the paper. He shook hands and exchanged hugs with everybody for a few minutes. Ruth squeezed him so hard he thought he might pass out.

"Mama," he chided. "Quit blubbering or you'll make me cry."

He turned and looked around and smiled as folks waved when he walked toward the security checkpoint. He'd shipped his books and most of his clothes to Durham, so he carried one small suitcase with things he didn't trust to anyone.

"Rory," someone called as he approached the security checkpoint. Ashley rushed toward him. "Wait up," she said.

"I couldn't let you go off to medical school without saying good-bye. I brought you something." She held out a package. "I don't know if they'll let you take this on the plane without opening it."

Rory asked the airport screener if he needed to open it.

"I'm afraid so," the woman said. "Either that or you'll have to leave it here."

He put his suitcase down and slit open the wrapping paper to reveal a box. He lifted the top off and stared at a stethoscope.

"You'll need one of those," Ashley said. "It's from Mama and Daddy and me."

"Lord, Ashley, I don't know what to say. It's beautiful. I was gonna see if I could find a used one when I got to Duke. They're expensive."

"You're worth it, Rory. Just think of me whenever you play doctor."

Rory laughed as he grabbed her in a one-armed hug, and they held on to all the memories of their shared childhood for a long moment.

"I'll call you soon," he said. "Good luck teaching. I know the kids will love you almost as much as I do."

He placed the box with the stethoscope on the conveyor belt next to his suitcase and stepped through the metal detector.

"Your girlfriend?" the screener asked.

"My best friend," he answered.

He slipped into his shoes, tucked the box containing the stethoscope under his arm and picked up his suitcase. Rory turned one last time to wave and tried not to cry.

The end.

ABOUT THE AUTHOR

Lissa Brown has been writing since she learned how to form letters and put them on paper. She's been a columnist, a speechwriter, a ghost writer for elected officials and corporate executives, and a media relations specialist for gubernatorial and state legislative campaigns.

After successful careers in teaching, public relations and marketing she retired to her present home in North Carolina's Blue Ridge Mountains. There she discovered the joy of writing for herself and quickly published *Real Country: From the Fast Track to Appalachia* as Leslie Brunetsky and *Family Secrets: Three Generations* under her own name. *Another F-Word* is her second novel.

Contact Lissa Brown through her website,
www.lissabrownwrites.com
to arrange readings, book club visits and signings.